CONTAGION PROTOCOL

By **Monsuta**

Autopsy Notes
An imprint of Ink Beyond

Copyright © 2025 by Monsuta
All rights reserved.

No part of this book may be reproduced, stored in a retrieval system, or transmitted in any form or by any means—electronic, mechanical, photocopying, recording, or otherwise—without the prior written permission of the publisher, except in the case of brief quotations used in reviews or scholarly works.

This is a work of fiction. Names, characters, events, and incidents are either products of the author's imagination or used fictitiously. Any resemblance to actual persons, living or dead, or to actual events or locations is purely coincidental.

References to real products, companies, or institutions, including but not limited to Subaru, St. Mary's Medical Center, KISS 101, KWCW, and named musical artists, are included solely to provide a sense of realism and setting. Their inclusion does not imply sponsorship, endorsement, or association with this work.

Contagion Protocol
First Edition – July 2025
Printed in the United States of America

ISBN: 978-1-969141-05-8

Published by Autopsy Notes
An imprint of Ink Beyond Publishing

DEDICATION

For Destinee.

I've watched you find your voice,
loud, brave, and unapologetically yours.
I've watched you embrace rebellion,
become a nurturer,
and grow into a hell of a fighter.

You're an amazing mom,
a kick-ass friend,
and the kind of daughter every dad hopes for.

From the day you were born,
I knew it would be you
who helped me shape a voice strong enough
to survive the end of the world.
And in this world full of noise and shadows,
you are the light I'd fight through any apocalypse to find.

I will never stop being proud
of the person you've become.
You are, and always have been,
my hero.

"We overlook the living from our room of the dead.
If you're hearing this, you're still alive.
That's mistake number one."
— *Monster, The Morgue Radio Show*

Author's Note

I wrote *Contagion Protocol* while living in Walla Walla, Washington.

It's a town where the pace is slow, where the fairgrounds come alive during the Balloon Stampede, and where people still wave at each other across the street. I wanted to imagine what would happen if the end of the world didn't start in a city or on a battlefield, but right at home. In quiet places. The familiar ones.

More than anything, I wanted to explore what those first 24 hours might feel like. Before the news got out. Before the military showed up. Before anyone outside of town even realized something had gone wrong.

This is the story of ground zero, of people caught in the noise before the scream.

A lot of it grew out of my own surroundings, places I still think about fondly, people I'd met, theories I've wrestled with. But the heart of this story, especially the character DJ, comes from someone much closer, my daughter.

At the time I started writing this, she was a teenager figuring the world out in real time; she was bold, sarcastic, tough as hell, and carrying more wisdom than she realized. DJ is shaped by that same spirit: someone learning how to fight, how to love, and how to survive when everything familiar feels like it is burning to the ground.

This book is fiction. But if you've ever lived in a small town, listened to late-night radio, or wondered what you'd do when the world cracks open, you might find something familiar in these pages.

Thanks for reading. And if you're still alive by the end of the book, that's mistake number one.

— *Monsuta*

00 – YOUTH GONE WILD

1989

"You are listening to KISS 101, Walla Walla's rock and roll station, broadcasting from the top of the Marcus Whitman Hotel! That was Guns N' Roses with 'Paradise City.' Up next, Skid Row's 'Youth Gone Wild.' Get ready to lose your mind!"

The radio DJ's voice cuts out with a twist of a worn stereo knob.

Jeff, slouched behind the wheel of the white correctional transport bus, scowls at the other guard fiddling with the dial.

"Dammit, Jeff," barks Skip, a round-bellied correctional officer standing by the cage gate. "That kind of music's the reason you're stuck on transport duty."

Jeff huffs, navigating the large vehicle down Poplar Street. "Come on, Skip, it was an accident. Tower Seven was a fluke." He glances at his coworker through the rear-view.

Skip chuckles, his belly jiggling. "You fall off the ladder 'cause you're spying on admin girls with binoculars. Fluke my ass."

Laughter erupts from the dozen inmates on the other side of the cage and finger-pointing follows. Jeff flips the blinker as he turns off Poplar Street into the back lot of St. Mary's Medical Center.

"Shut up!" Jeff snaps, glaring into the mirror. He eases the bus into the unloading zone. Air hisses as the brakes decompress.

Shotguns rack. Shackled inmates line up and are herded through the hospital's rear entrance and marched under armed supervision to the cancer wing.

One by one, the inmates are cuffed to examination tables in a room full of biohazard symbols, connected to patches with wires, stabbed with needles for blood drawing. The nurses collect urine samples and catcalls. Their vitals get taken and their physicals finalize with a final round of injections of sludgy looking fluid, not unlike tar. The process takes much of the afternoon.

Jeff and Skip wait in a fluorescent-lit lobby with Smiley Snacks from the vending machine, magazines from the end tables, and the drone of static-filled silence. Occasionally, they snicker over underwear ads or curse the clock.

After a long pause, Jeff lowers his magazine. "You ever wonder why they're doing all this medical crap on inmates? Feels...off."

Skip shrugs without looking up. "Hell, if I know. Been goin' on a couple years now, some federal thing. Cancer trials, maybe. Or immuno-boosters, they said once. They don't tell us much. Just drive 'em, cuff 'em, shut up."

Jeff frowns. "Yeah, but why the injections? And why here? St. Mary's ain't even a federal hospital."

Skip exhales through his nose and finally meets Jeff's eyes. "All I know is, the ones who get the shots come back lookin' worse than when they left. They look like wax dolls, man. Gives me the creeps."

Jeff asks, "And why the cancer ward? These guys don't all have cancer, do they?"

Before Skip can speculate, a nurse waves them down from the hallway. "They're done."

Jeff rises, abandoning his magazine on a table. The inmates line up again, same faces, same chains, but something is different. Their skin looks moist, almost spongy, and their eyes are vacant.

"Well, looks like we got our kids back." Jeff mutters to Skip, noticing the perspiration on more than one inmate, despite the chill hospital air. "Jesus, you're right. They don't look so good."

They re-chain the inmates, shuffle them to the bus, and begin the return trip. The bus rumbles across town in silence. The inmates do little more than stare at their shoes or out the windows, showing no signs of emotion or talking about what they miss in the world outside of prison, none of their usual conversation. Even the guards fall quiet. While Jeff focuses on the route, Skip continues to stare at the group of lifeless inmates, waiting for any activity but finding none.

As the bus turns right on Ninth street, he catches a glimpse in the rearview of one inmate, Davisson, wide eyed and lips moving, like he's ready to crawl out of his skin, despite his stillness. Jeff doesn't hear him speaking, just the sound of chattering teeth.

At the penitentiary gate, Jeff tries to shake the chill riding up his spine. The silence unnerves him, so he tries to break it, "Unloading's always more relaxing than loading."

Skip grunts and unlocks the cage. The inmates rise in unison, their movements are slow, uncoordinated, as if muscle memory, not will, drives them. Skip walks the aisle of the bus, ensuring the chains are properly in place before positioning himself at the rear of the transport.

Jeff leads the prisoners, and they shuffle into the holding pens like cattle, feet seldom leaving the ground. They offer no resistance and no recognition. Jeff returns the bus to motor pool while Skip begins the paperwork. The last hours of shift pass without incident. Jeff and Skip clock out and disappear into the routine of their life.

Within the prison walls, the sun sinks behind pink wheat fields. Dinner ends and for a few hours every night, cell doors stay open for socialization. Life behind the walls drags without meaning.

Before the inmates are herded to their cells for lights out, inmate Davisson collapses and shakes violently on the floor. Another inmate, not from the hospital visit, leans over to check on him, only to get his face raked.

Davisson's eyes snap open, red and raw. He clamps onto the inmate leaning over him, fingers like iron around the man's collar. The tug is sudden and violent, dragging the Samaritan down into his hungry mouth, teeth tearing into the man's neck. The man's jugular pops and a spray of hot blood fans across the floor as Davisson bites again, harder, chewing through flesh.

Each of the twelve inmates who visited the hospital shift from lifeless to rabid. Sallow turns visceral. They attack without hesitation, cellmates, guards, anyone nearby.

Blood sprays and saliva flies. Bones snap under feral strength. A scream echoes as a prisoner rips open another's throat. Another jabs a sharpened toothbrush into an officer's eye. Chaos erupts into violence.

Control room alarms blare, radios crackle with urgent voices, and the penitentiary's Emergency Response Team is enroute. Some cellblock guards run toward the riot with batons raised, others hang back, securing exits in case it is already too late.

One inmate gets thrown over the third-story railing, his body slapping the ground like meat on a butcher's floor.

When the ERT arrives, they form a barrier with shields up and weapons drawn, but the inmates, now berserk and unyielding, crash into them.

"Call SERT!" someone yells. Specialized Emergency Response Team, the state's special team for when backup needs backup. The ERT team holds the line, steadying while inmates, red with anger, assail the shield wall. Their view of their assailants slowly disappearing behind the red smears.

Minutes later, SERT storms the block with rifles ready. The pressure breaks. The inmates surge again, driven by instinct, not fear. Gunfire erupts and bodies drop on both sides of the rumble. Guards are torn apart, and prisoners are perforated by bullets.

The riot lasts less than ten minutes.

Afterward, silence returns. Then, the cleanup happens. Blood gets mopped, medical teams tend to the wounded, reports are filed. Officers who died are reverently removed while the inmates, or what's left of them, are bagged and tagged with the same care as someone would show while picking up stray dog shit.

The fallen inmates with families are processed through next-of-kin paperwork while the rest are wrapped like deli meat and buried in a back lot called Nine Wing; an inmate cemetery with no headstones, only bricks and ID numbers.

By week's end, no one remembers their names. And new inmates fill the empty cells, as if nothing ever happened.

01 – HIGHWAY TO HELL

Today

Smoke twists through shattered windows, billowing onto the main street of Weston, Oregon. Headlights flicker across the wreckage like stuttering fireflies racing the dawn. A brown sedan screeches, flips sideways, and crashes into a rusted-out pickup. Metal folds. Glass shatters.

"Oh my god! Watch out!" The shrill squeal comes from the redheaded passenger in the front seat of the crowded SUV as it careens down the destroyed street.

A ragged man stumbles into the intersection, his clothes are soaked in blood, and his hands tremble violently, broken fingers twitching as he waves frantically at the oncoming SUV.

"Stop! He needs help!" The passenger screams, but the driver ignores her plea.

Inside the vehicle, chaos ignites. Passengers jolt upright. A woman begins to sob. A boy buries his face into his mother's coat.

The man in the street freezes, determined to hold his ground in hopes they will stop.

The vehicle rocks as it swerves past the man, tires squealing. The sharp veer causes the SUV to bounce off a parked car and metal screams as steel kisses steel. The near collision causes the passengers to scream, and the driver yanks the wheel to correct. Bodies slam into seats and windows, an older woman in the back hits her head and drops.

"He's covered in blood, look at his eyes, they're all black!" another passenger screams from the back.

The front passenger turns to look back, checking on the man. For a moment, he stands there, his gaze vacant, and his jaw slack. Then, something barrels into him from the shadows and tackles him. Both figures skid across the pavement.

An eruption of glass and flame from a storefront pepper the SUV. The driver instinctively pulls the wheel and hits the brakes, sending the scared and wounded passengers to one side of the vehicle. The stench of burnt rubber and rot fills the cabin. Blood streaks down the emergency hatch. The child in the backseat cries.

The driver's breathing turns shallow. Sweat pours from his brow, staining his collar. It smells sour, chemical, wrong. A vein pulses dark along the side of his neck. The street swims in and out of focus.

He blinks, but the blur stays. "Where…are we?" The question falls from his mouth before he realizes he's speaking. He stares at the carnage around the vehicle, doing his best and failing at processing what is happening to his hometown. This street is usually so quiet. He thinks about the parade last month and how many smiling kids were picking candy up off the road. He watched his daughter dancing just down the street in her favorite flowery dress. Now its all glass and bone.

The man in the cargo area of the vehicle yells in frustration, "Keep this damn rig steady." He holds a large woman and juts the fingers of one hand back into the gaping hole in her neck while ripping the sleeve off his plaid cotton shirt with the other.

Outside the SUV, twisted hands slap against the passenger window, crumpling against the force. They smear blood, filth, and something oily with every violent assault on the windows. One of the people wears a cracked badge. The name is illegible, but the logo reads: Weston Foods Processing. To the side of the words is a cookie with a happy face and a bite out of it. The Smiley Snacks logo.

The mom in the back seat whispered, "I know that guy. He works the lunch line." His face presses against her window and she wonders, "Shit, what did they do?"

The woman in the front seat pounds the dashboard with both fists, her knuckles already bleeding, "Who cares?". She turns and screams at the driver, "Get us out of here!"

He doesn't respond, his stare is distant, pupils dilating. His foot slips off the brake and the SUV lurches forward.

The man in the cargo hold barks again at the driver, "Why don't you put a little speed on it? She's dying here!" He wads up the cuff of the shirt sleeve and presses it up against the void in her soaked neck, then wraps the remainder around her gurgling throat, and mutters, "She was clean. Five weeks clean."

"Why don't you back off?" Another passenger in the back seat fires at the man, "He's doing all he can!"

Outside, shapes move, staggering figures with twisted limbs and missing jaws. One crawls on all fours, entrails dragging behind.

The crusty man pressing the cloth to the wound opens his mouth to speak but is thrown forward as the SUV slams the brakes again, burning tire, and barely avoiding a maroon Subaru blasting through the intersection.

The driver of the Subaru tries to drift into a turn but oversteers, clipping debris in the road. The car tilts into the drift, flips, and slams into a truck. It ricochets skyward, ejecting the driver through the windshield, and landing bumper first into the pavement. The car tumbles end-over-end through a fence and into a creek bed.

Three passengers in the SUV scream. The woman in back seat and the angry man in the luggage area begin yelling at each other. The front passenger cries out. The driver, frozen in place, vomits across the steering column, and the stench forces dry-heaves from others in the car.

Grimy hands from outside the vehicle hit against the glass again. A half-mulched face snaps its jaws against the window, leaving blood-smeared streaks. Then more join, five twisted figures clawing, groaning, hungrily seeking entry.

The screams swell. In the back seat, the wounded father clutches a stump where his hand should be while his child wails in terror. He sobs through his pain, "What the hell is wrong with these people?"

"Go! Go! Come on, please?" the redhead cries, pounding the driver's shoulder. "Goddammit, please! Just go!"

A burned and bloodied woman climbs onto the hood, dragging herself closer to the windshield using the wipers.

She slams her fists down repeatedly. On the seventh strike, the windshield cracks.

"I don't want to die!" the passenger wails. "Please, just go!"

The driver gasps, shakes, and slams the gas pedal. The SUV jolts and the attackers slide off, except for the woman on the hood, who rides up the windshield. The wiper catches her tank top, tears through fabric, and gouges her abdomen. She snarls, her eyes vacant, and she continues pounding as if unaware of pain, oblivious that the wiper has embedded into her side.

The driver weaves through wreckage, swerving past a spilled load of logs from a tipped semi. At last, he reaches the open road and banks hard to the onramp, lurching the attacker on the hood to the side, snapping the wiper off the vehicle. She is thrown from the hood, smearing across the windshield and onto the roadside. She stands, then runs back toward the town.

The family in the back watches her fade behind them, eyes locked on the burning town swallowed by smoke. The hills, normally lush with growing wheat, are now burning ash. Confusion and disbelief stun them to silence.

The redhead clutches her shoulder, breath ragged, trying to see through the fogging windshield and ignore the stench of the bile, blood, and shit. Vomit curdles in the footwell beneath her, thick and sour, while a metallic tang clings to the back of her throat, like rust and electricity.

The man in back yells, "Now can we hurry up and get to the damned hospital? Misty is dying back here!"

The girl in the front turns toward the road, just in time to see the sign. Walla Walla – 17 miles.

Seventeen miles of hell-stretched hope.

02 – UNDER A DARKENING SKY

Somewhere inside Washington State Penitentiary, a battered radio hums in the corner of a shared cell. A cracked speaker spits static before settling into a voice as smooth as silk and equally dangerous.

"It's finally Friday and you're listening to The Morgue Radio Show right here on KWCW. As always, we are broadcasting live from our booth at the Whitman College Campus." The voice belongs to a woman known to listeners only as Violet. "Thank you for tuning in to the voice of the valley of misfits "

A ripple of chuckles runs through the cellblock, but not all are amused. One inmate slams a domino down hard enough to crack it, muttering, "Turn that shit off." His cellmate ignores him, leaning closer to the speaker like it is whispering freedom.

In the far corner, Anderson, the old timer who's been locked up since cassette tapes were relevant, leans back against the wall with his eyes closed. He doesn't care much for death metal, but he likes hearing Violet, and often says she reminds him of his wife.

Violet continues, her voice curling around every syllable like candle smoke. "We've got a full lineup for you degenerates tonight. But first, let's see who's still among the living."

A deep, rumbling voice cuts in. "Hey cadavers! It's your favorite decomposing DJ, Monster, back from the crypt with more noise than your ex's lawyer." the co-host growls. "Put your death masks on, because we have a lot of ground to cover tonight. I've curated a devious musical line-up, we've got some events you cadavers might actually care about, and I've got a fresh batch of listener mail that definitely didn't come from your parole officers."

Monster rustles some papers into the microphone, encouraging some laughter and cheer from the inmates. Someone in the cell block flicks a lighter while another inmate leans closer.

"First up, Otero from B Block wants to know what Violet's wearing tonight."

Violet lets the silence hang long enough to inspire fantasy, "Guilt and a little regret."

The cell erupts with laughter. Even the guards, who hear the radios they're supposed to ignore, can't help but glance sideways, trying not to smirk.

"We've got another from Rusty out in Richland," Monster says. "He saw an event online for a balloon stampede at the Walla Walla County Fair. Wanted to know what that's all about. Do you live under a rock, Rusty?"

"Oh, you know," Violet purrs, breezing past Monster's question, "It is Walla Walla's own pastel-colored apocalypse. Dozens of helium-filled demons loosed upon the innocent. A true marvel of suburban terror."

Monster adds, "Children crying. Old women trampled. It's a place where the old go to eat funnel cake and die." He chuckles. "A full-blown societal collapse in rainbow form."

"I will say, though, Monster, I'm honestly kind of excited for it. I know being around people isn't your thing, but I really like seeing all the hot air balloons. Plus, even you have to admit, the night glow is pretty fun to watch."

"I'd love to watch the night glow light up if it actually lit the balloons on fire and brought them down onto the crowd of sheeple like the Hindenburg." Monster responds with acrid humor which finds an unheard backing of support within the claustrophobic prison cell, not only Bartholomew's, but in many throughout the prison.

Unscathed by her co-host's response, Violet turns her songbird voice to another disembodied presence inside the small gray radio, "Butcher, do you plan on going tomorrow?"

"I'm going to try. Even if for a little while." The voice responds in one steady tone. "I just want some funnel cake."

"I know, right?" Violet chirps. "As long as it hasn't been affected by that Smiley Snacks recall I read about online today."

"What?" Monster's bassy voice raises an octave in sheer surprise. "Are you two effing kidding me?" The disc jockey's disbelief drools out the speakers and into the cellblock. Some inmates chuckle while others groan. Anderson scowls silently, thinking of ways to teach Monster how to properly speak to Violet.

Both the other DJs chime together with their own confused response to Monster's reaction.

"You two are on a metal radio show. We play the evilest music on the planet. We constantly give our listeners news about morbid death and mutilations. We find the latest and greatest kink to share with our cadavers and you're both sitting here, going on about funnel cake and hot air balloons! What's next, are we going to play My Little Pony while listening to Hinder?"

"Hey now!" Violet steps to the mic in defense. "You brought up the whole balloon stampede thing."

Butcher backs his feminine cohort, "She's got ya there."

"Well yeah, I brought it up because we got mail asking about it, and we're contractually obligated by the powers of the station to promote local events. I'm just doing my job."

His feelings of validation are quickly quashed with Violet's next question, "So, why'd you ask what I thought?"

"I certainly didn't do it so we could sing the praises of funnel cake!"

"Well," Her questioning melds into malicious jibing. "Be careful what you ask for."

"Alright." Monster begins to declare with vindication. "Here's the deal for all our cadavers out there with their ears stapled to the radio…"

Butcher mutters loud enough to be picked up by the microphone but apparently too soft for his male co-host to hear, "Uh oh, here it comes."

"Apparently Violet will be out and about at Walla Walla's little balloon fest tomorrow. For those of you that aren't locked up in the cemetery on the hill, go to the balloon stampede and try finding Violet. I will stay up here in the Morgue and will take your calls. The person to successfully find her after each set of songs will pick up a CD of my choice from our music vault."

The inmate audience groans at their missed opportunity. In various cells throughout the prison, some inmates share their fantasies of finding the serenading disc jockey with their cell mates.

"Monster," Violet giggles through her exasperation. "You are incorrigible."

"I know." The DJ confirms with satisfaction.

"But how will they know they got me? It's not like we have our photos up on our websites."

"Don't worry about that my dear deadite, I figured that out already. When they find you, they have to approach you and name the song playing exactly at the time they find you. If it is you they are approaching, you will call the station with their name, and we will get their swag to them."

"Well, now I guess I have to be there." Violet resigns.

"Which transitions us nicely into our next track," Violet says, her voice momentarily glitching, warped and digitized, for a second.

"What the hell was that?" Monster laughs. "Either Violet's possessed, or we are getting a call from beyond the grave."

The static smooths. Violet's voice returns, cool and composed. "Here's God Dethroned with 'Under a Darkening Sky.' A love song to societal decay."

The song begins and, before the lyrics start, Monster concludes, "Here's hoping that Violet sees you out there, cadavers."

Guitar shrieks from the tiny speaker. The inmates nod in rhythm, some mouthing lyrics, others simply feel the noise vibrate through their ribs.

03 – READY TO GO

The sun beats down on the dusty field beside the Walla Walla County Fairgrounds. Pop-up tents ripple in the breeze, and the smell of corn dogs, cotton candy, and sunscreen hangs thick in the air. Families drift between booths, hands sticky with lemonade and caramel.

Since morning, the stage has been alive with music and scattered announcements. Now, as the sun starts to hang low in the sky, a small group of martial arts students begin setting up off to the side, unrolling mats, arranging gear, and moving through warmups. One of the adults heads onstage to promote the school, while the kids stretch and get loose behind the scenes.

A girl in black workout pants sets down a battered personal stereo and tunes the radio to the Whitman college station, KWCW. The Morgue Radio Show crackles to life, already mid-broadcast.

"How can you listen to that show, DJ?" asks a thick girl with hair in a messy bun. She sits on the grass, pink-faced and scowling, reaching toward her outstretched foot. "They're gross."

DJ shrugs while stretching. She lifts both arms to the sky, then leans sideways until her silky black hair brushes the mat. "I think they're hilarious."

The other girl switches feet with a sigh. "It's all just yelling and noise. The music is growly and smashy." Her nose wrinkles as she watches people meander through the commons; past food stands, toward the bleachers, or aimlessly wandering. "I don't get why the station even lets them in the building."

She climbs to her feet, muttering.

"Lay off her, Rose," says a man in a matching uniform as he hauls an armful of punching mitts and martial weapons from a white van toward their camp near the stage. He sets the gear down with care, revealing a lean frame and fuzzy head with a receding hairline which seems premature for his age. "Not every girl has to like your taste in music."

Rose spins toward him, cheeks flaring pinker than usual. "What the hell is that supposed to mean, Steve?"

A younger man following behind drops another pile of gear onto the grass and joins in with a grin. "You know, your music's the kind you party to. Drink, smoke weed, get wild." His thick glasses slide down his nose as he chuckles.

Steve shoots a warning look at him, but before he can speak, Rose cuts in, copying DJ's stretch with more aggression than grace. "Go to hell, Eric. Jeez."

DJ smiles, her cheeks lifting until her mahogany eyes squint. With hands on her hips, she twists at the waist, back popping softly with each rotation.

"Be nice, you guys," she says, teasing as she transitions into jumping invisible rope, arms swinging for her warm-up. "I just like it, Rose. The hosts crack me up, especially when they argue like an old married couple."

Sweat beads along DJ's hairline, either from the heat or the rising pulse of pre-show nerves. She finally matches the shimmer on the rest of her classmates. "I know the music's heavy, but once you get past the noise, there's some really cool stuff in there. Some of those bands actually have amazing songs."

"Yeah," Rose mutters, "if you're into devil worship and goat sacrifices."

"Actually," Eric cuts in, straightening his glasses, "extreme metal encompasses a wide range of thematic material. Many artists focus on political rebellion, self-awareness, or philosophical detachment from mainstream ideology. Others dive into pre-Christian mythologies, Norse, druidic, or cosmic structures of time, space, and the shadow self..." He pauses. All ten martial artists are staring at him blankly and he blinks. "What?"

The awkward silence lingers, until a small voice interrupts it. "Pardon me."

A petite woman with straight brown hair and slender glasses approaches the group, gently leading a little boy in overall shorts with stark white hair. Her voice is soft, almost shy.

"Excuse me," she says again, this time aiming her words toward DJ, who's still locked in a blank stare at Eric.

The woman taps her on the arm. DJ blinks, refocuses, and offers a warm smile. "Yeah?"

"Are you all going to perform?" the woman asks, gesturing toward the stage beyond the huddle of young martial artists.

DJ nods. "Yeah, we're on right after The Little Theatre's set, probably in about ten minutes." She casually slides her foot over to the mini radio and taps it off with her bare toe, cutting the brutal metal mid-scream.

The woman barely glances at the now-silent stereo. "That's great. Benjy loves watching karate movies, and he's been really excited to see some real martial arts up close."

The mom jiggles the small boy's hand gently. "Boo Boo, say hiya!"

Benjy doesn't respond. His wide eyes are locked on the blonde girl nearby, who's spinning through high axe kicks and heel turns with practiced grace.

"Benjy," the woman says again, coaxing softly, "Hiya!" Still, he gives no response, only quiet awe.

When the blonde girl finishes her final spin and steps back into the circle, the little boy's face lights up. Encouraged by his mother's third gentle prompt, he pumps up one tiny fist, holds her hand for balance, and let's fly three wild kicks, each punctuated with a loud, earnest, "Hiya!"

DJ laughs. "Careful, tiger. Save that for the finale."

Benjy beams and throws his arms into the air. "Hiya!"

The group erupts into laughter and playful applause. A few "aww"s ripple through the crowd, and the mom lifts her chin a little higher, glowing with pride.

"Well, we better go so you can get ready. Thank you," she says, leading her little martial artist away. Benjy waves furiously as they head off.

"I think he's sweet on you, Kay," Rose teases.

The blonde girl blushes, chuckling as she shakes her head.

"I mean, I can see why," a third boy from their team adds with a sly grin, reigniting the awkwardness that had temporarily been banished by Benjy's charm. Kay's blush deepens into crimson and more laughter breaks out, peppered with playful commentary.

"Smooth, Tom," Steve mutters. "Real subtle."

"I'm just saying…" Tom mumbles, tugging self-consciously at his uniform top, but his protest fades as a new member cuts in from right outside the circle, an adult.

Their teacher who they all address simply as Ma'am, is a woman in a crisp black uniform, her dark hair is pulled into a neat braid, walking toward them with purpose. She exhales and surveys the martial arts team gathered around her. The kids, all in matching uniforms, stretching, fidgeting, and practicing.

Rose walks over and kneels beside two girls adjusting their belts. "Keep it tight, Rae," she says, helping with the knot. "If your gi flies open again, Steve's going to lose it."

From across the prep area, Steve looks up from a stack of bo staffs. "Hey! That was one time."

Ma'am grins, watching the students banter. The team's a mix, some new, some seasoned, but they've been working hard. This performance is supposed to be fun, a flashy demo for the fair crowd.

"Hey gang!" she calls out. She claps her hands together, beaming. "You all excited? You're on in just a few minutes!"

The students cheer and bounce to their feet, feeding off her enthusiasm.

"Are we ready?"

"Yes, Ma'am!" they shout.

She cups a hand to her ear. "Didn't quite hear that!"

"Yes, Ma'am!" they roar.

"Much better." Her smile widens. "Now, do you all remember your performance order?"

They give a chorus of nods and affirmations.

"And your gear's all set?"

Another wave of agreement comes from the students.

"Perfect. You've got ten minutes for final checks. Breathe, remember your forms, and whatever you do, don't drop your weapons. Unless you want Eric to lecture you on retention."

Eric, stretching by the fence, salutes with two fingers. "It's not a lecture if it saves lives."

The group burst into laughter while Ma'am returns to the side of the stage, talking to the show coordinator.

As they gather their gear, a distant siren echoes faintly from the highway, but no one reacts. It's the fair, sirens mean nothing here.

DJ shades her eyes and looks out over the crowd. It looks like a good turnout, dozens of families, couples, bored teens leaning against food trucks. At the far end of the grass, a toddler chases bubbles. A pig's squeals can be heard in the direction of the agricultural area.

The atmosphere is vibrant, full of music and movement, but DJ feels something off-kilter, an itch in the back of her brain that something isn't right. She scoffs at the thought and brushes it away.

Rose steps up beside her, arms crossed. "You nervous?"

She shakes her head. "Not really."

Rose glances at her. "That's not your lying face, but it's close."

She chuckles. "Maybe a little."

"Think this'll be the year our school makes it to the big leagues? Are new students going to pour into our school after this demo?" she asks.

DJ looks back out, past booths and banners, through the hum of conversation and the smell of fry oil. "Nah," she says with a grin. "But it's the year we steal the show."

She smirks. "Hell yeah."

Ma'am returns, her energy is electric, and the kids respond, springing to their feet and crowding in close. "We're up. Remember your practice. Watch the edge of the stage. But most of all, have fun out there! Bring it in."

She extends her hand. One by one, the students stack theirs on top until they form a solid circle, shoulders touching, nerves alive, hearts syncing.

Ma'am lowers her voice, steady and clear. "What kind of mind?"

A unified whisper, growing stronger: "A beginner's mind!"

"Why do we train?"

"To learn. To grow. To rise again!"

"What do we bring?"

"Focus! Strength! Respect!"

"And what do we leave behind?"

"Ego, fear, and excuses!"

Their hands burst into the air with a shout. Ma'am beams at them, pride glowing in her eyes. "Alright. Let's go be legends."

The person on the stage announces the school's demo team and the students line up before the crowd. They bow in unison and steps onto the sunbaked stage. The music starts and the crowd leans in. The world keeps turning in small town bliss.

04 – UNLEASHING THE BLOODTHIRSTY

"This heat is killing me."

The ambulance driver mops sweat from his forehead with the sleeve of his uniform. He glares through the windshield at the crawling traffic choking the street behind the Walla Walla County Fairgrounds. Sunlight bakes the asphalt. Pop-up tents and food trucks crowd the horizon. "Not even summer yet," he mutters, "and I'm dying."

The ambulance inches forward, only to stop again. He lurches, then stops, waiting for the rhythm of traffic to become steady. Pedestrians surge across the road in chaotic streams, ignoring signals, ignoring vehicles. They wheel their way between moving vehicles to cross the road and reach their destination, driven by want. They want food, music, novelty. They want to be first. They want what's theirs. They want.

The driver grips the wheel and barks, "Come on, people! Siren's on, that means get the hell out of the way!" He twists the wheel with frustration in a futile attempt to break out from the drudgery of festivity traffic. A woman pushing a stroller shoots him a dirty look before darting between bumpers. He scoffs, watching her shove the stroller through like a shield. Around her and all along the street, most people don't even take their eyes from their cell phones.

Further up Tietan Street, the driver sees a fire engine and two patrol cars, already at the scene he is trying to reach, which provides him both relief and distress. He is thankful there are others on the scene because that suggests it is under control, but he's upset that he's the last one to the call.

He lays on the horn, but the herd of fairgoers give it as much heed as they do the siren, and because the street is lined

"

with parked cars, the drivers in front of him have no place to pull over.

It takes a grueling crawl through the festival mess before Danny finally reaches the Jobsource parking lot which is oddly empty for a day like this. He knows why, the caution tape is also a dead giveaway.

Emergency vehicles barricade the entrance, their hulking frames positioned to block people hunting for fair parking. Police cruisers and fire engines form a makeshift wall, shielding something on the other side. Something big.

Danny steers the red-and-white rig into the lot and tucks it alongside the vacant fire engine, adding his piece to the improvised screen. Before the vehicle fully settles into park, he's out, with his black duffel bag in hand. A second EMT jumps from the rear doors, having silently prepped the patient area.

Danny doesn't stop to check in. He already knows where to go, past the blockade, and around the fire truck, but as he rounds the engine, a firm pair of hands plants against his chest. A uniform, Officer Ramirez. "Whoa, Danny. Hold up, buddy."

Another officer, Spreitzer, points at the EMT behind him. "Him too. Just…wait."

Danny's brow knits with impatience. "I'm needed," he snaps, trying to slip past. The officers shift with him, blocking his path with practiced ease.

"Yeah," Spreitzer nods, the muscles in his jaw tight. "We know. But…"

Danny squints past them, trying to peer around the firetruck. "Ramirez. Spreitzer. What the hell's going on? Let me through." He tries again to move, and again, is denied.

Spreitzer steps closer. His voice flattens. "Look, Dan…what you're about to walk into, it's bad." He exhales slowly. "Real bad."

Danny stiffens, one shoulder rolling under the weight of the duffel. "I know bad. I've been an EMT for years."

Ramirez shifts his stance. "Yeah, well…this is worse. Like, worse than any training video. Way worse."

Behind them, a third officer physically blocks the second EMT, staring him down with a silent shake of the head.

Danny gives the duffel a sharp jerk. "Yeah, okay. Gruesome. Got it. Now can I do my job?"

The two officers exchange a look. Neither finds the answer they want, only mirrored uncertainty. Finally, Spreitzer exhales. "Okay, bud. But don't say we didn't warn you."

They step aside, Ramirez following with a silent nod. Danny and his partner move past, skirting the edge of the fire truck, and then they see it.

A wrecked SUV, half-buried in the overgrown bushes at the far edge of the parking lot. Though the area around the vehicle seems mostly undisturbed, the vehicle is riddled with crumpled siding, shattered taillights, and a luggage rack dangling from the side. Danny slows and looks around the lot for anything that might have caused this much damage.

The rear side window is cracked in a spiderweb pattern, each line ready to turn skin into ribbons. The back glass is intact, but smeared over, thick with something dark and gelatinous. As he steps closer, the Brown-black sludge reveals red hues.

The stains glisten in the sun and as the paramedics close in on the wreckage, shapes in the smear become recognizable of dragged handprints and half-formed face prints. Someone inside, more than one, was clawing, pressing, pleading.

His head swims and the air turns syrupy. With each step toward the wreckage, the stench sharpens, sickly sweet and rotten, like spoiled fruit soaked in copper. His throat seizes. Years on the job haven't dulled that reflex. He stops, pulls a cloth from his uniform, and covers his face. He takes one breath, then another.

Through the smears, he sees them. Bodies, large and small, but not still.

"Hey!" Danny yells over his shoulder. "Hasn't anyone tried prepping these people?"

Ramirez calls back from behind the fire engine. "What's the point? They're all dead."

Danny shakes his head and mutters. "Didn't know dead people could move!" Then, he says louder for his partner, "Let's get them out."

He rounds the back corner of the SUV, skirting the gas cap, heading for the rear driver-side door. His partner moves to the opposite side. Every window is smeared with streaks of blood, spittle, and something else, something thick and pinkish, coating the glass like jam gone rancid.

Danny grabs the warped handle and shouts back again, "They're definitely not all dead! Maybe learn how to do your job."

"There was nothing moving when we got here!" Ramirez defends. "Hell, there wasn't enough of 'em left to move!"

What the hell does that mean? Danny tries finessing the bent door handle, wedging the twisted metal tab back into the frame. It clicks, but the latch refuses to budge. He leans closer, squinting through the grime-caked window in search of the lock mechanism.

It's jammed. Bloodied. He opens his bag to dig for tools. "Don't move," he mutters, but his hands are trembling. Something isn't right. It's Too quiet. Too still…until it isn't.

Something bangs against the door. The glass jolts under a sudden blow from the inside. Danny flinches, heart punching his ribs.

A mangled hand with three missing fingers slaps against the window. Blood seeps from open knuckles, not pumping, but oozing. A shard of bone juts from the wrist and scrapes a long, shrill line down the glass.

Danny recoils, swallowing hard. The hand slumps, leaving behind a fresh smear in the muck. "Oh Jesus," he gasps.

He lunges forward, yanking his bag open and digging through gear. "There's a survivor in there! I told you, dammit!"

Rescue workers crowd in behind Danny, confusion etched across their faces. He wedges the flat end of his bar into the SUV's door frame and leans hard, using the vehicle for leverage. The door groans while the metal bends.

Danny shouts through the grime-fogged window, "Hang on! I'll have you out in a second. Just stay calm!"

With practiced effort, he pops the locking mechanism, hooks the interior handle, and yanks the door open wide. The stench hits with a pungent sting. It rolls out in thick, choking waves, a mixture of burnt wiring, rancid meat, and sewage.

From the open door, sludge spills out and a filthy stew of bodily fluids, crumpled receipts, straw wrappers, half-digested food and something unidentifiable sloshes to the asphalt. A Smiley Snacks wrapper catches the air and flutters into the wind.

Danny doesn't stand a chance. He turns and retches hard into his cloth mask, the vomit pours out from the sides and spills across the pavement. It splatters on the hot tar with a wet hiss. Behind him, other emergency personnel recoil. A few gag, and one doubles over, adding his own contribution to the mess.

While the responders are unable to compose themselves, there is movement at the wreck. Bodies erupt from the SUV like pressure escaping a boil. The first out is a redheaded woman, scrambling over the driver, her face torn and jaw half-exposed. She leaps onto Danny's back, snarling, arms clamping down with inhuman strength.

An older man follows, missing an arm, his remaining hand clawing for purchase. He crashes into Danny, dragging all three of them to the ground with a wet, gargling moan.

More spill out, nearly half a dozen, including a young boy covered in bite marks and torn flesh, crawling, stumbling, and sprinting from the SUV with blood-slick lips curling back over gray teeth.

They slip and fall but they don't hesitate. The passengers lunge toward the responders who are reeling from the stench. Uniformed men and women frozen mid-vomit are tackled, clawed, bitten. Screams from the responders and the accident victims pierce the air.

Ramirez is the only one of the emergency responders still free standing, the only one taking full witness of the horrors unfolding before him. He fumbles for his sidearm, eyes locked on a massive woman barreling toward him, nightgown soaked with filth, flesh splitting across her arms.

He raises the pistol, hands trembling. "Stand down!" he shouts, voice cracking, breath sharp with fear. He knows it won't be enough.

The massive woman doesn't slow. She barrels toward Ramirez, arms outstretched. He fires, once, twice, three times. Chunks of blackened flesh burst from her chest and belly, but she keeps coming. He tries to move, to sidestep the oncoming collision, but it is too late.

She crashes into him, a forceful wall of reeking mass and raw momentum. They slam to the pavement, and his breath is knocked from his lungs. She's on top of him before he can scream. Her thick, drooling mouth buries into his chest, tearing through fabric, through skin. She bites deep, causing Ramirez to convulse and howl.

His hands push against her, but his efforts are useless. Her fingers bloated and stained, pry into his mouth, wrenching his cheek wide. The other hand lands hard on his abdomen, pinning him in place while she feasts on his chest.

Across the lot, a firefighter kicks the child attacker off his bloodied leg and limps toward the fire engine's open cab. He never sees the next threat, until it's too late.

A small, older woman with a shredded blouse and skin striped revealing deep cuts jumps on him from behind. Her body collides with his back, driving him forward a step before he stumbles but stays upright, barely.

The child returns, tiny hands clamping around the man's uninjured leg. One of the boy's arms is half-skeletal. He clutches the leg with both tiny hands and sinks needle-like baby teeth into the calf, severing muscle in a single jerk, bringing the firefighter to collapse.

The woman atop him plunges her face into his neck, tearing flesh with the ferocity of a starving animal. Her arms snake around his head and wraps one hand into his eye, which she twists. He doesn't scream, not anymore.

All three crumple to the ground twitching while the woman and child feed. All around them, the screams of the living fade and the chaos burns out into silence, broken only by the unyielding wail of the sirens from the vacated vehicles.

Ramirez gasps beneath his devourer, the final breath of a man who died long before his body stopped moving. The silence doesn't last.

One of the dead officers, a weathered man with blood-slicked hands, rises first. He tilts his head toward the wind, toward the fairgrounds.

The others gather, Spreitzer. Ramirez. Danny, and two other firefighters. They stand, broken bodies reanimated, gathering in a slow cluster near the wreck. Others lay sprawled across the pavement, twisted, torn, steaming in the sun.

A breeze cuts across the lot, riding in from the fairgrounds. It carries the scent of sweat, popcorn, the swirling aroma of the living. The wind taunts the half-eaten dead.

They move as one, not in sync but tethered by purpose. Sloppy, shambling, tangled bodies bound by shared instinct, a tattered procession of hunger.

Though the wall of emergency vehicles blocks most outside view, there are gaps, barely enough space for them to push through. Once they do, they run, onto the street, and into the crowd.

The festival traffic crawls with people, families, teens, and sunburnt couples thinking of little more than fair food and rides, all moving toward the festivities.

The dead follow. Whatever the living want, the dead now want too. The scent, the sound, the pulse of the fairgrounds. That single destination drives them forward like blood through muscle.

A few veer off, not out of choice, but by triggered impulse. One lunges for a teenage girl distracted by her friend. Another barrels into an elderly man carrying his wife's purse while she adjusts her sunglasses. Predation with none of the grace, only hunger and velocity.

The crowd screams. Not all at once, but in a ripple. Heads rise from phones, eyes widen, panic spreads faster than the outbreak. The fairgrounds are no longer a destination. They are a trap. And behind it all, the sirens keep flashing.

05 – SOMETHING FOR THE PAIN

Martial arts demonstrations are a staple for small town fairs and today, Walla Walla is no different.

A modest crowd circles the stage at the county fairgrounds commons area, drawn in by the sharp crack of wooden sticks and the coordinated movements of Beginner's Mind, a small, upstart dojo new to the valley.

At the front of the mat-covered clearing, two young men clash in rhythm. Steve and Tom wield long rattan sticks, striking and parrying in perfect flow, an elegant dance of muscle and control, each blow is a precise maneuver. When one scores three clean points, both fighters stop, bow to each other, then turn and bow to the crowd and applause swells from the audience.

From towering speakers flanking the stage, a bright, amplified voice calls out, "Give it up for Steve and Tom, who just performed a flawless demonstration of the Eskrima twelve-count and gave us an amazing impromptu stick match!"

The audience responds with scattered whoops and energetic clapping.

As the men exit stage left, five girls emerge from the opposite side, walking cool and unbothered. Their entrance is well-timed and confident. Behind them, vibrant hot air balloons rise into the sky, an unintentional, majestic backdrop none of the performers seem to notice.

"And now," the announcer purrs, "please welcome Rosey, Kay, Samantha, and our youngest student, Tessa, led by student teacher and drill commander, DJ! It's the girls of Beginner's Mind with their take on the advanced form!"

The crowd shifts and phones rise. The moment is still, then the music hits with an energized beat and electro synth, mixed with rock guitars. The performers ignite into precise action.

They move in perfect sync, their bodies snapping repeatedly from stillness into explosive motion. Each beat triggers a flurry of kicks, blocks, and dramatic turns, part traditional kata, part martial ballet, part Broadway spectacle. The choreography blends ancient technique with modern flair, punctuated by synchronized 'kiai' shouts that echo across the fairgrounds.

As the chorus swells, the girls launch into a set of spinning kicks, rising into the air with ballet-like grace, then landing in unison with one knee down, a fist to the mat, and an arm to the sky with a final, "Kiai!"

The crowd erupts and applause rains down.

DJ dares a glance into the audience and finds them. The little boy from earlier, cheeks glowing, hands clapping excitedly. His mom is beaming beside him, clapping through a teary smile. DJ smiles back and winks at the child.

Then, without a word, the girls rise into their next formation and the music drives on.

The students move with laser focus, their kicks and strikes slicing through the air in rhythm. Synth-heavy beats from the speakers drown out the background noise of traffic and chatter. All eyes remain locked on the mat, entranced by the choreography, and by the vibrant hot air balloons drifting behind the performers, glowing like floating stained glass.

At the far end of the green, behind the gathered crowd, something ruptures. Panic ignites beneath the vendor canopies as a mob of blood-soaked figures burst through the open-walled tents. They smash down tables, tearing through jewelry stands, handmade candles, and artisanal jam. Shrieks pierce the air as these mutilated rioters tackle people with feral strength, biting, ripping, devouring. They don't hesitate, they don't select targets, they simply consume.

Tents collapse under the weight of confusion and violence. Scattered limbs and overturned displays litter the ground. Behind the food trailers, more emerge. Mangled bodies pour between fried food trucks and BBQ pits, slipping on hoses and power cords as they lurch forward, jaws wide. Some sprint, some limp, all are hunting. All are hungry.

They tear into the back of the crowd gathered on the lawn. Screams rise like steam. People turn and phones drop. A child is snatched mid-step. A woman vanishes in a wave of snarling limbs, but on the stage, the girls continue, unaware.

The students spin to face the backdrop of the stage, continuing their form as planned, and strike through the final movements of their routine, performing for a world already ending behind them, believing the volume of the crowd belongs to them.

The swell of destruction reaches the thick of the crowd and everything erupts into chaos. The screams fall silent, some turn guttural. Something cracks, someone vomits, and blood flies. The audience begins to scatter.

The girls perform their last spin and land their final kicks. They freeze, locked in finishing pose, arms raised, chins high, in time to see the sea of brutality.

A hot wind rattles the mic, carrying a squeal of feedback across the fairgrounds.

Tessa is the first to scream. It's high, shrill, and animal, scraping across the air. Kay and Rose lunge toward her, forming a protective circle around the smallest girl. Samantha breaks rank and bolts toward the crowd, screaming for her mother, her eyes locked on a blond woman in pigtails now disappearing under a pack of gnashing teeth.

DJ doesn't move, simply stares. Her eyes scan for a pattern, for anything that makes sense, but nothing does. There are no sides being taken, no one is waving weapons or flashing gang colors. There's no sense at all, only humans tearing each other apart.

Not twenty yards from the stage, a striped hot air balloon dips low, its gondola slamming into the earth and crushing a knot of frantic feeders beneath its weight. A scream cracks from the basket and the pilot shoves a thrashing woman over the edge, her body hitting the ground with a sickening crunch. He clasps his neck, trying to stop the blood oozing through his fingers.

He fumbles with a yellow scarf, tying it tight to staunch the flow. A man sprints toward the sagging balloon, lifting his daughter up into the basket.

The pilot turns, startled, and sees the man climbing in after her. Without hesitation, the pilot punches him square in the face, multiple times, then yanks hard on the burner cord. The propane flame roars to life and the basket rises. He never seems to notice the girl in the basket

The father clings to the side for half a heartbeat, until a swarm of hands tears him off mid-ascent. He falls hard, and the crowd consumes him before his body fully lands. His screams end in a wet snap.

The balloon narrowly avoids the branches of two towering pines before floating up, past the reach of the dying.

DJ watches it all, transfixed and horrified. The pilot's trauma, the girl's escape, and the man's fate. She rips her gaze away and scans the field. Tessa, Kay, and Rose are still huddled on the mats. Steve and Eric are shouting, wrestling gear into the van while fending off attackers.

Then she sees them. Benjy, wailing in the crowd, his little arms flailing toward his mother. She is screaming and thrashing, locked in a tug-of-war with a man twisted in blood and madness, his fingers knotted in her hair. DJ's paralysis shatters and she bolts, leaping off the stage, racing to the mother and child. She drives her forearm upward, shattering the attacker's elbow from underneath with a loud pop. The man crumples, howling.

"You okay?" DJ barks, grabbing the mom by the shoulder.

The mom scoops Benjy into her arms, dazed. "Son of a biscuit, that hurt!"

DJ sidekicks another attacker in the gut, sending him flying into a knot of flailing bodies. "This way!" she shouts, turning the woman and gently shoving her toward the mats. "Go! That van's our only shot!"

The mom stumbles toward the stage, clutching her child. DJ hangs back far enough to protect their retreat. She spins on her heel and intercepts two assailants, deflects the wrist of someone trying to grab her, redirects another with an elbow trap, and slams a third with a brutal palm strike to the sternum.

Yet another attacker grabs her shoulder. She pivots and hurls him over her hip in a clean judo throw, sending him crashing to the ground.

"Rose! Kay!" she screams. "Get Tessa in the van! Move!"

Steve and Eric charge in with another teen boy, rushing the girls toward the van. Kay shoves the sliding door open and the boys hoist Tessa up. The third boy screams as a cluster of infected slams into him, their teeth flashing and hands clawing at the youth. Strips of hair and flesh peel away from his skull as he drops, twitching. One of the things bites straight into his neck and his scream becomes a wet gargle.

"DJ!" Steve bellows, "Let's go! Now!"

DJ glances toward the van, at the wall of gnashing bodies, at Benjy's terrified face in his mother's arms. She catches up with the mom. "We have to go, come with us!"

The mother stares wide-eyed at the field of carnage devouring the fairgrounds, she is shaken by the screams, snarls, and bone-cracking violence. Her mouth opens, but no words come. The taste of fear clings to her teeth and sears her sinuses. "I…" she starts.

"Come on." DJ grabs her arm and pulls her forward.

A blood-slicked attacker lunges in, but DJ ducks beneath the swing, slides her arm under his, and drives her palm into the assailant's chin. His teeth shatter and his head jerks back. Before he can recover, she strikes again, her hand slicing down into his throat. He drops, choking on his own breath.

The van roars to life behind them, coughing smoke from the tailpipe.

"DJ, move!" Steve's voice cuts through the chaos. "Let's go!"

The mother scrambles forward and DJ leads her toward the open cargo doors. She lifts Benjy high and the little boy screams as he's pulled into the van by waiting arms. He reaches to stay connected to his mom while she tries to climb after him, but the van lurches forward.

"No!" she cries, reaching. The older boys grab and yank her in as the tires roll.

DJ starts to run for the back doors, but she's cut off. A dozen violent hands shoot from the chaos, gripping her arms, her belt, her shirt. She swings hard, kicking, blocking, and throwing elbows. But there are too many. She disappears beneath a tangle of flailing limbs and gnashing teeth.

"DJ!" Eric screams.

Steve doesn't hesitate. He leaps from the van and charges into the swarm. He punches one in the face, kicks another in the shin, rips bodies away from the mass. For a moment, it looks hopeless, until he spots DJ curled on the asphalt in a defensive crouch, slamming her heels and elbows into anything that gets too close.

"I've got you!" he roars.

Together, they fight, backs pressed together, meeting the onslaught with bone-snapping rhythm. More figures close in, too many to handle, they defiantly brace for the end.

Then, there's a shift, one of the crazies stumbles backward, and another. Something crashes into the pack with precision, a blur of black uniform and sharp, practiced motion slices through the mob. Their teacher, Ma'am.

The black belt carves a path of pain through the attacking crowd, spinning, striking, and disabling with mechanical beauty. Her face is a mask of fury and focus while her fury carves an opening for the teens.

"Get to the van!" she shouts, dropping a brute with a spinning elbow. She slows the pressing wall of violent bodies to cover their retreat, but others fill in from the sides, creating a blood drenched rift between teacher and students. "Go! Now!"

"Not without you!" DJ yells over an increasing number of hungry heads.

"All of us," he agrees, defiant. "We leave together."

"No!" Ma'am launches into the air, the hem of her uniform snapping in the wind. A full-leg tattoo, a tangled tree, flares into view as her heel crashes down into an attacker's skull. The force jars her focus, but she steadies herself.

"I promised..." she growls, pivoting with fury. "I promised your parents I'd protect you! So go!" Her leg whips sideways, catching an aggressive elderly woman mid-lunge, sending her tumbling.

"But what about you?" DJ cries out, driving a series of straight punches into the chest of a wide man. The blows shove him backward into the waiting arms of other snarling lunatics.

"Don't sweat it," Ma'am calls over her shoulder, flipping a screecher from her hip onto the torn grass. "I'll be right behind you."

"No way, Ma'am!" Steve blocks a reaching hand, locks the elbow, and shatters a nose with a brutal strike. "I've seen too many war movies. That line means we'll never see you again!"

Ma'am grunts out a sharp laugh as she sidesteps another charge. "I've almost got an opening over here. We'll meet at the dojo, it's only a few blocks from here."

A tangle of greedy arms seizes her sleeves and belt, yanking her backward. She drops low, slithers through the hold, and lets her uniform top slip free. The hands rip cloth, but not flesh, and a few attackers tumble from the loss of grip. Clad now in a black tank top, she straightens with a defiant fire in her eyes.

"Once you're out, I'll give these crazies the slip," she shouts. "Nothing's stopping me over a few blocks. Now respect your teacher, Go!"

DJ mule-kicks a gangly woman reaching for her hair. Her eyes lock on Ma'am's. Doubt flickers. Then the teacher winks and grins, sealing a silent promise. "Yes, Ma'am!" DJ yells, grabbing Steve's shoulder.

Steve nearly rolls her reflexively before realizing who it is. Together, they sprint after the van, now dodging bodies and swerving toward the exit. The side door is open and Tom waves at them to hurry and catch up.

A flash of light to the side of the teens alerts Steve and he tackles DJ mid-stride, both tumbling to the pavement as a runaway ambulance blasts past, its metal frame barely missing them. Wind lashes DJ's leg as the behemoth barrels forward, smashing through food stalls and sending a kite of sparks into the air.

They scramble to their feet. Their dojo van swerves ahead, still reachable. The duo runs, not looking back. They don't see their teacher break from the fray, teeth gritted, fists swinging. They only run, because that's what Ma'am told them to do.

"Why did I even say yes to this?" Winston mutters to the battered table in front of him as he slumps into a creaky, well-worn chair. His right hand flops onto the tabletop, jostling a nearly empty coffee can and a wobbly, hand-painted Phi Beta Lambda sign that quivers like it's had too much caffeine. He exhales sharply and glances around the crowded pavilion.

People drift from one booth to the next, oblivious to each other, their eyes glazed with fair fatigue. Tiny display tables are packed together like prisoners, each offering something and each fighting for a scrap of attention. Winston picks absently at the signup sheet in front of him.

As time slogs on, picking becomes scribbling and Winston gradually tortures the sheet with the bored precision of a man dismantling a paperclip during a long phone call. He nudges a forgotten roll of raffle tickets out of the way, pushing it toward a dented cash box where it sulks in neglect. His fingers work the page like it owes him something, thumbs digging at the corners as if extracting confession from pulp and ink.

"Hey Win." The voice floats above his blond faux hawk. He doesn't react.

"Hey, Win." This time, the table jolts as a hand, not his, claps down, snapping him upright.

Across from him stands a petite woman in fashionable denim overalls that hugs her curves with practiced precision. Silky black hair frames her face and spills over her shoulders. Winston's expression snaps from startled to bright. "Hey Miku. What's new?"

"Just wandering the fairgrounds, soaking up the weird and wonderful," she says, waving a hand toward his sad little table. "What's all this?"

"Oh. It's a fundraiser for the business club." He taps the dull red raffle reel and manages a half-smile. "Want to buy a ticket? All you need is a dollar."

"What do I win?" she asks, raising an eyebrow.

"No prizes," he admits. "You buy tickets and vote for a teacher on the list." He taps the heavily abused paper in front of him. "The one with the most votes has to kiss a pig at graduation. On stage with the whole school watching."

"How...charming." She flashes teeth, but her tone is dipped in sarcasm. "Been a successful afternoon?"

He shrugs, gesturing to the nearly empty pavilion. "Nah. People just drift through like ghosts. Looking at everything and caring about nothing."

"I'm a little surprised to see something like this here," Miku says, gesturing around the pavilion. "Feels like what you're doing is mostly aimed at college students."

"Yeah, I know." Winston leans back in his chair, idly scratching at the scarred tabletop. "But I need to log volunteer hours, so here I am."

"Having taken the same course," she continues, casually propping her hip against the edge of the table, "I can't help but think this is a bad marketing strategy."

Winston's gaze lingers briefly, how the ledge presses into her perfect curve isn't lost on him, but he flicks at the ticket reel with feigned indifference. "Yeah, that thought crossed my mind too."

"So, why are you here then? I mean, what's the point?" She tries to sound curious, but the undercurrent of condescension bleeds through her polished tone. Miku has never noticed how obvious her superiority complex is, but Winston has.

"It was a club decision," he says with a sigh, bored with the dance.

"Oh?" Her mock surprise doesn't even attempt to be subtle. "The club chose this location? How forward-thinking."

"Yep." He leans forward, resting his arms on his knees. "And, because the club votes, we go with the majority decision." He pauses to smile and wave at a passing woman in a gray suit. "This fundraiser happens every year. The committee wanted to try something different, go public, boost visibility, maybe even draw in new members. Give the club a bit of a face."

Miku straightens, pushing off the table into her practiced power stance. "I guess that makes sense."

Before Winston can respond, a speeding ambulance bursts through a wall and rips the world of the pavilion open. The floor vibrates, then howls with an ear-shattering roar as the rig tears through the walkway, followed by a rolling concussion that peels paint from the walls and shakes loose mortar. Collapsible chairs flip and displays explode. A surge of dust, debris, and shrieking chaos stampedes across the opening, launching wood splinters, trash, and shattered cement in all directions.

Winston jerks upright in time to be slammed back into his chair. His vision doubles and his ears ring. The air tastes scorched. He tries to rise, only to find he has been pinned in place. A jagged steel rod has driven clean through his left knee and into the wooden floorboards beneath him, impaling him like an insect on cork.

The realization crawls up his spine in delayed horror. His breath comes in sharp, involuntary gasps as nausea coils behind his ribs. He stares at the embedded metal, wishing it to be a dream, but knowing it isn't.

Miku lies several feet away, blasted off her feet. She slowly gathers her legs beneath her and pushes upright, one hand gripping the floor, the other instinctively finding her hip. Her movements are shaky, but she's alive. Her hair, streaked with gray dust, spills debris as she rises. "Oh my god…" she mutters, barely audible beneath the rumble of settling destruction.

Winston gingerly reaches toward his impaled leg, fingertips brushing where steel meets flesh. His voice comes thin, strained: "Miku! Are you okay?"

He gives the rod a tentative pull, pain explodes up his leg through a detonated nerve, and the world whites out. Sweat beads on his forehead as he lets out a guttural moan.

Miku rights herself, trying to respond, when a blur of motion crashes into her. A tangle of ragged bodies with flailing limbs barrel through the settling dust, slamming Miku to the floor a second time. This time, she doesn't rise.

She's pinned beneath two bodies, one is a man in a scorched apron from the food booth, and the other is the gray-suited businesswoman Winston waved at minutes earlier. The vendor straddles Miku's legs and yanks her right hand to his torn face, clamping down with a gaping, exposed jaw. She screams.

The woman in the business suit props herself up on Miku's shoulders, staring down at her with blood-glossed eyes. The woman's mouth twitches into something that might have once been a smile and, with a head tilt like a broken marionette and a piggish grunt, she descends, mouth open, teeth gnashing.

Winston jolts. "Oh shit!" He grabs the rod and yanks, barely dislodging the bar from the floor. Agony rockets through his body, stopping his breath and curling his stomach into knots. His hands freeze on the metal, sweat slicking his palms. He can't look away from the scene playing out under the strobing emergency lights.

The suited woman lifts her head from Miku's face with a wet, sucking sound. Flesh clings to her teeth and Miku's cheek meat stretches like melted taffy. It finally tears loose and flings a red arc across her jaw and neck.

That image breaks the paralysis and Winston rips at the metal rod again. There is more pain, worse now, but he works more of the rod through his leg. His stomach heaves and this time, he can't stop it, vomit splashes across the toppled table in front of him.

The apron-wearing vendor keeps thrashing at his victim. He raises his skeletal fingers high, then stabs them into Miku's stomach, tearing through denim and parting flesh. He plunges his arm deep inside her abdomen, twisting until his elbow disappears into the wound, then pulls back with a handful of glistening intestines.

Rubbery strands slip between his fingers and slap against her hip and thighs. He gnashes down with cracked teeth, shredding the loops of flesh like overcooked pasta.

Winston retches again, the convulsion echoing through the ruined pavilion.

The sound draws the vendor's attention. He drops what's left of Miku and bolts forward, lurching with inhuman hunger. Winston, still pinned, frantically works the rod. His arms shake and his vision tunnels from the pain. The post rocks side to side but won't dislodge.

The man is nearly upon him so he braces his good foot against the table and kicks. The pain is unbearable and his body screams in protest, but the rod pops free from the wood of the chair. With a cry that breaks into sobs, Winston tumbles backward, the bloody rod skewering his leg. He tries to stand, but his leg collapses under him. He scrambles, dragging himself toward a nearby staircase.

Behind him, the cannibal cook crashes into the now-vacant chair. Winston flips onto his back and scoots away as the snarling monster rushes again. Winston has no choice and no time, he grabs the rod jammed through his knee, points it at his attacker, and braces.

The apron-clad man leaps and Winston braces for impact. The rod drives through the man's chest with a sickening crunch that vibrates down to Winston's knee. Ribs snap, tissue parts, and the pole erupts from the attacker's back, crowned with gore. He doesn't stop, though. The cook grabs the impaling rod with both hands and begins to pull himself forward, sliding himself relentlessly toward the college student.

Winston's arms shake. "You've got to be kidding me…"

The added weight on the pole makes Winston's escape impossible. He stops trying to pull the rod out and instead wedges it against the stairwell's edge, scooting closer to the steps. Bone grinds and muscle splits. Slowly, the bar pushes forward through his knee, meat and splinters of bone squeezing out with it.

But as the crazed man clambers down the pole toward him, the rod begins to shift, listing to the side under the strain. Winston reflexively shoves it away, which he immediately realizes is a big mistake.

The movement tears what's left of the tendons tethering his shin to his leg. The sound is splitting rope, leaving everything below his knee hanging on by little more than a resilient strand of flesh. With a howl of agony, Winston watches as the cannibal cook topples off the pole and crashes to the side in a heap of flailing limbs.

The suited woman's head snaps up and blood runs down her jaw like jelly from a sandwich. She rises without using her hands, knees locked, and head cocked at an unnatural angle.

Winston watches in stunned silence, until something worse happens. Miku stirs, then sits up, and finally, stands.

Her face is half gone. Her stomach is open, glistening intestines hang in loops from the hole in her abdomen, swaying as she begins to walk.

"No," Winston breathes.

Panic floods him. He twists and flops his broken leg behind him, dragging himself up the stairs to the pavilion's upper level, anything to get away. Behind him, the two monsters follow.

The pavilion erupts again, this time not from violence, but from the hysterical flood of incoming would-be rescuers. Screams rise from all corners as concerned citizens pour into the room. One woman in a floral print summer dress barrels down the stairs clutching a water bottle and a box of Kleenex, racing toward the suited woman, thinking she needs first aid. Two other attackers tear into her before she gets within five feet.

Winston keeps climbing, four steps from the top.

He hears the snarl before he sees it, the impaled vendor is back, storming up the steps with a bull's rage, hands outstretched, blood dripping from his apron. Winston claws forward, step by step. The cannibal grabs his flopping leg and yanks.

He screams. Pain is replaced by something colder, numbness. His ruined nerves don't register the bite anymore, only the weight pulling him down. He thrashes and kicks as the tension grows unbearable.

He turns to his back near the top stair and kicks at the cook with his good leg. He kicks again, this time, hitting the metal rod protruding from his attacker. The pole flips into the air, twisting the cook upright and backward, sending him tumbling down the stairs, clutching at the rod poking through his chest. Winston makes it to the top, sobbing. He sees only one way out, the blown-out second story window. He crawls through it to the overhang, bleeding, broken, and his heart sinks when he realizes the world outside is no better.

Chaos has spilled into the streets below. Bodies race, people scream, some fight, some flee. All of them are hunted.

To his right, a large white shuttle van slams into a gray pickup at the fairground's main exit. The truck flips end over end, crushing a stream of pedestrians before smashing into the entrance gate. The van veers sharply left, crashing through the wooden fence at the lot's edge. Right beneath Winston.

He watches from above as the van's windshield explodes outward, ejecting the driver and front passenger like ragdolls onto the road. They slide across the asphalt and stop, one doesn't move, and the other bleeds out silently.

Moments later, others climb out through the shattered opening. They help each other. No one gets left behind.

Winston's heart hammers. They're together and they're alive. They're his only chance.

He drops from the pavilion roof onto the top of the van. The impact sends a bolt of pain through his fresh stump, and he screams.

Below, the group is already sprinting across the street, heading toward the middle school beyond the tennis courts. Winston scrambles to the edge of the van. "Wait! Please!"

Winston yells again, "Please help!" he is alone, his life pouring out his leg onto the white van's roof. He knows he's dead, realizing no one will escape, and yet, he clings to a shred of fleeting hope when one of the girls manages a glance over her shoulder while running away. She slows and stares at him. Winston waves frantically, but she turns back and catches up to her group.

07– DARK SIGNS

Behind prison walls, dinner has been served and devoured. Some offenders are assigned to clean-up the cafeteria while the rest retreat to their cellblock's common areas for social time. A number of inmates prefer their individual cells so they can read or write, some of these residents click their radios on and tune in to their favorite broadcast.

"Welcome cadavers, to the Saturday night bloodbath that is the Morgue Radio Show!" The snarling voice punches through the small speakers throughout many cellblocks, filling them with chaotic energy. Laughter and jeers echo from the prison tiers as inmates hoot and whistle at the familiar intro.

"We've got a killer show planned tonight, brutal metal tracks, and grisly world news from our own Butcher!" The voice, known to fans as Monster, spits his enthusiasm with theatrical flair. "Oh, and for you bloodhounds at the Walla Walla Balloon Stampede, our roving reporter and busty mortician Violet is on the prowl! Spot her and win a metal CD from our musical tomb!"

Canned applause blasts through the airwaves, chopped off by a sharp audio click.

"Alright, cadavers, the night is young, the sky is growing dark, and in the studio tonight are all the freaks who make this show the spectacle it is. Yours truly is here, obviously, and our butcher of broken news, Butcher! Say hi."

"Hey." The voice is flat and gravelly.

"And we've got a full graveyard tonight. Back from the dead, it's Goblin. Stop drooling on the board, man!"

A new voice gives a chuckle. "What's up."

Monster continues introductions, "Blade is here with her beastly bodyguard, Ogre. Blade, maybe don't sharpen that knife by my head, though."

There are no words, only a grunt, deep and primal.

"The Morgue's own cursed couple, Fresh and Meat."

"Hi, Monster!" chirps Fresh, her bubbly tone jarringly upbeat.

"And finally, as promised, our own returning audio assassin… Ninja. What's up, Ninja?"

"Not much." The man gives a breathy, half-whistled reply.

Monster groans. "Seriously? I just hyped you all up and that's what I get?"

Half-hearted protests and chuckles rise from the group, but no real line of defense is drawn apart from Fresh who makes note of her own enthusiasm.

"Alright, except Fresh. At least you brought something. The rest of you? You're fired, get out!"

Laughter bounces around the mics. "You can't fire us," Goblin shoots back. "None of us work here."

"Yeah, we're all volunteers, including you," Butcher adds dryly.

"Po-tay-to, po-tah-to," Monster mumbles. "Look, remember, this is radio. Sound like you're waving!"

There is a momentary flicker of silence, broken only by Monster's next outburst, "Oh hey! First call of the night." Monster clicks the line to reveal crackling background noise. "This is the Morgue Radio Show, you're on with Monster."

Frantic, panicked noise surges through the radio speakers.

"Whoa, little fella, turn down your radio. I'm getting hellacious feedback."

Amid the garbled chaos, one voice punches through, "Oh my god! Oh god!"

"Yeah, you got me. Direct line to God. Are you calling because you found Violet, or just want to sing my praises?"

"Help me! Please God, help me! I'm stuck…"

Monster leans into sarcasm. "Sounds kinky. You find a knothole or something more in the agricultural side of the fair?"

"They don't, they don't see me yet. I need to get out! How do I get out, man?"

"How the hell should I know? You calling for a song request or what?"

A scream, raw and real, fills the speakers. "Ow! Son of a bitch bit me!" Then, the line drops, with a click.

Monster exhales, unfazed. "Well. That was colorful. Folks, you heard it here. Reminder, cadavers, we're not your emergency line. Don't call us for your bedroom accidents."

Butcher cuts in, voice low, flat. "That wasn't an accident, that was survival."

Monster fumbles with the mic, static buzzing. "Right, right. Survival. Which means lines are open so, if you're breathing and not bleeding out, give us a ring."

A radio silence follows Monster's impromptu PSA, until he snaps at his cohosts, "What?"

"What do you mean what?" Fresh's cuts in, shaken. "That sounded like a real emergency!" Other voices murmur agreement.

"If it was a real emergency," Monster insists, "he should've called 911. Last I checked, we're not the same number."

Inside the prison cell, the cheap speaker pops and fizzles before the show continues. A couple of inmates chuckle, but one man, tall, tightly wound, with eyes like knapped glass, leans forward on the edge of his metal chair. "Damn, you think that was legit?"

"Everything sounds real to you, Anderson," grumbles his cellmate, a burly, tattooed man who hasn't looked up from his chessboard. "Monster's always pulling crazy shit. It was probably a movie clip or someone he had call in."

"I don't know, Bartholomew," Anderson whispers. "That sounded pretty real."

The radio kicks back in and the speaker spits another snarl of laughter from the Morgue crew, followed by a guttural burst of noise, a grindcore song too harsh to be intelligible. The music causes the inmates to hoot, and one begins moshing alone in the corner of his cell.

The crackle of the radio jumps in pitch and the song stops less than a minute in, snatching the attention of every inmate within earshot. A breathless shriek cuts through the music. "...Oh man! Oh holy shit!"

Heads rise from bunk pillows and cards pause mid-game to listen. That unsettled voice, Violet's, doesn't sound like her usual velvet-and-vinegar self. She's breathless, jumbled, almost manic. Another burst of sound follows, overlapping voices, creating a chaotic mess of live mics when they shouldn't be.

On-air, Monster responds to the interruption, his voice deeper, trying to reel it in. "Welcome home, Violet. But aren't you supposed to be out there trying to give all my music away?"

A sharp thump, maybe a door slamming, followed by her barked reply, close to the mic, "Get that mic out of my face!" This draws the curiosity of even the most skeptical inmate.

She's panting, hard and desperate. The kind of breath that comes from outrunning something dangerous. "Oh my god, Monster... oh jeez..."

In the background of the radio, a voice, not hers, rumbles low, drifting away from the mic, "Someone following you? You alright?"

The inmates hear another door slam over the speaker, then quiet.

In the cell, Anderson points at the radio, "How about that? Does that sound staged?"

One cell over, Otero responds through bars, "I think Anderson's right, man. This might be real!"

Monster's voice returns, closer and clipped. "Butcher, cut us to music for a minute, will ya?"

Shuffling sounds emit from the speaker, and what sounds like plastic CD cases clapping together issues before dead-air panic. "Sure thing, Monster. Anything specific?"

"No, man. Just kill us."

There is another pause in the broadcast, then, "Wait." Violet again, breathy but firm.

The room on the other end of the radio falls silent, dead silent. Even the inmates stop breathing.

Then a soft crackle, like fabric brushing a mic. Violet speaks again, her voice is clear now, controlled, and tightly wound with dread. "If you are listening to this…do not go to the fairgrounds."

08– BALLS TO THE WALL

A few blocks north of the Walla Walla County Fairgrounds, the evening is calm, punctuated only by the sizzle of barbecue and the clink of ice in plastic cups.

"Damn, George. Maybe we should be over there," the man in khaki shorts says, raising his half-empty beer toward the commotion beyond the back fence. Sirens echo faintly in the distance, chased by scattered pops and crowd noise. "Sounds like a riot."

George, a broad-shouldered man built thick as a refrigerator in flip-flops, chuckles as he turns back to the grill. "Don't sweat it, brother. I told you, my backyard's the best seat in the house for the night glow. You get the lights without the lines, and the only people you're bumping into are the ones you choose." He grins as he sets his tongs on a spice-smeared tray and pulls a phone from his cargo pocket. His lips move silently while he reads the screen.

"Speaking of which," he grins, big and wolfish, "The girls just pulled up out front." He claps his meaty hands together to close his phone and does a half bounce on his heels.

"Really?" A skinny dark-haired guy at the patio table springs up, nearly knocking over his drink. "I, uh…I think I'll go see if they need a hand." He rakes a hand through his hair, adjusts his collar, and throws a smirk over his shoulder.

The two older guys sitting at the bench with him burst out laughing. He freezes mid-strut, strikes a pose, eyebrow cocked giving off dollar store Brad Pitt vibes. "What?"

No one answers, so he sprints for the sliding door and disappears into the house.

"This kid…" The bald man mutters.

"You think that's funny Chris?" George chuckles, pointing his wobbly steel spatula at the open glass door. He grins, lifting his beer. "You ought to see the stuff Brian does on social media."

Chris glances at the guys at the table, looking for clues, when they shrug, he looks back to George, "What? What's he do?"

George leans in, lowering his voice enough to make it sound conspiratorial. "You know all those girls on my friends list?"

Chris nods, wary.

"You know I've hooked up with more than half of 'em."

Chris gives another nod, slow this time.

"Well…" George glances toward the open door to make sure the coast is clear. "Brian goes through the list, my list, and follows every single one."

"What?" Chris laughs.

"That's not all." George's voice drops lower still. "Any time I add a new girl…pow! He's on her profile within seconds. Like some kind of thirsty-ass digital ninja, commenting all over her posts."

"Bullshit!" Chris denounces.

"No, it's true." One of the men at the table defends, "He does it to me too."

The other, older man exclaims, "I'm just glad he doesn't do that with my friend list."

The group laughs and the first man at the table retorts, "That's because all the women on your friends list are old enough to be his grandmother, Darren!"

"Fuck you, Terry." Darren growls, cracking open another beer.

Their laughter cuts short as Brian reappears, swaggering with grocery bags. With game show host bravado, he announces, "Gentlemen, and George," he says with mock ceremony, "I present…the ladies!" He pantomimes the word 'hot' with exaggerated flair as the women follow behind him.

Chris smirks and mouths his own word, 'smooth'.

Behind Brian follows a blonde with an eye-catching smile and proudly displayed cleavage. Her gaze scans the yard and lands squarely on George, who is manning the grill. "Hey big sexy!" she laughs, tiptoeing to kiss his cheek. "Sorry we're late. Ashley didn't know where you lived. We swung by her place so she could follow us here."

George wraps an arm around her shoulder, squeezing just enough to collapse her into him. "I'm glad you made it, Chastity. We were starting to get bored."

As flirtations continue at the grill, a taller, modestly dressed blonde steps out of the house, waves, and drops her bag on the table.

Terry greets her. "Hey, Caroline."

Following her, a thin blonde who looked too young to drink steps into the golden light, a girl in a denim skirt calls out a sweet greeting, and a freckled redhead in a sports jersey brings up the rear. Last in line, a broad-shouldered young man hauls a red picnic cooler through the door and sets it down beside the grill.

"Hope you don't mind I brought my brother Jason," Chastity says. "He's home from WAZU and had nothing else going on tonight."

"No problem," George replies with a nod. "The more the merrier. WAZU, huh?"

"Go Cougs!" Chris hollers from halfway across the yard, raising his beer. The cheer draws a grin from Jason, who throws a quick fist pump back.

Chastity breaks from George and hooks an arm through Caroline's. "Come with me."

"Where to?" Caroline asks.

"Bathroom. Emergency." They vanish into the house.

Jason steps closer to George, lowering his voice. "Hey man, you got another pisser?"

George grimaces. "That little house barely fits the one it's got. Sorry, buddy."

Jason nods toward the fence between the shrubs. "That gate lead to the alley?"

"You can't piss back there, my neighbors will see you!"

"I'll be discreet." Jason waves it off and ambles toward the gate.

Chris watches him go, chuckling. "Kids these days, huh?" He tears his gaze away from the balloons floating in the distance and back toward the grill, then to the blonde in denim.

Darren leans from the picnic table. "What's wrong, Chris? Already forgot what it's like to be young now that you're thirty?"

"Ladies!" Chris cuts him off, lifting his voice. "I don't think we've all met. I'm Chris." His gaze fixes on the younger-looking blonde.

The girls start to reply, but Brian barrels in, pointing at each. "That's Melissa and Rachael." He gestures toward them, then points at the last.

She beats him to it. "I'm Ashley," she says, her liquid blue eyes locked on Chris.

"Yes." He grins. "Yes, you are."

George grins and jabs a spatula in Brian's direction. "Hey Brian, you been surfing my friends list again?"

The rest of the guys chuckle while Brian scowls, flicking his hand dismissively. "Shut up."

George turns back to the grill, trying to maintain control of the flames as the backyard buzzes with separate islands of conversation. Chris and Ashley have nestled into a pair of patio chairs, while Darren, Brian, and Terry engage in a full-on peacocking contest at the table, each vying for dominance like aging lions before a skeptical pride. Rachael and Melissa split their time between being mildly impressed and mockingly amused.

A few minutes into the mingling, Melissa points toward the back gate, her voice uncertain. "Who...is that?"

Terry seizes the chance to flirt. "The only person I see is you." He grins, smooth as sandpaper.

Darren lowers his beer and leans forward, squinting toward the fence. "Uh…" His hand braces against the table as he begins to stand, rising enough to show concern. "George, who the hell…?"

Darren's concern causes heads to pivot and all eyes shift to the broken man crawling through the gate on all fours. He twitches left and right with a slack, sniffing head. He stays hunched, head dragging low, limbs spasming erratically to either side He sways and shudders with disturbing rhythm, a bloodhound catching scent, if that bloodhound had been hit by a truck.

A stunned hush ripples through the backyard, only broken by Rachael's audible gasp. George tries to reassert control, waving his spatula. "Hey buddy, this is a private party. Fairgrounds are that way." He gestures to the street alley and the gate. "Keep on moving, crackhead."

The man-creature jerks his head unnaturally sideways at the sound of George's voice, and behind it, a new terror arrives, scorched hands curl over the gate's edge and yank it open wider. Three more damaged people lurch through the opening in a confused tangle of limbs and ragged clothing. The tension detonates.

Voices crack like glass underfoot and George swings his spatula overhead with trembling bravado. "Hey! You need to get the hell out of here!"

Ashley clutches Chris's wrist, her eyes wide. "Go tell them to leave!"

Chris recoils. "Fuck that! I ain't going over there!" He flings his beer can into the air. It arcs cleanly, trailing a ribbon of frothy spray before cracking against the dog-man's hunched back with a dull thud. "Get out of here!"

The dog-man's shoulders twitch. His body launches upright, dirt and grass scattering. Behind him, others surge forward, bursting through the gate in a chaotic stampede.

Chaos erupts in screams and scrambling limbs as George's guests get up and scatter as the strangers descend upon them.

Chris stumbles back, tangled in Ashley's own frantic scramble, he hits the ground hard. She turns, eyes wide as a pair of mangled arms wrap around her head, lifting her clean off the ground and hurling her over Chris with terrifying ease.

George freezes long enough for the animated remains of a woman to lurch out of the chaos. A third of her face is missing and her abdomen hollowed to the spine. She slashes with manicured claws, missing only because George instinctively staggers back.

He swings and his spatula flashes, the edge slices across her eye, then arcs again, this time lodging in the bone of her cheek. As she falls, dragging the spatula with her, George recoils, stunned by his own brutality.

Behind her, more bodies flood the gate. The dog-like attacker leaps onto the patio table, landing with a wet rip as the flesh at his elbow splits open, exposing bone. Brian shrieks and drops to his knees.

Rachael reacts on impulse, launching a punch that cracks across the creature's jaw, sending him sprawling to the concrete. Another attacker slams into Darren, clawing into his chest with savage precision.

A third wave of intruders from the back gate crashes into George. Jagged fingernails rake across his chest, tearing his shirt and leaving thin trails in his skin. Another swing comes fast, but before it lands, the invader is yanked backward. The new guy, Jason, lifts the attacker in a crushing bear hug and slams him headfirst onto the concrete, the crack echoes.

Chris stares, frozen. Ashley's body is barely recognizable now, two women hunched over her, digging and feeding. The animalistic sounds, wet and sloshing, make him gag. One of the women slurps something from Ashley's open stomach.

His eyes dart to the grill, to the chaos at the table, to the still-open gate and he rationalizes there's no chance of saving anyone. He scrambles backward and disappears through the sliding glass door, slamming it shut behind him.

The assault in the yard collapses further into madness. The dog man lunges forward, grabbing Melissa by the blouse. The fabric tears, buttons flying as his yellowed teeth find the soft flesh of her chest.

Terry reaches for her, but two more figures crash into him, slamming the group to the ground and tipping the table on its side. Brian is exposed, curled and sobbing.

Darren hits the concrete hard, the attacker on top of him pounding into his chest with horrifying force, cracking ribs with each wet thud. Three other mutilated strangers dogpile them.

Another creature lunges at George, digging jagged fingers into his back. Before he can react, Jason snatches the creature by the back of its ragged shirt, yanking it off with brute force. With a roar, he lifts the snarling attacker high overhead and body-slams it down onto the grill. Meat sizzles, some of it human, as flames leap up around the thrashing form. George doesn't hesitate; he slams the lid down, trapping the writhing thing's head inside, severing it from the monster's body, nearly taking Jason's hand off before the younger man can pull free. The grill clangs shut, smoke and blood rising together.

"Jesus Christ…" George spits.

"Come on, man! Let's go!" Jason grabs George by the arm and pulls.

"Fuck that!" George jerks free, pointing with a trembling finger at the patio, which is now a battlefield of tangled limbs and torn clothing. "They need us!"

Jason turns him by his shoulders, locking eyes. "Dude, look at them! They're already gone!" He tugs again. "If we don't move now, we're next!"

"But that's…" George's voice fractures. "Those are my friends…"

More ghouls pour in through the back gate. Jason grabs George with both hands. "You want to die here? Decide now!"

The words snap George into motion and together, they race for the sliding door. "Shit!" George shouts, yanking on the handle. "It's locked!"

"Well unlock it!" Jason barks, glancing back at the swarm closing in. "Let's go!"

"I can't!" George slams his palm against the glass. "Who locked this fucking door?"

The horde surges forward in a wave of flesh and rage. Jason presses his back to George, knowing their options are vanishing fast. The monsters are nearly upon them, blood-smeared faces snarling, cracked teeth bared, when the door suddenly glides open behind them.

Both men tumble backward into the living room and the door slams shut again. Chris throws the lock with shaking hands.

George and Jason scramble to their feet, staring wide-eyed at the glass as a dozen gore-slick hands slap and smear against it. Mouths open and close on the other side like fish sucking at the tank wall. Jason curses under his breath, while George collapses into himself on the floor, his face buried in his hands.

Caroline and Chastity, fresh from the bathroom, emerge from the hallway and Caroline grins, oblivious. "What's up, guys?"

Chastity sees the nightmare pressed against the glass and shrieks, loud and long, shattering the brief illusion of safety.

09 – CHILDREN OF THE DAMNED

Blocks away from the backyard massacre, a door slams shut, rattling the wall as DJ throws the deadbolt with a sharp click. She yanks the shutters down, first on the glass doors, then the front windows, plunging the space into dimness before collapsing against the barricaded entrance, sweat dripping from her brow.

Rose and Kay tumble onto the mats with heavy breaths. Rose starts to cry, silent at first, then louder. Kay can only gasp, voice cracking: "What was that? What the heck happened?"

Benjy wails, piercing and unstoppable. His mother, visibly shaken, tries to distract him, pointing frantically at posters of martial artists frozen mid-kick or strike.

"Shut that kid up," Eric snaps as he stomps past.

"Whoa," Steve says, stepping between them. "Back off, man. They're just scared, I think we all are."

Eric's voice trembles. "No shit, Sherlock!" He reaches for the top shelf of a weapons rack, fingers curling around a sheathed katana. He pulls it down and slides the blade free with a metallic hiss.

DJ watches, alarmed. "What are you doing?"

Her question is drowned by Eric's rising anger. "What's it look like? I'm protecting myself." He jabs a finger toward the toddler. "That noise is going to bring all those crazies here!"

Benjy's mother clutches him tighter, rocking him, whispering soft reassurances into his ear. Her eyes remain locked on the blade. DJ notices the mother's concern and scowls at Eric.

He takes a few awkward swings of the blade, then slides it back into its scabbard. DJ crawls away from the door, pulling herself onto the mats. "Maybe you should put that back, Eric. Ma'am wouldn't be okay with that, and you know it."

"Well Ma'am isn't here right now, and I feel a whole lot better with it than without it." He straps the sword to his waist. "And I'd rather have it than not." He eyes the rack again and reaches for something else. "Don't worry. I'll pay for it."

Steve backs her up. "Hey man, maybe she's right. I mean, we're way past the fairgrounds, someone probably already called the cops, right? This is probably under control by now."

Kay jolts upright. "Oh geez. I gotta call my mom, she's going to freak!" She pats her uniform and her eyes grow wide. "Crap. My phone's in my bag. In the van."

The gravity of the situation hits the students, and they pat down their uniforms and pockets, each one coming to the same grim realization that no one has a phone. Panic flares in the room.

DJ digs through her duffel and finds her cell. She crawls onto the mat and prepares to offer it, but Benjy's mom is quicker to provide. "You can use mine." She swings a dainty purse off her elbow, with the Union Jack emblazoned across it, and digs out a sleek touchscreen phone.

Kay rushes toward her, nearly diving for the device. Steve and Tom aren't far behind, each hoping to hear the voice of home. Eric paces by the door, his eyes dart between the entrance and the weapons rack. He tenses at the sound of a distant siren.

"Don't you want to call your parents?" the mom asks him.

Eric sneers. "I'm nineteen. I don't need to check in."

"What about you?" she asks Rose, who hasn't moved from the center of the mat.

Rose tries to answer, but her words collapse into hiccups and sobs. DJ steps in and explains for her fellow student. "She moved here last summer and doesn't really have family." She hands her phone to Steve.

Kay's fingers hammer the screen as she dials. "Mom? Mom?" Her voice cracks from fear. "I can't. The phone's not working. It's busy or something, or not connecting at all…"

"Can I?" Tom eases the phone from her shaking hand. "My mom was supposed to pick me up right after the demo." He punches in numbers and presses the phone to his scruffy cheek.

While he waits, DJ turns to the woman. "Thanks, miss…"

"Lena," she says, offering a tired smile. She gives DJ a quick wave, then runs her fingers through her child's soft hair, calming the young boy. "And I should be thanking you, for saving us from…"

From the door, Eric snaps, "Everyone shut up. I hear something."

Lena hushes her child and rocks slowly, her cheek resting on his soft hair. Tom cups the phone so the sound of the tones don't echo while he waits for a response. Rose muffles a sob and Kay slides closer, wrapping an arm around her. DJ, Steve, and Eric stiffen, with their eyes trained on the double doors.

Through the silence, the students hear a grinding noise, something dragging along the walkway outside. It stops, then it sounds again. There is silence once more and Rose whimpers.

A thunderous slam rocks the door. Everyone jumps and Rose screams. It hits again, this time sharper. Eric bolts for the weapons rack. "They're going to break the glass!"

His hands fumble through the rack, sending eskrima sticks, staffs, nunchaku, and baseball bats tumbling to the ground in a clatter of panic.

"Don't be dumb," Steve snaps. "That door has double panes. There's no way they're getting through that." He balls his fists and takes a stance, staring the threat down through the blinds.

Another bone-shaking impact crashes against the door, causing Kay to gasp, flaring panic in the room again. Benjy starts crying again while Eric digs through the pile of fallen weapons, finally grabbing a baseball bat. DJ clenches her fists tighter, whispering "Oh no" repeatedly. Tom drops the phone without thinking and pulls his katana free.

A low moan follows the next thud.

Tom eyes the door. "Eric, just check. We need to know what's out there."

Eric flips him off. "Get wrecked, dude."

"Come on, man," Tom presses. "Just peek!"

"Fuck you, man." Eric growls, "You want to know so bad, go look for yourself!"

The students hear another moan, quieter now. Then a fragile voice cracks through the tension, "Help."

DJ bolts to the door, one hand on the handle, the other on the lock. Her heart hammers against her ribs.

Eric races to the door and slams his hand down on hers. "Don't you dare open this door," he warns, his eyes locked to hers with something fiercer than fear, but far from conviction.

She freezes. On the other side comes another knock, this time weaker. "Please."

She tries to turn the handle, but Eric tightens his grip, his strength crushing hers into the cold metal.

"Ow!" DJ cries out. Tom and Steve rush over.

"Let go!" she yells, struggling, but Eric doesn't budge.

Benjy's cries turn to screams.

Then instinct takes over. She twists her free hand into his, drives her thumb into the webbing, and pinches hard with her middle finger. Eric yelps as she peels his hand away, throwing it aside, so she can twist the doorknob.

The left door swings open as Eric's palm cracks across DJ's face. Her head reels but she quickly recovers from the strike to see Eric get tackled by Tom and Steve. She looks back to the opened door and witnesses a young man lying on his belly at the entry, damaged and abused, blood and grime staining his light hair. He is missing half a leg.

He looks up at her and smiles, "Thank…you…" before dropping into oblivion. Two ravaged lunatics race up toward the door.

"Help me!" DJ shouts back into the school as she charges outside. Her foot rockets into the chin of one of the approaching attackers. His teeth shatter, bone crunches, and the force flings him backward toward the alley.

The ratty-haired woman racing up with him lifts her gore-streaked face and hisses, blood and tissue dripping from her lips. She swipes at DJ who side steps the attack and hollers, "Get this guy inside!"

She spins, driving a sharp heel kick into the horrific woman's face. The impact caves in the intruder's nose with a nauseating crunch, causing an eruption of blood and mucus. Before the body recoils, DJ feels something awful beneath her heel, like stepping on gum over gravel. She flinches, a hot sting lancing her heel as if something sharp dug into her skin.

Her balance wavers and she grabs the door frame for support.

Across the wide alley, a massive woman in something between a toga and a bedsheet stumbles out of a poorly maintained shack, waving a broom as a weapon. "What the hell are you kids doing over there!" she shouts, eyes squinting at the chaos.

The male feaster climbs to his feet and lunges toward DJ. Her stomach churns from nerves and violence. Her foot already aches and she just wants to be safe.

She grabs the unconscious boy by his one leg and bolts for the door. Steve and Tom already have each of his arms. Together, they haul him inside as DJ yells, "Shut the door!"

Eric's already there. He barely slams it shut in time. The attackers slam into the door from the other side and glass bows inward from impact. Kay and Rose throw their weight against the doors while Eric wrestles the lock into place.

Lena rocks Benjy, her voice soft and steady. "It's okay, baby. You're safe now. I've got you." The toddler calms while his mom hums a lullaby. No one moves, stricken by fear, they barely breathe.

The two attackers pound on the door repeatedly for what feels like an eternity, then it falls silent outside.

As quietly as they can, the students drag the wounded boy onto the mat, all eyes remain on the doors. Slivers of dying sunlight cut through the blinds, showing two feral shapes smear the glass, slithering left and right, smearing trails of red in their wake from their hands and faces.

Across the alley, the broom-wielding woman screeches, "I'm calling the cops! You hear me? You little shits!" Her voice rips through the quiet like nails on a chalkboard.

Steve mutters, barely audible, "Man, I hate that lady."

One shadow slips away from the door, then the other. For a second, the students dare to hope. Then the woman across the alley yells again, but this time, her tone has changed. "What are you doing?"

The group in the dojo wait in silence, tension rising from fear. "Get away from me! Don't touch me!" The neighbor's voice cuts through the walls like they're made of paper. "Help me! Get away from me!"

Her words fall away to screaming, long, ragged, and animal. The carnage feels like it lasts forever before it finally dies.

The silence returns and even the air seems to wait, knowing that the simple act of breathing is too loud. The group of students find themselves closer than ever before, unintentionally timing their exhales in unison. Silence pushes against the walls of the building, collapsing the collective huddle with its weight.

Daring the peace, Steve whispers, "We need to figure out what the hell is going on out there."

Tom answers, voice hoarse, "I left my laptop here when we were loading the gear, Ma'am said it was safer to keep it in the dojo." He swallows, "I can check the news on that."

Steve nods. "Good idea." He turns to Lena and asks, "Miss, mind if I try calling the police?"

She hands him the phone without a word, gently rocking Benjy.

In the corner, DJ checks her foot where she smashed it against that woman's teeth and sighs with relief when she finds it is only bruised. She rubs the tender spot and catches sight of the radio in the corner of the room. She crawls toward it.

"No!" Rose hisses.

DJ turns, finger to lips. "It's okay. I'm just grabbing the radio."

She unplugs the small unit from its wall mount and scrambles back toward the mat, aiming for a safer outlet on the opposite side of the open room.

Steve frowns at the phone. "Damn. Lines are all busy."

Tom doesn't look up. "No one's said anything on my feed either."

Steve blinks at him. "Seriously? You're checking your socials?"

"It's not like I'm not checking other stuff. I've got CNN and the Union Bulletin open too," Tom says, his voice creeping above a whisper until the others shush him. He lowers his tune and continues, "I know that when I need to know what's up, it's usually on my feed right away."

Before the argument can escalate, DJ cuts in, "Hey! Hey, everyone. I got something!"

She turns up the radio a bit and a voice crackles through the speaker, low and guttural, "Welcome back cadavers…"

It continues but is drowned out by Rose's disbelief. "Come on DJ. Now's not the time to listen to that crap."

DJ silences her with a sharp look and nudges the knob higher.

She adjusts the dial, trying to fine tune the static from the signal. She finally hits a sweet spot and the voice comes through again, this time clearer, and cocky. She found Monster's voice.

"We've just gotten a phone confirmation on Violet's story, some kind of riot at the Balloon Stampede. Sounds like half the town's gone batshit and the other half's running for their lives. I guess we missed the party, huh, Butcher?"

Butcher's raspy chuckle trails Monster's words, but he doesn't say anything, so Monster continues.

"If you were down there and lived to tell about it, hit up your metal morticians on the Morgue lines. Just don't feed us any bullshit, because we can smell a lie like a fart in a car."

10 – BACK FROM THE DEAD

A few blocks away, on Morton Street, a one-story house sits behind a leaning chain-link fence. The curtains are drawn. The front yard is a graveyard of windblown junk and rusted gear.

Inside, the world is louder, and far more oblivious.

"Yeah, bitch, yeah!" The recliner lurches with every spasm of the chubby bald man inside it. His body jerks in sync with exaggerated arm swings, hands locked tight around a game controller, while his unblinking eyes stay glued to the massive TV across the room.

Screams and explosions erupt from the speakers. The soundtrack is pure chaos, guitars screaming like tortured machines. "I will blow your shit up!"

In the kitchen, a heavyset man paces in front of the counter, a limp slice of pizza dangling from his greasy, hairy hand. His focus shifts between his dripping food and the couple seated nearby.

"I'm tellin' ya, this town's going to blow the hell up," he says, flopping the pizza slice wildly. "Just because we're stuck in some backwoods Washington dump doesn't mean we're safe from the gang war coming."

The man at the table chuckles, dragging a square of sheepskin across the disassembled pieces of a rifle resting on the plaid tablecloth.

Beside him, a woman with a long blade pauses mid-sharpening to glance up. "All the little gangbangers in this town are sissies, Bud. They couldn't start a war if they tried."

"Au contraire, Brooke." Bud aims his pizza slice, pointing at her. "Think about it." He mounts an imaginary soapbox. "The shooting by Chase Street? Dead. Gangs. The one on Second? Dead. The guy behind Rosita's? Also, dead."

The man at the table grunts. "Not gangs."

"Not confirmed!" Bud fires back, spraying dough and spit. "All I'm saying is, we gotta be ready. They're going to start running through our homes like it's nothing!"

Brooke gets up and pushes past him toward the open pizza box. "I hear you. Cops ought to crack down. It's getting bad."

The seated man snorts.

Bud scowls. "What's so funny, Ollie?"

Oliver doesn't look up. "If anyone's going to storm your home, it won't be gangbangers, it'll be the government." He wipes down the rifle barrel with slow, methodical care, then sets it aside and picks up the receiver.

"Besides," he adds, "it's funny how you start ranting about defending your turf the moment I start cleaning a gun. Freud would have a field day."

The camo-clad couple burst into laughter but the man with the pizza grimaces.

A room-rattling yell erupts from the front room. "Take that, you noobs!" Which is followed by unprompted round of sound effects, "Kapow! Kapow! Right in the fucking head! Yeah!"

The debate in the kitchen fizzles for a moment, then shifts seamlessly back to government overreach versus gang violence, sandwiched between bites of pizza and slow swipes of oil on steel. The argument is heating up when a new voice floats down from a set of stairs that sounds like a cartoon jingle.

"Great googaly moogaly, you guys!" Ellie, a round-faced, dark-haired girl, wearing a bright yellow anime shirt, bursts into the kitchen with a comic in hand and an expression of wild astonishment. The room falls silent.

She breezes past the table of dismantled rifles and lands by the radio next to the coffee maker. "Hey Matt! Come in here!" she chirps toward the front room. Then she twirls the dial, chasing static and snippets of mariachi.

"Matt!" she calls again, more forcefully.

Matt stomps in from the front room "What, Ellie? I was totally owning those bitches! That game's cake. Zombies ain't shit." He spots the pizza box. "Ooh, pizza."

Bud blocks his path, arms wide. "No way, dude. I bought that."

Still polishing his rifle, Ollie mutters, "Bud, don't be a dick, be a dude."

Ellie keeps tuning the radio, bouncing lightly from foot to foot. "So, I'm upstairs, minding my own beeswax, reading my favorite comic book again while you two finish making out with your murder sticks…"

Bud snorts and Brooke raises an eyebrow, but concedes, accepting the assessment.

She continues to turn the dial until heavy guitars blast through the speaker "…when I remember it's Morgue Night!" Ellie grins and twists the volume dial with purpose. "You will not believe what they're talking about right now."

They all hover in the kitchen, drawn in despite themselves. The pint-sized girl stands in all her majesty next to the stereo, waiting for the speaker to buzz through the end of a metal track, before it settles into the velvet voice of Violet. "Okay, morticians, I've looked everywhere online to try to figure out what's going on at the fairgrounds, but I'm coming up with nothing. It seems like half the internet isn't even working."

Monster chimes in, voice gravel-thick and cynical. "So far, here's what we've pieced together. Some kind of panic hit the fairgrounds and there was a full-on stampede. Like Portland riot levels of chaos."

The monotone drawl of Butcher cuts in, "There've been a lot of injuries, based on eyewitness accounts like Violet's."

Violet jumps back in, breathless with memory, "Oh man! The guy who got on my car was covered in blood! But he didn't seem hurt, more like pissed off!"

Goblin's voice bubbles through the static, giddy and unhinged, "Don't forget the biters! Oh my god, that's hilarious! Can you imagine being so pissed, you just go around biting people?"

Blade groans. "Only you, Goblin, would think that's funny."

"No way, dude, that's great stuff!" He retorts.

Monster retakes the mic, his tone dry as bone, "We also know Walla Walla and College Place police showed up in full force, but so far there's no word on whether the riot's contained."

Butcher interrupts, "Our last caller said they saw Walla Walla's Gang Unit there."

"What happened down there wasn't gangs." Violet testifies.

"If it's as bad as you say it is," Monster takes the mic again, "I'd assume there are still raving lunatics attacking oblivious fairgoers, and unless you filthy perverts in radio land enjoy being brutalized, I'd stay away from the night glow."

Violet chimes in, half-laughing, "You know, Monster, I think you told our whole audience to go down there."

Monster chuckles. "Who said it was inadvertent?"

Ellie twists the volume knob down, silencing the chaos. Her grin is electric. "Is that totally cool or what?" A mischievous glint sparkles behind her icy blue eyes. "You guys want to go check it out?"

Bud answers without hesitation. "Hell no. I don't have a death wish."

"I'll go," Brooke says, practically bouncing. "Maybe we can pound a gangbanger's head in."

"Oooh," Matt adds through a mouthful of pizza, "or zombies." Laughter ripples through the room.

Oliver doesn't look up. "That game's made you legally brain-dead."

As the chuckling fades, Bud squints out the kitchen window. Something's caught his attention, flashing red lights accompanied by a faint siren, the sound increases as it draws closer.

He steps toward the glass; eyes locked on the flashing red reflection bouncing off nearby houses. His pizza crust drops onto the table, right onto Oliver's workspace. Oliver snarls, "Really?"

But Bud doesn't hear him. "Uh...you guys?" he says quietly, palm resting against the window. The others gather around.

Outside, the world feels wrong. A half-dozen figures lurch down the street, swaying like drunks at closing time, but something about their posture is wrong, they are too stiff and too hurried. "What the hell?"

Brooke squints through the kitchen window, scanning both ends of the street. "Was there a car wreck or something?"

"I don't know, man," Bud mutters. "But they look messed up."

"Should we call an ambulance maybe?" Ellie asks, uncertain.

Matt hops up with a jack-in-the-box spring. "No way, dude. This is it." He bursts into laughter, his hands gripping his gut.

Brooke shakes her head slowly. "Oh no…"

Matt steps forward, "It's the zombie apocalypse, man! Time to drop your cocks and grab your socks, my friends!"

He spins toward Oliver, who's still sitting at the table but trying to peer through the crowd out the window.

"Ollie, dude, hook me up with that gun. I'm about to own some motherfuckin' living dead!"

Oliver clutches his rifle tight, refusing to let go. "Um. No."

Matt throws his hands up and stomps back to the living room. "Fine! I'll be over here with my fake guns while you're choking on your real ones and your own failure."

Ellie grabs her phone. "I'm calling an ambulance."

Matt flops back into his chair, muttering half-jokes while explosions from his game continue to rattle the house.

Brooke gasps, fingers jabbing at the glass. "Whoa, hey! That's George!"

She turns to Oliver, tapping furiously. "Ollie, that's our neighbor! He looks terrible!"

Ellie swears under her breath, fighting through busy signals while Bud tries to pull Brooke's hand away from the window, whispering, "Stop that, you're going to get their attention."

It is too late, two heads snap toward the house, their distorted faces stretching into something difficult to see in the waning light.

"Oh shit," Bud says. "Now they're coming to the house."

Without a word, Oliver calmly scoops up his rifle and a few other firearms he had staged for cleaning. He cuts through the living room, Matt barely noticing him walk by, and he disappears down the hall as the pounding begins.

Voices outside rise in a chorus of screams and pleading. Bud presses his face to the glass, peering further down the way. "There's more coming, looks like they're chasing your neighbors!"

The pounding grows more frantic. "Holy shit," Bud mutters, eyes wide. "They're all messed up!"

Brooke acts first, rushing to the door and swings it open. She stands in the entryway, welcoming the chaos. "Hey guys, come on in! Need some help? You all okay?"

Five strangers barrel past her into the house, filled with panic and yelling, begging her to shut the door. She holds it open, staring outside at a second group sprinting down the street.

"Are these guys with you? Did you all get in a wreck or something?" she asks the neighbors. Then louder, to the oncoming trio, "You guys need help too?"

The stragglers turn toward the house and Brooke's eyes widen as the porchlight hits them, illuminating shredded clothing, and a thick layer of grime and dark, stickiness smeared across their bodies. In the early night hour, it is tough to tell if it is motor oil or mud, but Brooke recognizes they are covered.

The trio rushes through the small front lawn and the first one stumbles on the steps. In their nearness of the porchlight, Brooke stops cold, finally capturing a clear view of ripped flesh, faces twisted with rage, and eyes burning with something raw and hateful. Their grime is blood, and it is everywhere.

The first five newcomers inside scream at her, again and again, "Shut the door! Shut the door!"

She staggers back. The first of the attackers lunges through the doorway, only to get kicked square in the chest by Jason.

The blow launches the ravaging man backward. He crashes into the other two, and all three tumble down the porch steps in a heap of snapping limbs and growls, but they don't stay down.

Whether crawling or staggering, they rise again, eyes locked on the open doorway.

George surges forward, pushing Brooke out of the way and slamming his bulk into the door. It hits one of them dead center in the chest, but the body doesn't yield. It clings and pushes back. George growls, straining, trying to force the door shut.

"Open the door!" Jason yells.

George shakes his head violently, bracing with everything he has.

Jason shouts again, "Open the damn door, I'll kick him out!"

George grits his teeth, leans into the push, but inches the door open enough. Jason slams a front kick into the torso of the clinging man, and it lands with a rib collapsing crack. The attacker flies backward, down the steps again.

George slams the door shut, flips the deadbolt and the lock on the knob. The room plunges into a horrifying stillness. George and Jason turn to wide eyes and clenched fists, everyone frozen in stunned shock and disbelief.

Caroline, Chris, and Chastity lie on the floor where they collapsed after bursting through the entryway. Their chests rise and fall rapidly.

George manages a shaky smile "Damn, Girl Scouts are pushy these days!" he says, voice quivering. His grin doesn't quite hide the shine of fearful tears in his eyes.

11 – THE RISING OF THE UNDEAD

Orange light floods the prison cell, then passes, allowing darkness to follow. Then the light returns.

The cycle repeats, over and over, thanks to the spinning emergency beacon stationed outside the locked door. Its rhythmic wash of amber pulses through the bars, illuminating collages of scraps and graffiti showing a strange harmony of clashing worlds. Most cells are similar, tribal symbols scrawled beside Aryan emblems, handmade drawings, inner-gang affiliations scratched on concrete. In one of these cells, two men sway in a trance from the music of a battered stereo.

One is bald, his skin is a patchwork of jailhouse ink and racial symbols. The other has long, gray-streaked hair tied into a thick ponytail, his lined face catching every dramatic shadow the light casts. Together, they rock in time to the music pouring from the tiny radio.

Guitars shriek and drums pound in a relentless cadence. The sonic assault hits a peak, then drops into sudden stillness. That's when the voice comes. "Alright, cadavers," growls the unmistakable tone of Monster. "That brutal block of blackness brought you Marduk, Cradle of Filth, Zyklon, and finally Gorelord with their biting track 'The Rising of the Undead' which, it seems, is happening right here in Walla Walla, Washington!"

The bald man elbows his cellmate, grinning. "Hey, Otero, wouldn't it be the shit if this was real?"

"What, all this stuff about Walla Walla going crazy?" Otero nods at the stereo.

"Yeah." The man's teeth flash. "Like something in the water making people snap. Neighbors turning on each other. Friends tearing each other apart. Total fucking anarchy."

Otero snorts. "More like something in the wine, I'd say." Both men laugh.

The station rolls on as Monster circles back to the chaos outside. "So, Violet, why don't you educate the masses on what exactly is going on here in the valley of the misfits?"

"Certainly, Monster." She gives a breathy pause, then lets her velvet tone glide through the speaker, cool and composed. "Some kind of riot broke out under an hour ago at the fairgrounds. Walla Walla residents have begun attacking one another. The violence has spread beyond the Balloon Stampede, reaching all the way to Pioneer Park and beyond. It's accelerating. There's no sign of it slowing down."

Then, as always, Goblin crashes in with his own quirky commentary. "Don't forget," he giggles, "it's not just people attacking people, it's neighbors attacking each other! But, you know what they say about loving thy neighbor." He laughs at his own joke.

Goblin's giggles barely fade before the sweet, sardonic voice of Fresh bubbles up. "Seriously." She sighs with amused exasperation. "It's not like these people are running around beating each other up or shooting or something."

Goblin fires back. "Nope! They're running around biting each other!"

Violet tries to pull the discussion back on track. "Right, they aren't using weapons or yelling, they're just biting and clawing. What we've also learned is, though these people are basically mobbing together, they aren't organized in the way a person expects. It doesn't look like gang violence so much as packs of wild dogs."

Ninja chimes in, voice sharp and playful. "What do you mean 'what we learned,' Violet? Weren't you down there?"

Violet sighs. "Yeah, I was. But only for a few minutes." Her tone shifts, frustration giving way to reflection. "I didn't even get out of my car. By the time I pulled into the parking field across from the bleachers, people were already panicking. It looked more like a stampede than a riot, like bulls running wild. People were leaping on each other, tackling and trampling. I saw bodies flying over cars, people getting run over. It was chaos."

The others fall silent as she continues. "One guy, he jumped on my hood and started trying to punch through my windshield. That's when I decided to get the hell out of there. I'm pretty sure there's still blood smeared on the glass. I know it was there when I parked outside."

"…Whoa." Goblin's voice drops, suddenly serious.

Monster pushes forward. "Okay, so yeah, there was a panic at the Stampede. We've got that. What else is going on, Violet?"

"Wow, Monster," Blade snaps. "Way to be sensitive."

"Get off me, woman." Monster huffs. "We already went over this off-air, I was plenty sensitive. But now we're live. Our job is to inform or entertain, not cry on air like we're in therapy. Our listeners want answers. They want to know what's happening in Walla Walla, and since we can't pick up any other damn stations, that job falls to us."

Violet sighs, but her voice holds steady. "Monster's right. Even if he is an ass."

She clears her throat and shifts back to business. "Like I said, other than the guy trying to beat through my windshield, I didn't actually see anyone biting anyone else."

Monster jumps back in. "And the rest of the news?"

"Well," Violet replies, tone uncertain now, "as you said, Monster, we can't find any other radio broadcasts from the area. So for now, KWCW 90.5 FM is the only coverage anyone's getting about this...this event. The Riot. The Outbreak. Whatever we're calling it."

A chorus of answers flows from the radio personalities including "riot," "massacre," and "meltdown", but the final voice is the deep, gravel-worn tone of Ogre, silent until now. "Event is probably the safest explanation for now."

Violet hums in agreement. "Okay. 'Event' it is." She continues. "Internet access seems limited at best. And that depends on your provider. We've only seen two updates posted to our station's Facebook page so far. One says the Ice-Berg burger stand looks like a scene from Friday the 13th. The other claims people are wandering through Pioneer Park, attacking pedestrians or chasing the geese."

Violet pushes on. "Then there's the phone lines. At first, nothing, dead air. I know a lot of you cadavers probably noticed. Only recently have we been able to get a steady dial tone at all. And even then, that doesn't mean a damn thing if you can't connect. All we get are busy signals trying to call out, and so far, we've only received three inbound calls since this whole thing started."

Back in the prison cell, the two inmates glance at one another, their trance broken. Otero is the first to speak. "You think this is serious, Swecker?"

The bald man shifts, uncertain. "I don't know, man. You remember their Halloween show last year?"

Otero squints, then nods. "Yeah. That one about the Walla Walla vampire, guy stalking the parks, drinking people's blood."

"Exactly." Swecker nods again, slowly. "They went all in on that one. Fake obits. Fabricated news clips. Made it all sound real as hell."

Otero sighs. "So, you think this might be another stunt?"

"Every time I start to believe it, I think about October."

"But this one feels different." Otero shakes his head, hair swaying with the movement. "It sounds real."

"I know," Swecker mutters. "I can't tell anymore."

The sound of boots, heavy and quick, echoes down the hall. Both men freeze.

A squad of correctional officers rushes past the bars, eyes forward. One peels off and stops at their cell, flashlight beam slicing through the room. "Sound off."

Each man stands, stating his full name and DOC number.

Satisfied, the guard lowers his light. "Kill the radio and return to your bunks."

He jogs to rejoin the rest of the team, boots pounding toward whatever's waiting on the far end of the prison block. Otero flips a middle finger toward the now-empty cell door.

Swecker mutters loud enough to be heard. "Fuck you, Officer Joyce." Then quieter, to himself, "Fucking pedophile." The echo of retreating boots fades and Swecker steps to the urinal in the corner.

The sound of boots picks up again, letting the inmates know that Joyce is coming back. Otero shrinks toward the stereo, hoping to drown out whatever's about to happen, and Swecker either doesn't care, or doesn't seem to notice.

Inside the speaker, the sultry voice of Violet answers a call. "Morgue Radio, this is Violet. What news have you got for us?"

A female voice responds, hopeful, yet anxious. "Did I really get through? You guys, I got through! I did it!"

Monster grunts over the caller's celebration. "You going to say something useful or just shower us with adoration?"

The girl stumbles. "Yeah. Oh yeah. Sorry." Then she continues with a shaky voice, "Okay, so I guess I have news or something."

Violet softens. "Who is this, darlin'?"

"Oh, sorry. My name's DJ. I'm a student at Beginner's Mind Dojo, here in Walla Walla."

Monster growls, "Sounds like someone just scored free advertising."

"Sorry. I do a lot of demos for my school, I guess it's habit."

"That's what she said." Fresh quips.

Violet gently brings it back. "So, whatcha got for us, darlin'?"

DJ hesitates, then finds her words. "We were doing a demo at the Stampede when the mob came crashing into the crowd. They were actually biting people. Like…" She hesitates. "Like eating them. They looked crazy. Angry. We got away in our school van, well…most of us did."

She falls silent so Monster speaks, his voice less harsh now. "Hey, kid. Take a second if you need to, but we could really use whatever info you've got. If it helps you talk about it, pretend it's a class presentation or something. Just tell it like you saw it."

A few of the hosts groan at his bluntness, but DJ presses on. "Yeah…alright." She inhales sharply, then continues. "We made it out of the fairgrounds. But our van crashed, so we had to run. And I mean run. These people, they're fast. Super fast."

Violet jumps in before Monster can speak. "So, we've confirmed there are bitings and excessive speed. Anything else important?"

"Um…" DJ pauses, her voice smaller now. "Yeah, a lot of these people are really messed up. Not dirty clothes, but bruises, cuts...some of them are missing arms. Or chunks of skin. I think…"

She hesitates. "I think some of the ones who got eaten got back up, but it all happened so fast."

"That's insane." Blade breathes.

"It's true!" DJ snaps, then softens again. "Anyway, the reason I called is, we're stuck. At the dojo. We can't reach the police or our families. We have someone really hurt, he's missing half a leg. We need help." A murmur rolls through the broadcasting booth.

"What do you want from us, kid?" Monster asks, surprisingly direct.

"Do you know where we can go? Have you heard if the police have this under control?"

The mood inside the booth shifts, palpably heavier. Violet answers gently. "Sweetie, we haven't heard anything yet. You said you can't reach your families, are your instructors with you? Any other adults?"

"No." Her words are heavy as a stone, and she pauses. "Our instructor's still at the fairgrounds. We've got a lady here with us, but…she's got a little kid." The radio falls quiet.

Back in the cell, tension explodes. Officer Joyce, returning once again, hurls a baton through the bars, aimed at Swecker, who's mid-stream of his piss. The baton bounces off the wall and Swecker pivots to flip the guard off with a grin. The baton crashes against the radio, sending shards of plastic across the concrete floor, causing Otero to bolt upright. "Hey!"

The cell door slams open and Joyce charges the offender. Swecker meets him halfway, pants half zipped, fists already flying. They crash into each other, boots stomping, knees hammering, limbs flailing. Swecker doesn't care that he's exposed. He doesn't care about rules. He fights dirty.

The officer grunts, trying to wrestle him down, until Otero grabs a jagged chunk of the broken stereo. He drives it into Joyce's ribs. Plastic rips through fabric and flesh. Otero jabs repeatedly, each thrust pushing out a scream from Joyce, which drives him to strike faster.

12 – LEFT FOR DEAD

"Seriously, dude," Matt says, planting himself in the kitchen doorway. He blocks Oliver's path. "Hook me up with one of those sweet pieces you got, and I'll save the motherfuckin' day!"

Oliver exhales and shifts his weight, cradling a steaming bowl of water in one arm as he nudges Matt aside. "No, dude. You're not going to shoot anyone. This isn't funny."

He pushes through the doorframe and steps into the living room, moving with the speed of a slow rolling boulder. He lowers the bowl to Brooke, who's kneeling beside George. She takes it without a word and begins dabbing at the sticky red smears on George's face.

The cloth makes two gentle passes before Chastity, her legs cradling George's head, reaches over and snatches it from her hand. Without a word, Chastity cups George's chin, lifts his head into her lap, and resumes the cleaning with focused tenderness.

Brooke stares with astonishment at the other girl, then stands. She shoves the bowl onto the cushion beside Chastity and stomps away without a word. If anyone notices the interaction, no one comments on it.

The three bruised attackers slam against the door with mindless persistence. Most of the group tries to ignore it, but Bud doesn't.

He's pressed to the window near the door, watching the trio through the glass. He narrates every twitch, every swing, every smear they leave behind. Nobody listens. "That one blinked, I swear he blinked," Bud mutters, voice shaky.

On the sectional couch, Chris, sweating and pale, sits with Caroline curled into his side. They take turns breaking down, struggling to piece together what's happening. Caroline wipes blood and dirt from Chris's scalp whenever she's calm enough to move.

Chris finally lifts his voice. "Has anyone gotten through to the cops?"

Oliver looks down at the stranger on his couch. "All the 911 lines are busy."

Jason and Brooke both echo with muttered, "Yeah."

Still watching the window, Bud gestures at the strangers. "So, you never told us what happened. Who the hell are these people?"

Jason, standing by Ellie, replies quietly. "We were attacked."

Bud snorts. "Obviously."

Jason doesn't rise to Bud's sarcasm. He keeps going. "We were having a barbecue at George's place. Just hanging out. Then a bunch of crazies crashed through the back gate. Before we knew it, we were surrounded."

Bud squints through the window. "These three?" he scoffs, but even as he asks, the scene changes, and more bodies approach.

Joining the original three slamming the door, now a handful more emerge from down the street. One limps across from the house opposite. Five come trudging up from George's backyard, crossing the lawn like drunken shadows.

Each one is wrecked, bleeding, and filthy. Some look like they've crawled straight out of hell. Bud staggers back, his eyes wide. "Holy shit!"

He staggers into a side table and it tips, spilling three potted plants across the floor. One metal base slams against the large front window with a sharp, ringing crack. Every head inside turns and Caroline shushes him angrily.

The room fills with panic as the metal base rolls across the tile, sending dirt and leaves scattering across the floor. The scratching against the front door increase and build into pounding thuds, all accompanied by moans.

Outside, the new arrivals throw themselves against the window, clawing, biting, and smearing gore-streaked face prints across the glass.

Fear takes over. People inside scramble for cover, under tables, behind couches, and around corners. Oliver rushes into the hallway toward his room.

"Shut the curtains!" Caroline screams from behind the sofa.

"Fuck that!" Bud yells. "I'm not going near that window!"

Chris fires back. "That didn't stop you from banging on it and bringing them here in the first place!"

"It was an accident!" Bud snaps. "It's not like I was trying to flag down a bunch of psychopaths!"

Ellie jumps in. "I don't think they're psychos!"

Brooke scoffs, "Psychos, criminals; what's the difference?"

"You don't get it," Ellie exclaims, pointing wildly at the window. "That one's missing his jaw! She's missing half her arm! That lady's got a dang hole through her chest!"

Matt screeches from his recliner fort. "That ain't pink eye, they're the living dead!"

"The hell?" Jason cocks his head at the overly excited stranger.

"Everyone shut up!" Oliver's voice explodes from down the hall freezing everyone in place. The only sound inside the house now is blood pounding in everyone's ears, broken only by the wet smack of fists and heads against the walls and glass.

Oliver returns from the hall. He cradles a double-barreled shotgun, thick and heavy, in his left hand. His right hand points toward the entry window, where streaks of red and pink ooze down the glass like war paint. "The cops aren't coming. That means it's on us."

He glares across the room. "As long as they stay outside, there's no need for violence, but if they break in, if they come into my house, that's it. I'll defend what's mine. And I suggest the rest of you do the same."

Matt lights up like a kid on Christmas morning. "I'm hella down! Hook me up and we'll defend the shit out of this place!"

His manic grin actually stuns Oliver. The big man starts to say no, until a crack echoes through the house, then a thunderous slam on the window shuts him up. Oliver hesitates and scans the house for his options.

Eyes turn toward him, tense, pleading, and desperate. He imagines being a contestant on a game show, staring at a simple question made impossible by the pressure. Another would-be intruder hits the glass, harder than the others. He shakes his head and mutters under his breath. "I'm going to regret this."

Before he finishes the thought, Matt vaults over the back of the recliner with wild glee. "Come to poppa, you sexy little bitches!"

He vanishes down the hall to Oliver's room for guns with the energy of a rabid chihuahua and Oliver calls after him. "Only because I've shot with you so many damn times."

The rest of the house hears the exchange, and they want weapons, too. Chris, Chastity, and Bud crowd around Oliver before Matt even returns, eyes wide and pleading. Oliver exhales, watching his last thread of order snap. "Don't even think about it."

Before anyone can argue, glass explodes. Ellie screams and everyone's heads whip toward the shattered window, while they back away in the other direction.

Jason dives away from the front door and the broken window, vaulting past bloody hands reaching inside. He crashes onto the carpet, rolls, and pops to his feet near the TV. "Oh damn!"

Oliver steps forward, raising his shotgun and taking aim, waiting for something more than a hand or a shadow. One of the intruder's heads comes in from the other side of the large window, then the shoulders. It's a skinny man with a popped collar and dark spiky hair, he begins to crawl through.

"Brian?" Chastity's eyes go wide in horror at the attacker in the window, "It can't be!"

Oliver's finger tightens on the trigger. Chastity rushes with hands out, trying to reach the big man with the gun. She collides into him, knocking his aim wild. The blast tears into drywall instead of the attacker's skull, showering dust and deafening the room.

Matt returns, blurring past Oliver, pistols drawn, a lunatic's grin painted across his face. "Yippie-ki-yay, motherfucker!" He unloads three rounds into the intruder who collapses halfway in the broken window, jerking with each impact.

He howls, "Come get some!" Standing mere steps from the shattered glass entry point, blasting with a pair of pistols.

Oliver herds Chastity through the chaos, tears streaking down her round cheeks. Her wide, crystal-blue eyes search for safety, and he helps her find it in the huddled group. Ellie opens an arm and pulls her in tight. Oliver stands between them and the new entry, between survival and slaughter. "Get in my room. All of you."

That's all the direction they need, the group rushes for the shadowed bedroom. The hallway seems to narrow as they squeeze together, elbows and knees jamming, breath coming fast. They become a human knot clinging to hope. Oliver backs up to the hallway but doesn't leave the living room. He kneels and holds his aim at the window and yells at his excitable friend. "Hey, jackass! Get back here!"

Matt doesn't hear him, he can't hear him. His pistols bark round after round into the oncoming wave.

"I can't believe this!" Matt howls, caught somewhere between euphoria and madness. "This is epic! You mad, bro? You mad?"

He fires until his fingers ache, shells clattering to the floor. "Come at me, bro!" he screams, standing against a tide of rot and rage.

Then the trigger pulls, but the gun no longer fires, merely sputtering out clicks. "I'm out!" he barks, stumbling backward. "Reloading!"

Oliver fires past Matt into an intruder, sending it back outside. He stands so he can retreat to his bedroom, watching in horror as the crowd begins spilling into the house, tripping over furniture, clawing past one another to be the first to feast. He yells at Matt once more, "Get over here, numb nuts!"

Matt turns to run, but his foot catches on the edge of the couch. He tumbles hard, landing on his shoulder, his pistols flying in opposite directions. "Shit!"

A feral shape lunges over the couch toward him. Oliver fires once and the creature explodes backward in a cloud of blood and shredded meat, crashing near the door.

Another attacker scrambles forward, too fast for a clean shot. Matt pushes himself upright, dazed but grinning. He throws both thumbs in the air at Oliver. "I'm good!"

He limps toward the bedroom, but the creature closes the distance. Matt makes one step, then another, and a third, but the fourth never lands.

The creature tackles him and the horde immediately swarms. Their mouths rip into him. They claw through cloth, shredding skin, and snapping through bone. Matt vanishes beneath a frenzy of bodies.

His screams echo through the house, ragged, high-pitched, and full of pain. Oliver curses loudly and retreats down the hallway to his room, slamming the door.

Matt's cries die with him and the silence that follows is louder than his screams. Inside the room, no one moves, no one breathes. The horror of his death lingers in the air with the hanging stench of reality

Then, a thump comes from the other side of the bedroom door. One of the intruders is on the other side. In a moment, it is no longer one, but many. The pounding grows louder, more desperate, causing Chris and Jason to shove a dresser against the door.

"Shit. Shit. Shit." Caroline's whisper becomes a prayer, repeated and ritualistic.

Panic sparks in the room. People scatter, scrambling, searching for defense or sanctuary. Brooke moves fast, rifling through closets, cabinets, and drawers. She finds a green military canvas sack and starts filling it with blades, firearms, and ammo.

Oliver sits on the edge of his bed, shotgun ready and aimed at the door. His expression is carved from stone but his hands tremble. Both Chastity and Caroline are sobbing now.

Bud breaks the silence first. He slaps his thighs, hands trembling. "Seriously, what the hell is wrong with those people?" He jabs a finger toward the door. "Did you see that?

They were still trying to break in after Matt shot them! People don't do that?" His panic starts to spiral, pushing tears into his fury.

Brooke, hunched over her bag of weapons, joins the crying.

Chris steps forward, trying to steady his breath. "We gotta get the hell out of here, man." He turns to Oliver. "You got a back door or something?"

Oliver gives a stiff nod but doesn't speak.

Chris throws his arms up. "Okay? Where is it?"

Before Oliver can answer, Jason cuts in. "Where do you plan on going, man?"

Chris turns on him. "What?"

"If we leave, where are we going?"

Bud jumps in. "Anywhere, dude. We gotta move!"

Jason keeps calm. "Okay, but where? What if this is happening everywhere?" He glances around the room, expecting someone to answer. "The cops aren't answering. Phones are dead. Nobody's coming. Where would be safer than right here?"

Chris fumes, his fists clenched. "You want to stay here? With them?" He points at the door like it's radioactive. "Sure, man. Hang out. Grab a beer. Me? I'm leaving!"

Jason raises both hands. "Easy, man. I'm not saying stay forever. I'm saying, let's not go running blind."

Chris stares, jaw tight, anger flushing his face. Then a soft voice cuts through the tension. Ellie steps between the two men, "I think I know where we need to go."

Nobody hears her at first. Bud waves her off. "Man, screw that. My battle wagon is parked across the street. We jump in and haul ass."

Another pound cracks the door, making the wood splinter. The dresser blocking the door shifts an inch. Oliver straightens, shotgun rising. "We're going to need to figure it out real quick."

Ellie tries again, a little louder. "Guys?"

"What's this 'battle wagon'?" George asks, already shifting into survival mode.

Bud looks wounded. "My ride, man."

Ellie raises her voice, a little louder this time. "I heard on the radio there's a place…"

Chris cuts her off. "Wait. You don't mean that piece of shit station wagon that's always parked down the street?"

"Whoa, dude!" Bud points, indignant. "That is not a piece of shit. That car's taken me to hell and back, twice! It's a legend. In fact…"

"Who fucking cares?!" Ellie explodes. Her voice cracks through the noise loud as a thunderclap. "They're about to break down that door and eat us like fucking fried chicken! Can we please live long enough to argue another day?"

That's enough to spark movement. People start standing and scanning for gear. Chris's eyes dart to the back door on the right side of the room.

"Fine," He mutters. "Screw it. Let's go die."

"I can't." George stays kneeling. "I've got to get my car."

Ellie rolls her eyes. "Seriously? You're that worried about what you ride in?" She throws her hands up. "Men."

George lifts his chin, more solemn now. "No. My dad gave me that car before he, you know, passed." He exhales slowly. "I'll get it and I'll follow you."

Any response is lost as the bedroom door takes one final crack and explodes inward. A wave of bloodied flesh and broken teeth surges through what's left of the barrier. Caroline screams.

Brooke grabs her bag and runs to the other door and the others follow. They scramble through the master bathroom into an adjoining bedroom, then use that room's door to cross the hall to the back door, shoving it open, nearly ripping it off its hinges in their rush to escape. The screen door swings wildly with each body that flies through, until it catches Caroline's skirt.

The hooked handle snags her fabric, yanking her backward as the others vanish around the corner. She cries out and pulls, but it's too late, the first attacker slams into her. His bloodied arms bash against her torso and the impact rips the skirt down her thigh, the hook yanking her off balance. She stumbles, then falls down the concrete steps. Her head smacks the pathway beyond, and her body sprawls on the ground.

The screen door creaks open again, and the attacker leaps forward, his jaws wide, but instead of finding her flesh, the twin barrels of a shotgun fill the monster's throat. His bloodshot eyes widen, some primal awareness flickering behind the rot. And on the other end of that steel is Oliver.

His face is grim, and his teeth are clenched beneath a thick beard. His feet are planted on each side of the prone woman. He shoves forward, jamming the hooked biter deeper into the press of other oncoming invaders. He uses the maddened monster at the end of his gun to block the door, bottlenecking the pursuers. The creature swings repeatedly at Oliver but falls short in the distance between them. The other intruders press forward, and their combined weight pushes the hooked one further onto the barrels.

"Run," he growls to the woman sprawled across the walkway at his feet. Caroline scrambles, hands and knees scraping concrete as she rounds the side of the house. Behind her, the monsters scream, not with words, but hunger.

They claw and swing at Oliver, desperate to get through. The one caught on his barrels glares at him, a twisted rictus of hate. Fingers claw at the gun stuck in jagged teeth and Oliver knows the stalemate won't last.

He yanks the barrels upward, angling the creature's skull in line with the heads of two more behind him, then squeezes both triggers, releasing a stuttering flash of fire and an eruption of shredded teeth and bone. The viscera explodes backward through the screen. The blast rocks his arm and his shoulder screams, but he holds steady.

The doorway is painted red. Oliver wrenches his shotgun free and bolts, sprinting around the side of the house, shaking the gore from his shotgun. He shoves over a pair of dumpsters as he runs, blocking the alley behind him. Stumbling into a dive, he crashes through a gathering of wild-eyed neighbors, their faces twisted in confusion, hunger, or both.

The station wagon is waiting, its engine growling and reverse lights glowing. The back hatch is wide open. Inside, a pair of hands reach out and Brooke yells, "Come on! Come on!"

Oliver throws himself into the cargo space, boots kicking at the bumper. He looks back long enough to see George sprinting across his lawn, trying to unlock his own front door with a horde nipping at his heels.

"Go, George…" Ellie screams from the front of the car, but the horde crashes in, consuming him in the flood of violence.

Oliver stares. The hatch slams shut, Brooke's hands shaking as she pulls him close. The wagon lurches forward with a roar.

In the escape, Bud plows into a person running at the car. A mangled shape bounces off the hood and into the street. "He's toast, man!" Bud screams from the front. "I'm so fucking out of here!"

13 – FUCKING HOSTILE

The battlewagon roars down a cracked suburban street, its dented frame rattling with every pothole it encounters. The engine growls, choking on adrenaline, the shocks groaning with every bounce of the oversized tires.

Inside, the radio hums low, tuned into KWCW and the ramblings of the hosts of the Morgue. A jagged crackle splits the silence, "...And we're back, cadavers," Monster growls through the static, "broadcasting from somewhere between the end of the world and your neighbor's basement and it sounds like the basement is the safest option, at this point."

The passengers in the battlewagon are silent as the grave. Their only sounds are the wheeze of panicked breath and the occasional curse from Bud behind the wheel as he wrestles the station wagon through the chaos of a street turned feral.

Brooke sits rigid in the cargo hold, one hand braced against the hatch, the other latched onto Oliver's thick arm hoping it might anchor her to reality. The big man is half-slumped, recovering from the sprint, sweat pouring down his temple, the front of his shirt streaked with dried blood and, though not his, it's fresh enough to remind them all how close death had come.

In the passenger seat, Ellie curls into herself, arms wrapped tight around her knees, trying to stay small and invisible. Chastity sits beside her, trembling, her lips whispering silent prayers or maybe the same word over and over. Chris and Jason are at each back seat side window, peering through the glass into darkened lawns and driveways, eyes flicking between porch shadows and silhouettes that might be movement, or simply tricks of the light. Caroline is sandwiched between them.

"Where the hell are we going?" Chris finally asks, his voice dry and brittle.

"Anywhere but back there," Bud mutters. His jaw clenches. "We keep moving. We find a way out."

"We need a real plan," Jason says, scanning. "Someplace to hole up and regroup. We need to lock it down."

"Yeah, well, maybe once the mob stops trying to kill us," Bud snaps, hands tightening on the wheel.

They hang a sharp right onto Chase Avenue, the tires barking on loose gravel. The street dips slightly downhill toward Chestnut and dim porch lights glow, exposing barred windows and empty lawns. Some houses are dark altogether, abandoned, or too afraid to show life.

They don't quite make it to their cross-street before realizing something's wrong. Figures fill the road up ahead, moving in tight, twitchy patterns. They've gathered, but not like their attackers did, they aren't shambling or chasing. These people are postured, and their movements are charged. Two groups have gathered across from each other like old rivals at the edge of war.

One side wears blue rags tied around their wrists, elbows, or stuffed into back pockets. A few have their faces covered in bandanas with skulls or horns painted across them. The other crew rocks red sashes and faded letterman jackets now marked with angular letters and demonic symbols scrawled in hasty layers. The number 13 appears more than once.

Each group has bats, chains, or other makeshift weapons. And at least one handgun glints under the flickering streetlight.

"Is that...a gang fight?" Ellie whispers, her voice barely audible.

The wagon stops in the middle of the street and Bud's grip turns bone-white on the wheel. Jason leans forward from the back seat, gaze narrowing. "Don't stop," he growls.

Bud nods stiffly, easing forward slowly. They try to coast past unnoticed, the battlewagon crawling with the care of a mouse past a distracted cat. For a second, it works, until a glass bottle smashes against the side of the car, sending shards scattering across the pavement.

The car is assaulted again, this time it's a rock. Caroline winces as the back window shatters. "We just left a house full of lunatics, and now we're driving into a damn turf war?"

"Yeah," Jason mutters, "Same old Walla Walla."

One gang member shouts, "Yo! What set you reppin', fool?" His focus is aimed directly at Bud. "That's 9 Kings tagging! You lost?!"

A chunk of concrete slams into the rear fender with a deafening clang, sending a metallic screech echoing through the wagon's frame. Chastity screams and Chris ducks low, instinctively shielding himself with an arm.

"What the hell?!" Bud yells, nearly swerving. "I didn't do anything!"

"You need to, though!" Jason mutters, pushing off shards of glass from the side window.

"Turn the wheel!" Oliver barks, bracing himself with the back seat head rest.

"What?!"

"Turn!"

Bud jerks the wheel hard to the right and the battlewagon screeches as it veers off the main road. Tires skid on pavement as the bulky car lurches into a narrow alley lined with graffiti-tagged dumpsters, sagging wooden fences, and half-toppled recycling bins.

A few gang members chase behind, shouting curses and threats, but their voices are swallowed almost instantly by a new sound, snarls and screams. Something else enters the fray.

Shadows flood in from the far end of the block. Jerking, hunched silhouettes with flailing arms and tattered skin, sprinting with unnatural hunger. The gang fight explodes into panic.

"Dammit," Jason curses. "Can't we catch a break?"

In the rearview mirror, the gang rivalry disintegrates into a massacre. Members of the red and blue crews scatter as the infected swarm the street, ripping bodies down like wolves on a carcass. The screams change, rage turning to terror, then to agony.

Up ahead, the alley narrows, pinching between a cinderblock building and an overgrown tree, barely wide enough for the battlewagon to squeeze through. The side mirror snaps as the car clips an open gate.

"Where the hell are we going now?" Brooke asks, her voice tight.

Bud's knuckles are bone-white on the steering wheel. "Dead end?"

"No," Ellie says, suddenly leaning forward and pointing out the windshield. Her eyes are wide. "There, the Beginner's Mind Dojo. I know that place."

Oliver squints and the sign comes into view, a faded wooden placard above a low concrete building with bamboo latticework framing the door.

"Karate?" he asks.

"Yeah," Ellie nods. "Could be weapons or gear. I don't know. But it's a building. And it locks."

"We'll take it," Oliver growls. "Pull in."

Bud jerks the wheel one last time and they whip around the corner into a tight, three-car parking lot tucked between a building and a fence.

Two infected already stagger aimlessly in the lot, one is missing an arm and the other is dragging a mangled leg behind him. The wagon plows straight through them. One disappears under the front bumper with a sickening crunch, and the other launches up the hood and smears across the windshield in a wide arc of red before rolling off the passenger side in a tumble of ruined limbs.

"Jesus!" Chris shouts, shielding his eyes.

The battlewagon skids to a stop and Bud kills the engine, which hisses from exhaustion.

Before the dust can settle, Bud glances into his side mirror, the one that's still functional. His voice drops. "Something's wrong. There's tagging on the side of my car. I think that's why they hit us."

"What kind of tagging?" Oliver asks, already grabbing his shotgun.

Bud swallows hard. "It's a 9 Kings tag. It wasn't there when I parked at your place. Someone must've hit it when all this shit went down."

Caroline leans forward between the seats. "Wait, that's why they started throwing stuff?"

"Looks like it," Bud says, knuckles white on the wheel. "They thought we were rolling with the Kings."

"Great," Chris mutters, glancing out the window. "We're meat to the psychos and bait to the gangs."

Oliver opens the back hatch and climbs out, chambering a shell in each barrel with a decisive movement. "Then we dig in," he says. "Everyone inside. Now."

From the mouth of the alley, more infected pour in, drawn by the screeching tires, the smell of blood, and the promise of fresh meat. They run on broken legs, stagger with open wounds, but keep coming.

The last thing Bud sees in the mirror is the first of them crawling over a dumpster like a spider. Then the mirror cracks and Bud flinches.

14 – EAT OF THE DEAD

A guitar screech bleeds from the radio into a brutal musical outro. In an apartment somewhere in the valley, two men sit eagerly at their kitchen table, both staring at the cell phone in front of them.

Monster's growl slithers through the final notes. "…And we're back, cadavers. Broadcasting from somewhere between the end of the world and your neighbor's basement and it sounds like the basement is the safest option, at this point. Let's go to a call."

"I don't think this is a good idea, Monster." Violet warns.

Monster doesn't acknowledge his cohost. "Seems we've got a real treat for those of you still among the living. Apparently, a couple of our loyal listeners put one of the lunatics down permanently and they say they've got something to share."

An excited murmur hums across studio mics before the low thrum of Butcher breaks through. "You ready?"

"Yeah," Monster replies.

With a click, the call connects. "You've got The Morgue. This is Monster. What've you got for our cadavers tonight?"

A piercing squeal of feedback rattles the airwaves. "Hey, friend," Monster says dryly, "You want to turn your radio down? We're gettin' a lot of reverb."

In the cluttered kitchen, a round man in a stretched-out white tee and short-cropped black hair walks to the radio and twists the knob on the radio. His wiry companion leans toward the cell phone on the table, his voice buzzing with excitement. "That better?"

"Yeah, man," Monster replies, "So I hear you got somethin' for us."

The seated man, gaunt and scruffy, leans forward, nearly shaking with manic pride.

"We killed one of those bastards. He's lying in the living room. We thought, 'What would Monster do?' So, we carved some off, and we're going to eat it. But then we were like, 'what good is it if nobody hears about it?' So, we called you guys. So everybody would know exactly what the dead taste like."

The radio gives a beat of silence, then Violet's voice cuts through, all pretenses gone. "What?!"

The studio erupts in laughter. "Do people really think I'd do that?" Monster mutters.

Fresh and Meat answer in gleeful unison, "Yes!"

The sharp-edged tone of Ninja pierces through the chaos, "Wait, you killed one of these people, a real person. And the body's lying in your living room?"

"Yep," replies the wiry man, nodding fast.

His friend chimes in, "Right there. On the carpet."

Ninja asks again, "And you're about to eat part of it?"

"Oh yeah."

The radio hosts are silent for a beat.

"Alright," Ninja says finally. Flat, almost impressed.

Monster interrupts. "Alright, alright. You can't just drop that kind of bomb and then wing it. You're on air, so conduct yourselves. Start from the top. Give us names, what happened. And slow the hell down."

"Okay. Hi everyone…um," the caller stammers. "I'm Locke. From here in Walla Walla. Uh, me and Paul, we killed one of these cannibals wandering through town, and, well…it felt like a very Morgue thing to do to give it a taste of its own medicine."

"Right," Paul cuts in, "We figured, hey, these things are eating people, right? So, how would they like it if we did the same thing back? Kinda like a revenge scenario."

From the studio speaker, Ogre's disdain rumbles through. "These guys can't be serious."

Locke responds, tone calm but shaking a little. "We are. And to be honest, I'm kind of anxious about it. You know? Like, a little excited, but mostly scared."

"Or maybe mostly excited and a little scared," Paul adds, too quickly. "It's tough to tell."

Locke agrees. "Anyway, we've got photos and everything. We're trying to upload it to our blog, but the connection's slow. Hell, it took us forever to get through to you guys."

"Yeah, and once it's up," Paul says brightly, "just go to paullocke.blogpit.com. You can see for yourself."

"More shameless plugging," Monster snorts. "We should start charging for ads on this show."

Locke doesn't seem to hear him. "Look, we've even got his driver's license here if you want us to read it to you."

"No, man," Monster sighs. "Just go ahead."

Paul giggles, high-pitched and giddy. "This is great."

"Alright, you pair of weirdos," Violet says, her voice trying to shake the disbelief out of her otherwise sultry cadence. "Remember, this is radio, not television. You'll have to walk us through this…thing you're doing."

The men pause, then nod at each other, struck by sudden clarity. The roommates begin handling the raw chunks more deliberately, inspecting the texture, examining their bites like food critics on a grotesque cooking show.

"Smells really strong," Locke says. "It smells very…"

"Smells like pig," Paul finishes.

"Yeah," Locke nods again. "You know, that good kind."

"So," Monster breaks in, dry as a bone, "are you going to eat that shit, or talk it to death again?"

"Monster!" Violet snaps.

"What? I'm bored."

"Not that," Violet groans. "Your language…"

"What, shit?" Monster volleys back, unfazed. "Come on, Violet. With everything burning through Walla Walla right now, I seriously doubt the FCC are going to dropkick us off the air. Besides, I think I recall a few other slips since this all started."

Finding no protest from the other deejays, he continues, "Alright guys, get to it."

"Right, okay. I'm delaying now," Locke admits, holding a strip of flesh to his lips. He inhales deeply, his shoulders are tense.

Paul smells the meat and grunts. "Three. Two. One. Go."

Both men shovel meat into their mouths.

The next sounds transmitted over the airwaves are wet, sticky chomps punctuated by sharp rips of flesh and frantic slurps. Their chewing is amplified through the phone, distorted and grotesque, bouncing across the Walla Walla Valley on the back of the Morgue's signal.

In the studio, multiple hosts gag, laugh, or shriek in revulsion. "Well?" Fresh coos, half horrified, half intrigued.

"It tastes like bacon," Locke says between hurried chews, meat pulping in his mouth.

Next to him, Paul breaks into a short coughing fit. "Went down the wrong pipe," he wheezes. "It slid right back there."

They both laugh, with near hysteria. It's the kind of laughter that always feels one breath away from gagging.

"It's actually really dry," Paul says, pressing a knuckle to his lips.

"Like eating smoked leather," Locke agrees, voice thick.

"You know," Paul adds, eyes wide with sick fascination, "Worthy gain. It is incredibly hot, though."

"Yeah, surprising heat," Locke confirms, now actively licking his gums.

"It's stuck under my tongue," Paul complains. "Back of my mouth too."

"What'd you season it with?" Blade asks, cautiously.

"Nothing," Locke replies flatly. "We didn't even cook it."

That image, brief and horrific, is shattered by the studio's reaction of gasps, curses, and mock dry heaving.

"You guys are seriously foul," Monster says with no trace of irony. "Pretty sure even I wouldn't do that."

Paul slurps again, trying to unstick meat fibers from between his teeth. "It's everywhere, man. My teeth. My cheeks." His eyes go wide.

"It's got a spicy burn," Locke pants. "It's like it's digging into my tongue."

Paul wheezes, gesturing frantically in circles along his jawline like he's sculpting an invisible beard. "It's coating everything."

Locke nods, barely managing a breath. "Ohh."

A burp rocks Paul's body. He grips his neck. "It's moving back…into the throat now." He drags his fingers along his neck like tracing a noose. "Sliding down."

The Morgue crew is howling in the background, some with laughter, a couple in disgust.

Locke staggers up from his stool, sniffling. "My nose is running. I need…" he vanishes from phone range before finishing.

"Oh, the drool…" Paul sighs, slipping into a groan. "Ohhh, it's bad."

Locke returns, toilet paper roll in hand and wads of tissue stuffed up both nostrils like twin torpedoes. The visual sets both men off again, raucous, wheezing laughter bouncing off linoleum and Formica countertops.

"Are you guys serious?" Fresh asks through peals of laughter on the radio. "Seriously, this is bullcrap, right?"

Locke wipes his chin, eyes wide. "My lip's going numb. And it's tough…not to drool everywhere."

"It's a real drool maker, isn't it?" Paul snickers, wiping his chin with the back of his hand.

"I need some fresh tissue." Locke flings soggy pink wads across the counter and tears savagely at the roll, desperately unspooling fragile sheets.

"It's actually painful to breathe," Paul wheezes.

"Yep," Locke agrees between labored inhales. "It's because it's dry, and there's bits literally lodged in my teeth. And my gums. And the…"

Paul interrupts, flailing his hands around his flushed cheeks. He swallows hard. "I feel like I swallowed glass."

Locke groans. "Yeah. My hands are tingling." He holds them up and starts shaking them like malfunctioning toys.

"I got the ol' fuzz feeling coming in. Great." Paul exhales through pursed lips, cheeks pale under the sweat.

"Oof." Locke winces and rubs his throat. "Back of the throat's lighting up now…" He clamps his jaw, shakes his head violently. "But…" He jabs a finger toward his temple. "My left ear is starting to burn."

He digs into his ear canal with his pinky and pulls it back, inspecting the red-stained fingertip like he unearthed something unholy. "Oh shit."

"Damn, it burns!" Paul croaks, clutching his skull with both hands.

"My ear is bleeding!" Locke wipes his messy hand on his shirt, then resumes fanning his mouth. "It isn't stopping."

At this point, both men are barely holding themselves together. Their audio feed is a nightmare of sniffing, slobbering, coughing, and questioning. Each sound punctuated by more cackling from the studio.

From the other end of the call, Violet's smooth voice cuts in with cautious disbelief. "I don't understand. You didn't season it at all, but you're both reacting like it's on fire? Sounds like you're pulling our leg."

"Oh god," Locke replies, with a pained sob. "I wish we were. My ear is bleeding, and I feel like I drank a bottle of scorpion pepper sauce." The two wince through their own torment.

"I wish it would stop." Paul flicks his tongue against his molars, searching for words. "It's not funny anymore."

Locke draws in another wheezing breath. "Oh Christ, I can feel it coming back." He clutches his gut with both hands, swaying slightly. "It's like it's eating me from the inside."

Paul bobs his head. "It hurts." He stops, his throat gurgling audibly through the radio. "Oh, Sorry," he mutters.

"The burn in my ear stopped," Locke offers, like it's some kind of small victory. "That's a good sign, right?" He continues, oblivious of the deep red stream trickling down his neck. His ramble collides with a throatful of bile.

Paul, unfazed or simply not listening, mutters, "I want to throw it up."

Violet's voice cuts through their heavy breathing and slobber-slick narration. "You two are clearly going to end up in the Darwin Awards. Just so you know."

Laughter from the other female hosts follows, and Monster backs her up with a scoff. "I'm usually down for some high-octane stupidity, but I think the lovely Vee's right, these two are certifiably brain-dead."

"Yeah, but it's not..." Locke doesn't finish. Instead, he retches and unloads his stomach all over the countertop. A thick, wet splatter echoes across the radio waves.

The hosts groan in collective revulsion.

Butcher pipes up. "Are you two okay?"

They don't answer. Instead, a thick, gurgling burp fills the line.

"That's it, I can feel that coming through." Locke goes pale, visibly blanching. His face twitches as another wave of nausea shudders through him. He grips the counter and powers through. "God, make it stop..."

They laugh, but not from humor, the jittery snickers are of two men realizing they've gone too far.

Locke suddenly doubles over with a dry, hacking cough. A fleck of something wet and dark slips down his chin unnoticed. Then he releases another cough, this one is wetter.

Paul hums vaguely, unaware.

"You breathe out," Locke pants, "and it's like you're exhaling fire."

Paul winces, rubbing his eyes. "Yeah. Pain's kicking back in."

"I mean, oh..." Locke's groaning falters. Something shifts. His voice sharpens.

"Paul? Fuck me, mate." Locke's eyes go wide. "You're bleeding out your eyes, man!"

"What?!" Paul's hands scramble up to his face, smearing crimson across his cheeks. He stares at his hands. "Oh shit, man!" he yells. "What the hell is this?!" Panic detonates with pipe bomb force.

Locke's voice rises in a ragged scream. "Paul, it burns!"

More groans and coughing fill the phone line, then something crashes, and one of the roommates shrieks.

The radio picks up every detail, the whimpers, the slippery footfalls, the blubbering terror. Obscenities flood the airwaves like a broken sewer main.

Then Paul's voice cuts through, a final scrambled warning, "Locke's… Locke's puking black! It's bubbling."

"I'm fucking dying, Paul!" Locke howls. "Call an ambulance!" The line goes dead.

Static hums briefly until an eruption of laughter issues from Monster and Goblin. "Oh my god," Goblin manages between howls, "He said black bubbling puke! I'm going to die!"

Fresh tries to bring some gravity to the moment, but even she's caught between disbelief and morbid fascination. "I mean…" she says slowly. "What if that was real?"

Blade steps up, her voice small behind the mic. "Should…should we call an ambulance or something?"

Ninja's tone is flat. "Where would we send them?"

They all pause and Violet sighs, clearly torn. "I don't know. But honestly?" She pauses for a beat. "They kind of deserve it."

15 – FLESH STORM

"That's unbelievable!" Rose's whisper cuts through the stillness of the dojo. "I told you that show's stupid!" She storms away from the group huddling around the radio, the growl of electric guitars and snarling voices begins to echo off the walls.

Eric and Steve snicker behind her. Tom rises from the mats, brushing off his pants, and wanders toward the far corner where Rose now sits perched on a fallen punching bag. She stares into the mirror ahead, her thick hair hanging over her face. She pretends not to see him, but their eyes had already met.

Tom hesitates just beyond her feet. Then he mumbles, "Hey," and nudges her slipper with the toe of his shoe. She pulls her foot back dramatically, squeezing her arms across her chest as she turns away.

"You alright?" he asks, gently.

Her chin drops, and she slowly turns to look at him, up through her lashes, her eyes are red-rimmed but steady. His awkward smile softens her a little, and she shifts toward the edge of the bag, creating space beside her without saying a word.

Tom accepts her unspoken invitation. He sits beside her and slides an arm cautiously across her shoulders, his palm settling on her shoulder. "I think that show's pretty stupid, too," he offers.

Rose doesn't speak at first, her eyes remain on the mirror. In the reflection, she watches the young mother holding her toddler in one arm while tending to the strange boy with a severed leg.

The mats beneath them, once a place of laughter, movement, and practice, are now stained with blood. The same mats where she learned to fall without fear. Her gaze drifts toward the window where Kay peers outside, one finger holding the blinds open a crack.

"Who would do that?" Rose finally murmurs. "It's so freaking gross."

"Sickos," Tom mutters. He gives her a reassuring squeeze. "I'm here if you want to talk. Or, if you just want to punch someone, I volunteer."

She snorts despite herself. Her shoulders slump and her head drops against his chest. "How long do you think we'll be stuck like this?"

The scent of her shampoo curls into his nose. He inhales, stupidly, then answers, "No clue. Hopefully not long." His cheek brushes the top of her head. "Maybe those people will wander off."

"I don't mean how long until they're gone," Rose says softly, looking up at Tom. "I mean…when are the cops going to come and fix all this? When do we go home? When do things go back to normal?"

Tom stares at the ceiling, as if the answer might be written in the water-stained tiles above, but there's nothing but the stale breath of uncertainty. The question hits harder than it should, cracking something in his chest. He holds her a little tighter, blinking back with sudden heat in his cheeks.

"I don't know if this gets fixed," he says finally. "But I do know we'll make it through, together." He cringes at how it sounds, cheesy, like something out of a teen drama, but Rose doesn't flinch.

The sudden thud at the front door makes several students jump. A groan follows, muffled and hungry. Then another slap issues against the glass. Kay doesn't move. She stands frozen at the blinds, watching. Her shoulders stiffen at the groan but soften again as it fades. She tilts her head, listening. "They're back," she says, her voice flat with resignation.

Rose leans back and brushes her hand along Tom's half-grown beard, a sad smile tugging at her lips. "Thanks, Tom. You're the best. I mean, why can't I ever meet someone like you who's straight?"

Tom opens his mouth, brain stumbling over itself. "Wait, but…"

Whatever he was about to say drowns under Kay's sudden voice, "I see headlights."

The groans outside turn violent, screeching as if they sense what's coming and the sound of an engine roars louder. Most of the students scramble toward the windows with wide eyes, hoping for sirens.

A boxy, blood-smeared station wagon barrels into view, its front end already mangled from impact. It plows through two of the lunatics, bones crunching beneath its wheels, before it skids to a stop inches from the front doors of the dojo.

The occupants are moving, but don't get out. The dead swarm, slamming against the old beater, peeling at the doors, ripping at the trim, clawing to get inside.

The back hatch bursts open, and a towering man emerges with a shotgun. He fires point-blank into the snarling face of a woman clawing near a taillight, blasting her skull into ruin. A side door flies open, and people spill out. A tall blonde, bare-legged and wild-eyed, races toward the dojo's entrance.

On the driver's side, a stocky man crashes out of the back seat, shoving away a small cluster of infected, then grabs another one and throws him back into the alley.

Inside, the dojo erupts into chaos. The pounding at the doors, the shrieking child, the stench of blood, it's all too much. "They're trying to get in!" Kay shouts.

"Don't open it! We don't know who they are!" Eric yells.

Kay argues, "She's screaming! She's not one of them!"

The force of another shotgun blast shakes the glass.

"Let us in!" the woman outside cries, fists hammering. "Please! Open the door!"

DJ ignores the arguing behind her and bolts to the doors, unlocking them with shaking fingers and yanking them open. "Come on!" she cries.

A flood of adrenaline-fueled survivors bursts through the entrance. Caroline stumbles in first, half-dragging Chastity behind her. Chris fights through next, helping to hold the door open as Oliver and Brooke lay down cover fire, mowing down the snarling horde with lead and fury while Jason and Ellie rush inside.

Bud clambers out of the driver's seat, slamming the lock button on the wagon before skirting around the crumpled front end. He dodges a pair of snapping jaws and dives through the dojo entrance. Oliver nudges Brooke inside and follows, yanking the doors closed behind him. His back hits the glass, chest heaving, streaking the window with sweat and grime. "Holy shit," he gasps as the dead slam against the glass, howling in frustration. The blinds tremble against the glass. Inside, the dojo falls deathly silent. Even little Benjy is startled into silence.

For a long second, everything holds.

On one side, the reeking dead rage. On the other, a room full of stunned teenagers stares down blood-soaked adults with guns smoking. Chris speaks first, his voice sharp. "Where the hell are the adults?"

Lena lifts one limp hand from her child's head and gives a weak wave. No one laughs.

Bud starts to stand. "Wait. What…?"

The glass door explodes. Shards shower the room as the door bursts inward. Bud is covered in fragments of glass and blinds, rocking him off balance. He stumbles back with a howl. One of his arms is dragged outside by unseen hands, tugging his body with it.

"No!" he bellows, grabbing the ruined door frame, trying to brace himself, glass embeds into his palm. Fingers, gray and twitching, clamp onto his shirt, his skin, even his hair. The grabbing hands multiply and pull. He kicks against the doorframe, legs spread wide in desperate resistance, but it's not enough. Nails sink into his flesh. Skin tears. Chunks are ripped away. The sound, wet and gurgling, echoes off the dojo walls.

Oliver and Steve lunge to help, but they're too late. Bud is yanked screaming into the night, his blood smeared across the doorframe signals a warning. Oliver roars and fires at the nearest corpse. The head disintegrates. "Get that bookshelf over here!" he yells.

He fires again, then reloads while another body hits the pavement.

Tom and Steve rush to the edge of the mats and slam into the heavy shelf, their muscles straining to push it over, but the dojo's polished concrete sitting area offers little traction. Jason joins, grunting wordlessly, and together they drag the weight across the floor.

Two more shells are discharged, emptying Oliver's shotgun again. He tosses it aside without hesitation and draws a pistol, rapid firing over the bookshelf as soon as it thuds into place in front of the shattered door. He fires until the pistol clicks.

Oliver doesn't stop yelling. He slams the trigger again and again, voice cracking with rage. With no other option, he hurls the pistol through the opening at the ghouls still feasting on Bud's remains.

It bounces off a shoulder and lands in the street with a dull clatter. The dead barely flinch.

Not content with a shoulder-high barrier, Eric, Tom, and Steve pool their strength to drag over a cabinet full of training gear and stack it on top of the bookshelf barricade. They add free weights in front of the blockade and prop long, heavy punching bags against the growing tower of improvised defense. Soon they run out of both viable material and energy.

"Well, this is just great!" Chris snaps, pacing along the edge of the blue mats, careful not to trip on the raised lip between the soft flooring and the exposed concrete. His fingers jab at the cluster of teenagers scattered around the studio. "This was a great idea." His mocking voice turns high-pitched and biting. "Hey guys, let's hide out in a karate school with no damn adults and fucking glass doors. What could go wrong?!"

His sarcasm cracks against Ellie hard as a whip, and her expression crumples, stunned first, then pained, and she turns away in shame.

The studio erupts. The boys bark at the stranger in protests. DJ throws Chris a snarl and shouts, "Why don't you shut the hell up?"

Nearby, Caroline rummages through a canvas bag hanging beside the wall of wooden training weapons, price tags still fluttering on their strings. She yanks out a folded martial arts uniform and begins sliding on the pants, pointedly ignoring the argument.

Chastity storms across the mat and jams a manicured finger in DJ's face. "You better check your mouth, bitch, before I slap it sideways."

DJ flinches, not from fear, but disbelief, and her fists clench at her sides. Before she can fire back, a thunderous impact crashes against the barricade. The wall of stacked gear quivers, and several books topple to the floor.

Tom steps between the factions. "Hey! Why don't both of you shut up!" He gestures toward DJ. "She let you in. She probably saved your lives. Show some damn respect."

Chris growls, "Or what? You're just a bunch of kids."

From her corner, Lena lifts a single hand and gives it an exhausted wave, silently reminding them she is not a kid.

Steve swaggers forward and pops his neck with a sharp tilt. "Yeah?" he says, squaring up to Chris. "Well, we're kids that can kick your ass." He grins with a sharp brow raise, not quite bluffing.

Another brutal slam hammers the door. The barrier shudders violently and more books scatter. Oliver, shoulder braced against the blockade, doesn't flinch, but he does bark at Chris. "Hey man, why don't you back up, they're scared kids."

His eyes cut to Chastity. "And you, whatever your name is, this ain't the time to run your loud mouth." He points to DJ, "She let you in. You could be dead right now."

He looks to DJ, voice roughening with earned apology. "I'm sorry. We came into your sanctuary and brought the storm with us. But you've done nothing but help us."

Another slam jars the door and Oliver presses harder, voice rising. "But this place is no longer safe."

Caroline, now fully dressed again, edges closer to Oliver as he scans for exits.

A sharp crash interrupts everything, one of the tall building windows near the parked station wagon shatters, and mangled arms reach through the broken glass. Fingers flex and grope with mindless hunger.

The room locks into a fresh silence, thicker than before. Hostility melts into instinct and whatever lines divided them seconds ago are gone. The dojo boys make the first move. They bolt for the weapons rack, yanking down wooden eskrima sticks, dulled swords, and other martial gear. Their eyes are wide, but their hands are steady.

Chris watches, arms crossed, shaking his head with disbelief.

Kay and DJ lift Lena to her feet, steadying the tired mother as she clutches her son. Winston stirs on the mat, groaning, propped on one elbow, pale and confused. He blinks slowly at the activity erupting around him.

Tom and Rose inch closer together, whispering between breathless nods. Their fingers lace and they're ready to bolt.

Brooke plants herself between Oliver and Caroline, her body tense. She nudges the newly dressed woman away from Oliver with a thick hip and asks, "Ollie, what do we do?"

Oliver reaches to his boot, draws another pistol, and points toward a single door on the far wall. "Hey," he says to DJ, "where does that one go?"

DJ follows his finger, her face tightening. "Just outside. Leads around the building. There's a private residence next door, but that door doesn't help. No way through."

"Damn," Oliver mutters. He braces one arm on the barricade, the other on the cabinet stacked atop it, and draws a long breath. "Alright, here's the play, we go back to the wagon. Once we're inside, we make a run for the police station."

A hum of cautious agreement buzzes through the circle of teens and blood-smeared survivors. "We don't have a better option," Oliver continues. "We run together. We cover each other. We make it fast."

The door jolts again, this time harder. A punching bag tumbles from its perch and slams onto a pile of scattered books. Oliver grunts and braces against the cabinet. Brooke rushes to his side, driving her shoulder into the barrier beside his.

Once the pounding stops, Oliver grits out, "Let me get out there and start the car. When you hear the engine, run."

"No," Brooke snaps. "You lay down cover. I'll drive."

He opens his mouth to protest but stops. Her eyes tell him it's not up for discussion.

"…Fine," he says. "Brooke drives. I'll clear the way. As soon as I get those doors open, everyone books it."

Another round of solemn nods and murmured agreement follows throughout the room.

From the back, Kay's voice cuts through. "Can someone help me with this guy?" She's crouched beside Winston, trying to lift him, but his one working leg won't hold. His face is pinched with pain and fear, but he's trying.

Eric spins an electric blue bo staff in his hand and mutters, "He's a goner. Leave him."

"Oh my god, Eric!" Rose barks. A chorus of disgusted groans and scolding glares echo her disgust.

"What?" Eric shrugs. "Look at him, he's toast. He's going to slow us down. I'm just saying, one for the many."

Chris shakes his head in disbelief. "Damn, dude. That's cold."

Ellie doesn't let it go. "That's incredible. You, sir, are a deplorable excuse for a human being."

Eric slams the base of the staff against the mat, throwing his free hand in the air. "What? I'm not trying to be a dick! I don't want to die and carrying him is going to make that more likely."

Ellie raises her hands to match his. "That's weakness, man. What's next? You want to use the kid as bait? Who do you plan on tripping so you can run away?"

Chris clears his throat and mutters, "I mean…that's kind of a good idea."

The entire group stares at him. Even Eric gets a moment of relief from the heat.

"Kidding!" Chris raises both hands defensively. "I'm just kidding."

"Pretty. Funny." Winston's voice is thin, wheezing between shallow breaths. He leans heavily on Kay, each syllable a slow climb. "I like. How. All of you. Talk. About me. Like. I'm not here." He takes a single hop. Blood darkens the bandage at his thigh. Chunks of tissue slip loose and splatter the mat.

Rose rushes forward, looping his limp arm over her shoulder. Tom presses in from the other side, relieving Kay and helping prop Winston up.

"Enough," Oliver growls as the cabinet perched atop the barricade topples forward, crashing into Oliver's head and cracking wood. The heavy doors burst open on impact, spewing gloves, mouthguards, wooden knives, and plastic training pistols across the concrete like spilled guts. The cabinet itself explodes into splinters with a final crash.

"Shit!" Steve yells. A crusted, half-rotted figure crawls through the breach. He steps up and swings an aluminum bat into the invader's temple. The sound rings through the room. Bone and blood spray across the frame as the thing reels forward, still coming.

He lets loose another swing. This time he crushes the monster's face inward, its mouth collapsing into the mangled cavity that used to be a skull and teeth scatter like gravel. The body slumps, twitching as it drops.

"You okay, man?" Chris shouts, rushing to Oliver's side.

Oliver groans, swipes blood from his forehead and sees the red stain on his hand. "Yeah, but we gotta move. Now."

He grabs the top of the bookshelf, muscles burning, and heaves it aside. Books fly as the shelf topples over the punching bags with a loud thud, clearing the exit.

Steve is already swinging again, slamming his bat into an infected woman clawing through the breach. Her face collapses and she flies backward into the horde.

Oliver reloads his pistol and fires outside. He misses, but it's enough to draw attention from nearby threats. He grabs the shotgun he threw earlier.

Brooke leaps over the debris and dashes for the wagon. She vaults the car hood and yanks at the driver-side handle. "Shit, it's locked!"

Oliver lumbers behind her, cursing as he stumbles through the mess. He makes it to the passenger fender and fires a shot at a figure lunging toward his wife but doesn't check to see if it lands before taking aim at another aggressive target.

Steve barrels into the fray behind Oliver, swinging as though he is possessed, his bat cracking bone and splitting flesh with every furious arc. Warm bodies spill out from the dojo like floodwater through a breaking dam. Winston limps between Tom and Rose while others push forward. Desperation covers the survivors in a shroud.

"Look out!" Oliver bellows at Brooke. One of the infected leaps at her and she turns, punching it square in its ruined jaw. She strikes again and again. Her fists land with fury but only stall the first attacker while another closes in from behind. Oliver starts toward her, but his path is blocked by a trio of infected. Steve grabs his arm, pulling him back toward the passenger side.

Behind them, the others scramble. Eric, Chris, Chastity, and Ellie pile against the locked car. DJ ushers Lena and little Benjy across the lot. Tom and Rose haul Winston between them. Panic pours from the dojo like smoke from a fire.

Brooke vanishes beneath a collapsing heap of bodies. Her scream curdles the air. Oliver roars and lunges, but Jason and Steve slam into him, dragging him back. He flails against them, fists wild, even as the last glimpse of his wife disappears in a mound of snapping teeth and thrashing limbs. Her cries break into a wet gurgle, then silence.

Kay runs. She makes it halfway across the parking lot before her foot hits something slick and unnatural. She slips hard, crashing flat onto her back with a sickening slap. Her hands instinctively brace, but the ground beneath her isn't ground at all.

It's Bud, or what's left of him. She's fallen straight into the shredded rib cage of the man who locked the door. Panic surges inside her. She twists and tries to push up, but her hands sink into something soft and jagged, bone and meat. Her arms buckle beneath her, and she collapses forward, face-first into a mound of pulped organs.

"Kay!" DJ screams from the car.

Kay gags, twisting her head sideways, trying to breathe. Her fingers scrabble through the remains for leverage, then stop.

Something cold and hard, wedged under Bud's shredded beltline. She feels a keyring. The car keys.

She rips them free as something lands on her back, something heavy. Her ribs scream in protest and a second weight crashes down, pinning her into the carnage. She can't wiggle free, she can't even breathe.

The keys tremble in her hand. "DJ!" she rasps, summoning the last of her strength. The weight presses harder and a jagged pain cuts through her shoulder. With a final cry, Kay flings the keys to her friend.

DJ snatches them from the air with a jingle, "I've got them!"

Kay's face is already pressed into the pulp of Bud's chest. Her lungs convulse as they take in blood and slop. Her body quakes for air. Another hand claws at her back, fingers digging into her spine.

DJ knows there's no hope.

She unlocks the passenger door and climbs to the driver's seat, crying. The engine roars to life and the rest pile in frantically.

As Kay's world narrows into darkness, her final breath escapes into the hollow cavity of a man she never knew, knowing the others still have a chance because of her.

16 – REVOLUTION

A flaming streamer sails through the air, tethered to the last shreds of a toilet paper roll, an airborne bathroom comet trailing fire and smoke. The chaos within the concrete hive of Walla Walla Penitentiary reverberates from every darkened corner and behind every steel bar. Smoke thickens like judgment day fog, and sparks rise from impromptu pyres across the wings. Somewhere above, automatic fire cracks out. Below, something wet and heavy crashes. The riot is no longer escalating. It has fully bloomed.

Shots crack like thunder. Debris answers back. Correctional Officer Joyce swings from the third-story catwalk, his face blue and swollen. The belt-made-noose is cinched so tightly around his neck it cuts through the skin. Blood drips from his boots, pooling on the floor far below his slowly spinning corpse.

Nelson from third tier, shirtless and sweating, emerges from his busted cell with the steel toilet he spent twenty minutes wrenching free from the floor. He hoists it above his head, piss and rust dripping down his arms, and with a primal shout of, "Fuck you pigs!" he hurls it over the rail. The metal monstrosity crashes down toward the clustered Emergency Response Team officers gathered below.

"Incoming!" one of them yells, and their shields rise in time to provide protection. The toilet smashes against the polycarbonate barriers and bounces off with a shattering clang. They push forward, boots stomping through smoke, providing enough space to make room for their backup, Special Emergency Response Team.

From behind them, the SERT unit marches in, black-clad and faceless, visors down and weapons ready. One steps forward and fires his grenade launcher. The canister arcs upward, trailing a lazy spin.

On the third tier, Otero backpedals toward his cell as the gas bomb bounces off the catwalk railing and clatters through the open door. The hiss begins immediately, followed by thick white vapor billowing outward.

"Mask up!" Swecker yells, his voice muffled beneath a sweat-soaked shirt wrapped over his nose and mouth. Otero rips his own shirt off and ties it around his head as Swecker charges forward and punts the canister back out of the cell. It tumbles end over end, trailing a stream of choking smoke as it disappears over the edge.

"Come on!" Swecker grabs Otero by the wrist and yanks him out of the gas-clouded cell. The two dart down the catwalk, skirting coughing inmates and ducking the occasional flash of light or explosive report.

Down on tier one, Insane Lane snakes through the madness. Bodies crash and surge around him, feet stomp dangerously close to his head, but he keeps low, crawling on elbows and belly, a hardened soldier in a dirty warzone. He grins through cracked lips with a prison-made knife clenched between his teeth.

He slides beneath the riot line as a guard swings left to bash a charging inmate. Lane drives his blade deep into the back of the officer's knee. The man howls, dropping to the ground. Lane makes another thrust and rips into the tender flesh between the legs of another officer. He keeps stabbing, red mist spraying his face. One guard falls, then another.

The formation buckles, and like floodwater through a burst levee, the inmates surge. Screams rise from both sides. Shields crack and batons swing. It's not a defensive line anymore, it's a brawl.

Some of the guards retreat, some fall. A few stay swinging, surrounded.

A tier above them, Bartholomew sees the shift. He stands at the railing, watching the tide turn, and mutters to his Native cellmate, Anderson, "They're breaking."

One of the guards below shouts into his radio: "Where the hell is everyone?!"

Another, swinging a baton with a wild look in his eyes, shouts back, "Half the staff left! Their families are in town, man! They're gone!"

Behind Bartholomew and Anderson, Swecker clambers down the rail from the third tier. "Told you, man! Told you the world was cracking open!" He lands next to them, dragging along his barrel-chested cellmate Otero, who scoffs and mutters something about who predicted what.

A man falls from the third tier above, flailing and screaming. His body hits the railing, bounces, and then tumbles limply to the cement floor. He doesn't move.

The group looks down at the carnage. A dozen inmates have gathered now, many bleeding, most shirtless, but all are furious.

Swecker doesn't wait for a plan. He runs, full sprint, and leaps from the catwalk. Gas swirls below and screams rise. A choir of the damned. He sails through it all like a falling god, arms wide. Then he makes impact, his body hits two guards and the whole knot of men collapse.

For a heartbeat, the riot bows to him alone, then the rest of the inmates follow. One by one, two by two, they leap from the rails like diving birds, crashing down upon the stunned defenders. The tier erupts with battle cries as the second-floor empties. The riot has become war.

Warden Felix Rourke stands alone in his office, surrounded by flickering monitors and the creeping scent of smoke leaking through the vents. His white shirt clings to his back with sweat, and his sleeves are rolled to his elbows in a futile defiance of the heat. The speakerphone crackles with static before the voice returns, calm, distant, and terrifyingly composed.

"We will not risk personnel on your site, Warden. The National Guard has been rerouted to civilian sectors. The threat vector from Walla Walla is no longer contained."

Rourke presses a shaking hand against the desk, his knuckles whitening. "The hell are you talking about, threat vector? I'm trying to contain a prison full of violent criminals!"

"Understandable, Warden, but with all due respect, your little prison problem pales in comparison to the larger issue at hand. Uncle Sam has a loose end to clean up." The man on the other end of the line pauses. "I've already divulged too much, but I'm doing this out of respect to you and your service. You need to know, our current plan includes an aerial strike."

He leans forward slowly, like gravity has shifted against him.

"A what?" he croaks in disbelief.

"Low-yield incendiary. You've read the scenario briefs I forwarded. Priority is containment, not recovery."

"I've got nearly four thousand people in here!" His voice surges. "Staff, inmates, the medical wing. Minimum security. You can't just…"

"You have until midnight, Warden." the voice cuts in. Cold and final. "I suggest you use that time to evacuate essential personnel. I think it's safe to say our strike will take care of the rest."

The line goes dead.

Rourke doesn't move. The silence hangs heavily, only the soft hum of the overhead lights remains. Somewhere in the distance, an alarm begins to wail.

On the wall, one of the monitors fizzles, then stabilizes. The west courtyard gate is breached. Another video feed shows flames pouring from the chapel window. Inmates, some now armed, some bleeding, move through waves of smoke.

He lowers himself into his chair, not out of defeat, but because the weight of what comes next demands grounding. From the drawer, he pulls a framed photo of his daughter in her graduation gown and arms around her long-buried grandparents. His thumb hovers over her smile. Then, his jaw tightening, he reaches across the desk and punches the facility-wide broadcast button.

"All personnel. This is Warden Rourke. Abandon all non-critical posts. Evacuate if you can. Do not wait for backup. There is no one coming."

He releases the button and breathes. For the first time in years, he prays, not for forgiveness, but for time. The monitors flicker and flare. One shows the cafeteria, another watches the warehouse stores, all of them are on fire.

In the control booth leading into C-Wing, Officer Marquez curses. "Shit. I'm leaving," he rips the Velcro of his vest open with shaking hands. The black body armor hits the floor with a thud, echoing louder than it should.

"You…you can't walk out!" a younger guard stammers, his voice cracking. His eyes are wide, and pale with shock, he holds his baton awkwardly.

Marquez whirls on him. "I've got a daughter in Richland with Cystic Fibrosis," he growls. "She needs me alive. I'm not going to die here for a pension that'll never come."

On his way out, he presses a ring of jangling keys into the rookie's trembling hands. "You want to be a hero? Lock the fucking gate."

The younger man clutches the keys like they burn and follows him into the hallway.

Control rooms across the compound unravel as well. Some officers grab weapons. Others take only car keys and cell phones. One guard drops to a bench and breaks into sobs, hands in his hair. Another kneels in the corner, muttering the Lord's Prayer under his breath, repeatedly.

A few officers remain upright, reluctant and grim, loyal or too scared to move. Final lines are formed in corridors. Some officers create hallway barricades of trembling breath and white knuckles. Others work to hold the passage, enough to die buying time.

Out in the yard, Officer Grant stands alone behind the inner fence, his exit path cut off by a mob of inmates. Their mass slams against the other side of the locked gate, fists pounding, bodies writhing in a living tide. He doesn't flinch. Doesn't raise his weapon.

He closes his eyes and reaches slowly into his chest pocket. He pulls out a worn photograph of his wife and his son, standing in front of their first snowman last winter. They wear matching mittens and smile like they've never had a care. He knows he will miss this life.

He stares long at the photo, his other hand dropping to his sidearm. With a hand that doesn't feel like his own, he brings the weapon under his chin, exhales once, then pulls the trigger. The shot throws his head back, sending the photo fluttering into the wind.

Back in C-Block, inmates storm past the last line of defense, trampling boots over black uniforms. Swecker and Bartholomew storm the empty control booth like mad prophets. "Hit the main!" Swecker barks. "Third switch left of the screen, then twist the override panel!"

Otero hesitates at the console long enough for Bartholomew to push him forward. "Do it!"

His fingers fumble and the switch clicks. A deep hum fills the block. All locked doors slam open, creating a drumbeat of doom.

In B-block, the battle between guards and prisoners remains deadlocked. In minimum security, a man laughs from his bunk. In the A-Wing, screams echo as the inmates break the final defense of the system, the sound of running feet fill the halls. All of General Population is on the loose. Freedom tastes of metal, blood, and adrenaline.

In the dim stillness of the segregation unit, far from the screams and smoke of the riot, an old man sits cross-legged on his cot. His name is Elijah. His jumpsuit is clean, his Bible is worn, and he hasn't spoken in three days. A sound breaks the silence, a soft metallic click. Elijah lifts his eyes. The door swings open.

Across the hall, a shadow moves. A tall figure steps into the light, hovering in the doorway. Vega, a lean man inked to the jawline with gold teeth flashing like fangs in the dark, meets Elijah's eyes with burning clarity.

He cracks his knuckles. "Told you, preacher. God answers, eventually."

Elijah doesn't flinch. He closes the Bible, runs one reverent hand across its cover, then sets it down, leaving the relic before standing to join his companion.

Around them, other doors swing open. More inmates step into the corridor, all of them are men the system forgot. Some blink like moles surfacing into sunlight. Others wear grins carved from old wounds. They don't all run, some walk with vengeful intent.

Vega nods once and turns. "Let's go. It's time to make this place ours."

Elijah and Vega join the exodus of criminals. They don't flee, they march out of confinement, and into purpose. Behind them, the gospel lies still on the bed.

Outside the administrative building, a group of five freshly freed inmates spray paint a concrete wall.

The tag reads MCR in jagged crimson, flanked by crude skulls and a snake. "Mill Creek Raza," one growls. "We're taking this town."

Another laughs. "9 Kings ain't going to know what hit 'em."

One inmate lingers, watching the paint drip. He lifts a cigarette to his lips and mutters, "Welcome to the new world."

The battlewagon roars eastward from the Beginner's Mind Dojo, a wounded beast, bloodied and rumbling. Inside, a tense quiet fills the space between the panicked breaths and groaning suspension. DJ grips the wheel, her elbows locked and eyes fixed forward, leaving the blood-smeared dojo in the distance.

Jason rides shotgun, scouting the dark neighborhood while Chris sits between the two in the bench seat. Behind them, Caroline stares out the side window while Chastity mirrors her on the opposite side. Lena clutches Benjy tight in her lap, next to Steve who is squeezed in close to make room. Winston is bleeding against the cargo hatch next to Oliver who has become a sobbing mess. Ellie does her best to tend to each. Pressed against the back seat, facing the wounded and broken are Tom, Rose, and Eric. The car is a mess of bruises, sweat, and frayed nerves.

Spray-painted in bold, slanted lines, the mark of the 9 Kings glares from the rear panel, a crooked crown above a snarling skull, scrawled in red and black. A warning.

DJ turns north up Second Avenue, the tires squealing slightly as DJ avoids a blown-out sedan in the middle of the road, leaving the horrors of Chestnut Street fading behind them.

That's when the tail appears. "Two bikes," Jason says, watching the side mirror. "And a car behind them. They're coming up fast."

DJ exhales through her nose. "What do I do?"

The bikes close in, flanking the wagon. The riders wear leather jackets patched with a crooked red crown. One rider taps on the window with a length of rebar, grinning through a cracked helmet. The car behind them speeds up to block their path.

DJ hisses, "They're herding us."

The battlewagon is forced down a narrow side street between two brick apartment buildings. Ahead, a blockade waits. A rolled pickup with missing wheels, sits sideways in the road. Behind it, four more 9 Kings stand in front of a graffiti-tagged wall, weapons in hand.

DJ slams the brakes two car lengths before the truck. Jason's already half out the door. "Let's do this."

"No!" Chris growls, grabbing his arm and yanking him back in. "They outnumber us, and they've got guns. We don't. Not enough."

One of the 9 Kings steps forward. He's tall, rail-thin, and covered in ink. A stylized 9 tattoo bleeds across his cheekbone.

"You're riding in our colors, but you ain't us," he says. " That mark on the back? That means tribute. Gear, gas, flesh. Whatever's inside." His eyes scan the car's interior, then settle on Caroline.

DJ keeps the engine idling, ready to bolt. The battlewagon groans beneath them like it's holding its breath.

The inked 9 King with the face tattoo taps the hood with the butt of his pistol. "Let's not make this ugly. Pay the toll."

Jason grips the door handle again. "We should run 'em over."

"Shut up," DJ growls through clenched teeth.

Another gang member steps forward, shorter and bulkier, dragging a bat wrapped in what looks like copper wire. He peers in through the broken back window. "We'll take that gear bag you got back there." He flashes a broken grin and nods at Chastity. "And her."

She spits at him through the window. "You'd have better luck fucking a chainsaw."

The leader laughs. "Spicy. Maybe we keep her mouth after."

Jason lunges again, but Chris keeps hold of his arm. "No. Not like this."

DJ looks at the blockade, then to the bike beside her. The rider grins, licking his lips.

She flicks the shifter and her foot slams the pedal. The battlewagon screams in reverse, tires shrieking in a drift. DJ whips the car backward into the alley, clipping a biker and sending him sprawling.

Gunshots crack the air, scaring a cry from Benjy. Lena clamps a hand over his mouth, eyes wild with fear. Winston groans in pain, clutching the blood-soaked cloth wrapped around his stump.

"Hold on!" she yells, shifting the car back into drive and stomping the pedal to the floorboard, catapulting the wagon back into the street. DJ whips the wheel, clipping a dumpster and barrels into another rider. He tumbles over the hood and disappears off the side.

She makes a sharp turn to bypass the rolled truck, then another to cut through the nearest street. She accelerates down the street and banks left at the next street. The bikers give chase, but only for a few blocks. The battlewagon passes through the intersection of First and Poplar, the riders pull back, slowing before turning around.

Jason cranes his neck to look behind. "They're pulling off."

"Why are they stopping?" Chris pants.

"Too close to Mill Creek Raza territory," Eric mutters. "9 Kings know better."

"Yeah, Poplar is a territory line," DJ mutters. She's silent for a moment, thoughtful, then she speaks, "We aren't far from the Armory, maybe it's safe there." No one argues.

The battlewagon limps along the road with one mirror gone and a side panel flapping loose. DJ's eyes are dry but alert, her jaw tight, as she scans every inch of pavement. The station wagon groans under its own trauma, metal grinding in protest with every pothole and turn.

Behind them, the street looks empty, but it feels like every building, every shadow has eyes. A flicker to the right, a kid in denim and a blue bandana, bolts across the street and disappears behind a parked car. Jason mutters, "Did you see that?"

"No one's chasing us," Chris says.

"That's worse," Ellie whispers.

Winston's head lolls against the backseat window, blood blooming fresh through the towel Ellie is pressing to his thigh. In the rearview, DJ sees Oliver pressed to the far corner, eyes wide and blank, muttering silent curses to himself. Jason has stopped looking out the window and now stares straight ahead, lips pressed together in hard thought.

They reach Alder Street and DJ realizes she passed her turn. She jerks the wheel, forcing the wagon onto a new path.

To their right, the pale bulk of the city library sits quiet, blinds drawn, windows fogged. Beyond it, a strip of brick buildings stands crooked and hollowed. Next to the church across the street, there's a flicker, a figure.

They round the block and glide past the back of the Armory. Across the street on a brick wall, sprayed in jagged navy and black paint, the symbol screams loud- MCR. The graffiti isn't new, but on this night, it sparks a new emotion, a warning. Rose shivers in the back seat. "We're still being watched."

DJ's hands twitch around the wheel. She doesn't say anything, she doesn't need to. She feels them. She turns right again, skirting the Poplar side of their destination.

Up on the rooftops. In alley mouths. Behind shattered windows. Mill Creek Raza is watching.

And they're not the kind to chase, they're the kind to wait.

18 – HOSTAGE

The Walla Walla Armory looms ahead, a fortress of red brick and rigid symmetry lit by moonlight and the distant flicker of a failing power grid. Twin towers frame the entrance like watchful sentries, their narrow windows dark and silent. The arched front doors sit atop a broad flight of stone steps, flanked by sturdy railings worn smooth by decades of boots and ceremony. A flag stirs overhead, half-lit by the streetlights and flapping limply in the night breeze, while above the main doors, the emblem of the National Guard is illuminated from a light near the top of the building.

For a moment, the Armory looks untouched, stoic and preserved, but in the stillness there's a quiet warning. No lights burn behind the windows, no movement inside. Only rows of blank panes, staring like empty eyes.

The battlewagon coasts to a stop in the parking lot across the street from the majestic building, its engine a fading growl. Inside, the survivors sit in silence, wrapped in blood, sweat, and fear.

"Think the doors are locked?" Ellie murmurs, her voice almost swallowed by the crunch of gravel under the tires.

From the rear, a soft whimper escapes Oliver, spilling his devastation over his lost wife. Caroline strokes his shoulder, whispering something the others can't hear.

DJ tightens her grip on the wheel. "I'll let it roll a little more before braking," she says, then twists around in her seat. "How are we doing this?"

Eric peers out his window, glasses askew. "It looks quiet. Why don't we all go?"

Jason frowns. "We're half a lot away. What if they're locked? What if we get swarmed? We should send two. Recon-style."

Eric shrugs. "Sounds like you just volunteered."

Jason starts to climb out, but DJ raises a hand, steady and firm. "I'll go with you," she says, putting the car into park, her lips twitching. "Steve, you get behind the wheel in case we need to get out of here."

Jason hesitates. "I don't think that's smart."

DJ slides out the door, her shoes crunching against loose glass. "I'd rather move free than be packed in this sardine can." She glances at the looming armory, its facade cracked and lifeless.

"Besides," she adds, flashing a grin, "I'm almost a black belt. Let's go." She illustrates her point by jumping into an exaggerated guard stance with her fists up mimicking an old-time fisticuff boxer.

"Alright, alright." He chuckles, "Let's go then." The two sprint toward the broad, brick building on the other side of the street without so much as a glance backward at the group of grieving survivors.

DJ and Jason vanish into the armory's shadows while the others wait like coiled springs. Inside the battlewagon, Steve repositions to the driver's seat and Eric keeps watch on the surrounding buildings, scanning for movement, living or otherwise. Ellie whispers excited encouragement, barely audible under her breath.

Caroline hums soft words to Oliver, whose trembling sobs fill the rear bench. Rose nuzzles into Tom's chest, seeking what little comfort she can find in his heartbeat. Chris, as always, flirts with the end of the world, leaning in close to Chastity with a grin too alive for a place like this.

Then Ellie squeaks. "They're in!"

Jason waves from the top of the armory steps, while DJ hops and gestures frantically for the group to follow. That's all it takes.

The station wagon springs open, and a can of pressure-packed survivors tumble out, racing across the street. Lena clutches Benjy to her chest and follows, her face ghostly pale. Steve opens the back hatch and loops Winston's good arm over his shoulders and half-drags the limping boy toward salvation.

Ellie makes it halfway to the steps before she stops. Her eyes snap back at the wagon. She sprints back to the open rear hatch, Oliver and Caroline haven't moved.

"Hey, Ollie. Let's go."

Oliver doesn't respond, his face buried in Caroline's shoulder, the weight of grief pinning him in place. She strokes his hair and murmurs, "You don't have to move. Not yet."

Ellie scowls. "Come on, Oliver. We need you. You're the biggest thing in this group besides that damn car."

Caroline spins, flashing fury. "Mind your own, you tubby bitch. If he wants to stay here, he damn well can."

Ellie adjusts her glasses with unsettling calm. "I don't need to watch what I say, harlot. I'm watching out for my friend. He belongs inside the armory, not velcroed to your tits waiting for a walker to chew through the glass."

Caroline swipes at her, but Ellie dodges with surprising grace and draws a slim, glinting blade from her hip.

"Ollie was always the gun nut," Ellie says coldly. "But Brooke? She liked her blades." She narrows her eyes. "Touch me again and I'll give you a slit nobody wants to fuck."

Something in the air shifts. Maybe it's the sound of his wife's name, or maybe it's the sting of guilt cutting through the fog, but Oliver moves. He lifts his head. "Ellie."

"I'm here, Ollie. Your friend, Brooke's friend." She's already collecting the gun bag. "Let's go."

Together, the three of them bolt from the car, sprinting toward the ancient redbrick stronghold.

Inside, the others are already filing through the arched front entrance into a long, echoing hallway. Tom flicks the light switches instinctively, and to everyone's surprise, the fluorescent fixtures buzz to life overhead, bathing the sterile corridor in pale white.

That's when the voice hits. "Freeze."

It's everywhere and nowhere, cold and mechanical, "One more step, and you're all dead."

The stillness hangs heavy. Legs are half-lifted, backs bent, muscles frozen mid-twitch. Slowly, cautiously, the survivors begin to lower their limbs, hoping not to draw fire from the invisible menace. Nobody dares speak. Breath comes in shallow gulps.

Then the front door slams open behind them. Ellie barrels in, followed by Oliver and Caroline, crashing into the frozen group like bowling pins. Rose shrieks and goes sprawling, others curse or groan as they're knocked to the floor.

"You've gotta be kidding me," someone mutters.

A sharp crackle from the speaker overhead returns. "Well, you fucked that up, didn't you?" The voice is cold and amused. "Now walk, slowly, across the hall and into the gym. No sudden moves, or I'll blow a hole in you so big an elephant could fit in it."

The crew look around in stunned silence, then Rose barks, "You heard him, let's move! You want to get shot?" She's glaring at Ellie, as the whole group begins to shuffle forward. Caroline sticks close to Oliver, clinging to her new security, eyes darting to every corner.

The double doors to the gym swing open without resistance. Pale light from beyond the windows on the far wall glints off the glossy wooden floor. Shadows pool in the far corners and the group moves like one with soft feet, searching eyes, and hammering hearts.

"This is stupid," Chris mutters. Jason and Eric grunt in agreement.

They reach the gym's interior and hesitate. The voice returns, sharper now through an intercom speaker on the ceiling, echoing hard through the expansive room. "Get to the middle."

"What?" Chris starts, but the group obeys, herded like livestock.

"Good," the voice hums. "Now, men to the right, women to the left."

For a moment, they stare at each other, hoping someone can dispel their shared confusion. Then, like lost students on the first day of school, they start to shuffle and rearrange themselves. A moment passes, then the voice continues, "Perfect. You, with the little kid."

Lena stiffens and points to herself. Her arms tighten around Benjy.

"Yeah, you. Hand the boy over to one of the guys."

"No," she whispers, clutching her son. A tremble swells in her body.

Oliver steps forward, gentle. He reaches for the child, offering a small nod and a hand to her elbow. She trembles but lets Benjy go. Oliver folds the boy into his arms as the two groups settle fully into place.

"Excellent," the voice sighs. The next command changes everything. "Now you women. Strip."

The silence is thick and the air buzzes. Rose starts to unbutton her shirt but pauses when she realizes she's the only one moving. DJ shakes her head defiantly.

"What the fuck is this?" Jason roars. He steps forward. "You sick bastard! You want to abuse someone, come down here and try it face to face, you fucking coward!"

A gunshot fills the room, but the echo masks the source. Jason jerks back with a howl, hand clamped to his shoulder. Blood pools through his fingers, painting a red trail down his arm. He drops to his knees, swearing through gritted teeth. The message is clear.

With trembling hands, the women begin to remove their clothing and the only sound filling the shocked silence is fabric sliding across skin. Chastity glares up toward the speaker in the ceiling. Ellie turns her back to the group as her shirt hits the floor. Rose undoes her bra with shaking fingers. Sweat beads on DJ's brow as she feels the bile rising in her throat.

When they hesitate, hovering at the edge of full exposure, the voice grows impatient. "Any day now, ladies."

Another voice issues from deep within the building. This one is real, raw, and not a speaker. "David! What the hell do you think you're doing?!"

A beat of static silence follows. Then the PA crackles again, this time the tone has shifted, less smug, more defensive. "There's intruders, man!"

The second voice, calmer and older, fires back. "You mean survivors. People seeking refuge."

A shuffling sound follows over the intercom. Then a muffled grunt. The second voice issues again, sharp with disgust, now broadcasting over the PA as well. "Why the hell are they naked?"

The first voice, David, answers with indignant pride. "We had to check for bites."

A sharp feedback squeal cuts the speaker off. The system dies and a beat of stunned silence hangs in the gym. The women hastily pull their clothes back on, hands fumbling in panic. No one speaks.

Then, the far wall door swings open and two men emerge. One limps heavily, half-carried by the other, a bald man with cold eyes and a steady gait. From the corner of the gym, a third figure steps out from behind a rack of folding chairs, rifle raised and ready.

That sight is all it takes to wake Oliver from his daze. He gently lowers Benjy to the floor, then raises his pistol with shaking but practiced hands, pointing it squarely at the sniper.

The rifle shifts toward him instantly. Benjy bolts back to Lena, who kneels to catch him, holding the boy tight.

Across the room, Ellie quickly pulls a pistol-grip shotgun from the duffel. She trains it on the two newcomers near the wall.

"Easy, miss," the bald man says, one hand raised in a calming gesture. "We're not here to escalate."

Lena snaps, her voice is raw. "You had women strip at gunpoint!"

Jason's already storming forward, blood trickling from his shoulder. "I'm going to break your fucking face!"

The man doesn't flinch. His hand drops smoothly to his belt and rises with a Beretta, the barrel trained straight at Jason's chest.

"Stop right there," he says, smooth as glass. His voice is steady, but the gun speaks louder. Jason halts, breathing hard, fists clenched at his sides.

"I don't want violence," he says. "But you're strangers in my building, and I won't die for your comfort. You understand me?"

Ellie doesn't budge. "Tell your buddy with the gun to stand down. Or I swear to God, I'll redecorate this gym with your insides."

To punctuate her promise, she pumps the shotgun, shell clacking with finality into the chamber. The man with the pistol flicks a glance toward the rifleman. "Howard, lower it."

"No fucking way, Bruce." Howard snarls. "That guy's got me dead to rights."

Bruce exhales, glancing at Oliver and Jason. His Beretta sways slightly between them. "Then maybe your men lower their guns first. Meet halfway. Or we all lose."

Ellie snorts. "That'd put us at a disadvantage."

"Miss, that would put us on more even ground," the man says, smooth but firm. "As it stands, we're the disadvantaged team. Your group outweighs us four-to-one."

"Ollie," Ellie snaps.

Without a word, Oliver lowers his pistol. The quiet command from his friend is all he needs.

"Excellent," the bald man says casually. "Howard. Stand down."

The sniper eases his aim toward the floor but doesn't let go of the rifle. His eyes stay sharp, replacing the iron sights. Still, it's enough.

The Armory leader lowers his own weapon, slow and deliberate, then holsters the Beretta at the small of his back. "Alright," he says. "Just a bunch of strangers now, eager to get to know one another."

That comment draws immediate scowls and mutters from the women. Jason, clutching his bleeding shoulder, jabs a finger at the man being dragged. "The only thing I want to know is how my foot looks lodged in that bastard's ass."

"Not to worry," the man says, brushing the tone aside. "When things settle down, David will be dealt with accordingly."

He squares up, posture military clean. "Bruce Snyder. Navy. MA Chief." His voice dips into authority, not arrogance. "Came home from Miramar on leave. Landed hours before this nightmare started."

"MA Chief?" Ellie frowns.

Oliver answers before Bruce can. "Master-at-Arms. E-7 pay grade."

"Who gives a shit?" Jason spits.

Bruce doesn't react to the insult. "I figured a little transparency would go a long way, if we're going to share a roof."

Chris steps forward, face tight. "Who says we want to share anything? What if we'd rather beat the hell out of the guy who humiliated these women and shot our friend?"

A chorus of agreement rises behind him. The room pulses with angry energy.

Bruce holds up his free hand, voice steady. "You're angry. Justifiably so. I get that. But we're all breathing in here, and out there?" He jerks a thumb toward the exit. "Out there's a whole damn town ready to finish what the dead started. So maybe instead of tearing each other apart, we work toward staying alive."

He draws a breath and smooths his voice. "Let's focus on solutions, practical ones. The kind that keeps everyone breathing."

The survivors grumble. The swollen tension slowly recedes.

Oliver finally speaks, his voice gravel thick. "We'll agree. For now."

"Fantastic," Bruce says, clapping his hands once with a dry smile, releasing David's arm and letting the shaken man slump backward. "Jeff," he calls, looking past the group, "would you mind locking up the front door?"

Heads turn to see who Bruce is talking to and find a paunchy man with an M16 who has stepped into view at the edge of the gym, emerging from the entryway. He's been watching quietly, weapon at the ready. With a silent nod, he turns and strolls toward the front entrance, casually flipping the locks into place.

"You've got wounded. And kids." Bruce looks to Lena, who's cradling Benjy in her arms. "Let's tend to what matters first."

He gestures warmly toward the hallway. "Kitchen's that way. Infirmary is with Jeff. Rest, eat, regroup. After that, we talk."

19 – SEARCH AND DESTROY

The riot roars behind them, a distant thunder of screams, alarms, and splintering metal echoing through the crumbling heart of Walla Walla State Penitentiary. Cellblocks are no longer locked, they have become proving grounds.

But here, in the administrative wing, the chaos thins into a tense, echoing quiet. The sterile corridors, once scrubbed and orderly, now wear the grime of rebellion, with blood-spattered floor tiles, overturned file carts, discarded handheld radios hissing static. This was the brain of the institution, where clipboards decided fates and uniforms signed away years. Now, the inmates stalk the halls like foxes in the henhouse.

Boots slap down the hallway in syncopated rhythm, half march, half hunt, Swecker leads the group.

Smoke snakes through the air like lazy ghosts, clinging to the ceilings. Fluorescent lights flicker overhead, casting sickly pulses of white across linoleum floors smeared with ash, blood, and discarded desk contents.

Swecker struts, sleeves rolled and face shining with sweat and soot. Behind him, Bartholomew walks tall, his expression unreadable beneath the prison grime. Nelson limps along beside Anderson, who's muttering to himself, voice rising with each step, and a length of broken pipe swings casually from his fingers, red and slick from earlier work.

"Ten goddamn years," Anderson growls. "Ten years for weed. Whole world goes to hell and I'm still in a cage for something you can buy at the corner store."

"Should've sold harder drugs," Nelson snorts, chuckling. His teeth are flecked with red.

"I did," Anderson replies flatly. "Didn't get caught for those."

Bartholomew glances over his shoulder, voice even. "Save it, you'll see the free world again soon. Focus up."

They round a corner where a security gate used to stand. It now lies twisted on the floor, sparks sputtering from the wall where it was torn loose. A guard's body is slumped nearby, his eyes open but vacant. No one stops, but Nelson kicks the body as he passes and chuckles.

At the end of the corridor, the brass plaque gleams, SUPERINTENDENT F. ROURKE. The door is closed, but the light inside shines from the crack underneath. Swecker slows and the others do the same.

"Boys, we found the Warden's office." He grins and knocks once with the metal pipe, then steps back. "Showtime."

The door to the warden's office is kicked open with enough force to splinter the frame. It slams against the wall with a thunderous clap, revealing Warden Felix Rourke inside, sleeves rolled, tie loosened, one hand clutching the receiver of a dead phone, the other frozen mid-pour over a crystal glass of whiskey. His eyes snap up, wide and wild.

Swecker crosses the threshold as though the office was always his, and behind him, the others flood in. Bartholomew rolls a loosened shoulder, his jumpsuit torn and smeared with someone else's blood, Lane dragging a bent metal stool in one hand that he found in the hallway. Nelson rolls his tattooed neck like he's cracking his knuckles. Anderson is the last to enter, closing the door with disturbing care, sealing them all in a tomb.

"Well, well," Bartholomew says, taking in the fine leather chair, the mahogany desk, the polished wood-paneled walls. "Looks like someone's been living real comfortable while the rest of us choke on tear gas and boot leather."

"You boys are making a mistake," Rourke says tightly. He sets the bottle down with a faint clink. "You're escalating this beyond redemption. You want freedom? You had it. Don't throw it away."

"You think we're free?" Swecker spits. "We're shadows in this place. Numbers. You sign your papers and call it justice, but you don't see us. You don't even know our names."

"I know exactly who you are," Rourke growls, his fingers twitching near a drawer, reaching for his service pistol. Anderson spots it and slams his fist down on the desk with a sound like its own gunshot.

"You don't," Anderson says flatly. "Because if you did, I'd be out of this shithole. I've been in here a decade for possession. That same green shit your buddies are selling in stores."

Swecker walks slowly behind the desk, watching Rourke, a predator circling wounded prey. "Tell me, Warden," he murmurs, picking up a half-smoked cigar from the ashtray and lighting it off Rourke's own desk lighter, "What were you doing while we were getting gassed? Taking notes? Calling in the cavalry?" He leans in close, "Masturbating?"

Bartholomew grabs a folder from the desk and flips it open to reveal handwritten notes, names, and coordinates. "Looks like he was getting ready to evacuate."

"Smart man," Nelson says. "Shame he didn't leave faster."

Rourke tries to stand, his chest puffed. "I gave you order! Food, beds, a chance to make something of yourselves."

Lane flings the stool across the room. Glass shatters and books tumble. "We made something of ourselves. You made enemies."

Anderson draws closer, knuckles white around a broken pipe. "You kept us locked away while the world burned. You let your men treat us like animals, you knew. Now you want to lecture us about chances?"

There's a silence that hangs heavy. Rourke looks from face to face, and for the first time, it hits him, there is no negotiating. There are no guards coming. He has no escape plan.

This has escalated beyond riot, it's a reckoning, his reckoning.

Swecker steps up and leans in close enough to smell the whiskey on Rourke's breath. "Don't worry, Warden. We're not going to kill you. That'd be too boring."

He picks up a bottle of the warden's top-shelf bourbon and takes a swig. He hands it to Nelson and grins, "But you're going to feel everything you made us swallow."

Rourke doesn't get the chance to speak. The room erupts.

The bottle crashes into his desk, splintering against the wood, causing a cascade of glass and alcohol. Bourbon sprays across paperwork and photos, soaking a half-written evacuation plan as if mocking its futility. Nelson's laughter is raw and animalistic, fueled less by joy and more from release.

Bartholomew tears the Warden's nameplate from the desk and hurls it at a shelf of commendations. Frames shatter and medals clatter to the floor. Lane topples a filing cabinet, kicking it until drawers spill their contents in metallic howls. Anderson, pipe in hand, brings it down on the TV mounted to the corner wall, sparks flashing like fireflies in a thunderstorm.

Rourke stumbles back, tripping over his own chair. "Stop!" he croaks, no one outside the room hears him, but the inmates do, and they simply don't care.

Swecker grabs the lapel of the Warden's shirt, jerks him upright, and slams him against the wall of accolades. "This is where you watch us rot, drunk on your own power." he growls. "Now you get a front row seat to your own downfall."

The Warden cries out as a framed certificate is shattered against the side of his head, glass embedding in his temple. He slides to the floor, clutching his face, bleeding and stunned, but breathing.

Another motley crew of inmates saunters into the room, Vega who leads Elijah. For a moment, everyone stops, ready to rumble, but like sees like and members of the first group nod.

Elijah slides into a leather chair in the corner and watches in silence, unmoved. Vega walks past Nelson. The men bump fists and Vega lights one of the stolen cigars, then blows smoke over the scene. He walks slowly to the Warden's oak bookshelf, selects a framed photo of Rourke shaking hands with a senator, and calmly drives a sharpened toothbrush shiv through the glass and into the wood behind it.

With the Warden's own fountain pen, plucked neatly from the scattered debris, Lane steps to the white-painted wall behind the desk. In bold, deliberate strokes, he scrawls, 'FREEDOM IS BLOOD.'

He casually walks to the Warden and jabs the pen in his shoulder, then returns to his graffiti and dots the final letter with a smear of Rourke's blood. Vega exhales another slow puff of cigar smoke over the trembling man on the floor, watching as Swecker reaches down and repeatedly hammers the warden with angry fists.

Amid the wreckage, a torn folder that was knocked from the desk lays scattered across the ground, containing some half-soaked napkin notes, government stationery, and black marker scribbles. Anderson picks it up. He reads, cocks his head and reads it again.

"Hey," he says, his voice low but rising, "You all need to see this."

Swecker wipes blood from his knuckles. "What is it?"

Anderson holds up the page. "They're going to napalm the whole city. Tonight." The inmates stop dead.

Silence returns, but it's different now. Not rage, but focus. The energy in the room shifts.

Moments ago, it burned with vengeance, shouts, fists, the shatter of glass and ego. But now it simmers, tension retreating into something colder, sharper.

Anderson holds the file like scripture, hands trembling, jaw tight. His voice cuts through the haze. "The fuck is this?"

He flips another page, eyes scanning. "Evacuation orders for high-level personnel. No mention of inmates. No mention of guards. Simply acceptable losses."

Lane snorts. "I Guess we're finally acceptable."

Bartholomew picks up one of the scattered documents and scans it. His face hardens. "Walla Walla is listed as a containment zone." His voice goes flat. "That's military talk for no survivors."

Nelson taps his pipe against the floor and exhales, "Damn."

Swecker looks down at the broken man bleeding on the floor. "You knew this?" he asks, voice level, but pulsing with threat.

Rourke wheezes through swollen lips. "They didn't tell me. Not at first. Maybe an hour ago."

"You knew before we did," Nelson snaps. "You didn't warn a damn soul."

"I…" Rourke tries to sit up, but his back scrapes the wall, and he winces. "I was trying to figure a way out. For staff. For my family."

"Not for us." Anderson's voice is flat.

There's a pause, a stillness like the moment before a match strike. Vega spits on the carpet and flicks the cigar at Rourke. "So, what now? We burn him? Use him as a message?"

Bartholomew shakes his head slowly. "He's not worth the fire."

Anderson's eyes stay fixed on the folder. "This changes everything. People need to know what's coming."

Swecker growls, "No one is going to listen to felons. How the hell are we going to tell people?"

"Swecker," Elijah calls, without looking. "You trust the Morgue?"

The man blinks once, slowly. Then nods.

Elijah gestures to the phone. "Then they make it known. They're going to napalm a city, and we're going to tell the world before it happens."

Lane whistles low. "You think anyone's listening?"

"It doesn't matter, there's a town full of people that don't deserve to die." Anderson mutters. "We should try anyway."

Rourke groans again, reaching weakly for a weapon. Swecker stomps his hand. "No more secrets, Warden."

"First, we tell the prison." Swecker lifts the microphone from Rourke's desk and fiddles with the buttons until his voice cuts through the compound speakers. "To anyone still roaming the halls. This is the warden's office. The prisoners are loose, the guards are gone, and your government just signed our death warrant. You don't have to go home, but you can't stay here."

Elijah moves toward the room's old radio in the corner. He dials into the Morgue and hears the hosts rambling on-air. Static fights with a voice mid-monologue.

Swecker moves toward the corner of the room, where an old, corded landline sits half-buried under a fallen stack of binders. He picks it up and dials a number he's memorized from years of listening.

It rings twice, then a voice cracks to life, filled with gravel and amusement. "You're on The Morgue. This is Monster. Don't be boring."

Swecker warns, his tone cold and clear. "Get your soundboard ready. This isn't a prank call."

The line pauses, then Violet chimes in, "Who is this?"

"Inmate 45713," Swecker replies. "Walla Walla State Penitentiary. This is Swecker."

There's a beat of silence over the phone, then Monster laughs. "The hell it is."

Swecker doesn't wait. He opens the folder again and begins to read, "Effective zero hundred hours, per Directive Echo-Four-Alpha-Two: Walla Walla has been designated a compromised zone. All civilian structures within perimeter are declared expendable. Aerial incendiary strike authorized. MK-77 delivery package confirmed. Priority: Containment. Collateral acceptable. No recovery expected."

The inmate delivers no punchline and the hosts offer no snark. The line stays dead quiet. "This a joke?" Monster finally mutters, voice thin.

"No," Elijah says, gently taking the phone. "We found the orders in the Warden's desk. We're not warning you because we like you. We're warning you because they're going to burn this city."

Violet asks, "You expect people to just believe…"

"You think anyone believed this prison could fall?" Elijah asks calmly. "It has and the rest of the valley is about to fall with it. Looks like the government fucked something up and now they're cutting the thread."

There's some distant scuffling, off-mic voices. The Morgue doesn't mute the feed this time. Finally, Violet asks, "You got proof?"

Swecker takes control of the phone again and states flatly, "This came straight from the warden's desk. Whatever has happened in the valley, the government doesn't want a paper trail. I suggest you get your asses off the airwaves and out of town. At the very least, into a bomb shelter. Time's running out." The line disconnects.

Back in the Warden's office, the fire is growing. Nelson has tipped a bottle of bourbon into a metal waste bin. Anderson drops a handful of pictures of the warden into it. Swecker lights it with a twist of torn curtain and a book of matches bearing the state seal.

The Warden groans against his gag, his eyes frantic. Bartholomew stares down at him. "You made your choices."

The flames kiss the curtains and glass pops in the heat. Swecker watches it spread without blinking. "Let it burn."

From the radio Elijah turned on, the Morgue's broadcast signal flickers briefly into chaos. The music cuts to an abrupt stop and Violet's voice cuts in, shaky and unfiltered. "This is The Morgue. If you're in the valley and you hear this, you need to get out, now. This isn't a test. We have confirmed government orders for a city-wide incendiary strike. This is Walla Walla, and we are being erased."

20 – WOUNDED VEINS

Jeff's key ring jingles with the rattle of a dozen lost doors. The middle-aged man with the beer belly and greying mullet thumbs through the brass collection until one small, pitted key catches his eye. He feeds it into the lock slowly, carefully. With a faint click, he twists the knob and eases the door open to reveal the armory's old infirmary, housing two clunky exam tables, a battered metal cart of supplies, and a cot dressed in hospital-white linen that seems to glow in the low light.

Without a word, Jeff steps aside, letting the procession shuffle in. Jason leads, with one hand over his bleeding shoulder. Steve and Eric carry Winston between them. He is half-conscious, his pant leg soaked in red, the crude bandages around his stump already failing. The cot welcomes him with clinical indifference.

Jason grunts as he hoists his frame onto one of the exam tables, his legs dangling like a kid on a dock. He winces as he probes the gunshot wound. "What the hell is wrong with you people?"

Jeff closes the door, setting the lock again with a quiet turn. "Don't go lumping me in with them," he mutters, slinging his rifle against a nearby cabinet. "I ain't thrown in with David or Howard. I'm just here to live."

Jeff's statement gets their attention. Jason's eyes narrow. "You pointed a gun at us like they did."

Jeff sighs, opening a cabinet full of gauze, tape, and antiseptics with practiced hands. He gathers what he needs while the air thickens with unspoken tension.

"Just 'cause we wear the same DOC badge don't mean we see the world the same way," he mutters, wrist-deep in supplies. "Those two? Still trying to swing their dicks like it's a yard fight. Me? I've done nearly thirty years. Some of it in the pen, some in the green."

Eric frowns. "Wait...you were a guard at the prison?"

Jeff glances back, nodding once. "Still am. But on weekends I wore camo and boots like everybody else. Until they stopped calling."

"You're not even military?" Eric presses, incredulous.

"Not no more." Jeff cuts the bloody sleeve from Jason's shirt, exposing the torn flesh beneath. He starts cleaning the wound with steady hands, no flourish, no theater, only tired precision.

Steve joins the effort, rummaging through the drawers for supplies. The clatter of metal tools and plastic vials fills the room.

Eric paces the length of the infirmary feeling cagey. "Then what the hell are you doing at the armory?"

On his next pass, Steve kicks him lightly in the shin and tosses him a pair of nitrile gloves. "You want to bitch or you want to help?"

Eric hesitates, then slides the gloves on. Winston groans from the cot, his head rolling toward the wall.

Jeff begins probing Jason's gunshot wound, hands steady, voice low. "We were on our way to work when all this shit broke out. Live up on Roosevelt, me, David, and Howard. Not with each other, we are close enough that we carpool most days."

He pokes around the torn flesh on Jason's shoulder with practiced fingers. Jason grits his teeth, stifling a hiss as the pain bites back. Once satisfied with the assessment, Jeff dabs away blood, cleans the wound, and begins wrapping gauze around the raw, pulpy mess. "Took Alder to the convenience store, right up the road," he continues. "Came up on a mob smashing out store windows. Glass everywhere. Looked like a riot."

Eric and Steve pause their efforts on Winston's leg, drawn into the story.

"We stopped. Howard and David jumped out to try and calm folks down. I was calling the cops. At least, I tried to." Jeff tugs the bandage snug. "David fired a warning shot in the air. People froze, then they charged."

He sits back on a stool with a sigh, the memory weighing on him. "They came at us, biting, clawing, like something from a nightmare. We fought back best we could, but it wasn't a fight we were going to win. We ran to the car, but it was already covered in 'em. Half those people looked wrong. Torn up. Rabid."

He shakes his head slowly and inspects his wrap job, hands stained with blood. "We didn't plan it, but we all ran the same way, like our guts knew where to go. Two blocks from the Apex to here, and it was hell. Every corner, someone was trying to tear our faces off."

His hands gesture animatedly, painting the memory in the air. "We lost count how many times one of us almost got grabbed. We kept moving, heads down, swinging like crazy. We took some hits but we made it here, barely."

The room settles in his silence, letting the weight of it land. Then Steve breaks it, voice dry. "So, your job knows you're not clocking in tonight?"

Jason snorts and Jeff smirks.

"We tried," he says simply. "For over an hour. Couldn't get a signal anywhere, home, dispatch, emergency services. Nothing. Eventually, we got a dial tone. By that time, it was nothing but busy lines, every single one. Eventually, they started ringing and ringing. No one answered."

He glances toward the window. "Felt like the world went quiet all at once."

Jeff leans back, eyes scanning the bruised faces and bloodied clothes of the young men around him. His gaze settles on the cot, and on the mangled stump soaking through its second layer of gauze. He lets out a low whistle.

"But I think the real question is…" he nods toward Winston, "what about you?"

Steve and Eric glance up. Even Jason, pressing his shoulder, follows Jeff's gaze.

Jeff gestures loosely at the cot. "They did a number on you, kid. How come you ain't one of them?"

Winston shifts. He's pale, slick with cold sweat, and wrapped tight in a shivering kind of silence. It takes him a second to speak. When he does, his voice is quiet, but steady.

"I was working a booth," he says. "Fairgrounds. Business club, Phi Beta Lambda. We were doing a fundraiser. Then people started screaming. An ambulance burst through the wall and a metal rod tore through my leg."

He closes his eyes for a moment. "Didn't see the first attack, but I saw the aftermath. The blood. The panic. I watched a girl I…I know…she got attacked. She should've died, but got back up…" His throat tightens. "It wasn't right."

"Had to tear my leg up just to get away. It wasn't fully gone yet." He winces, pain in his every breath. Eric and Steve steady him as he leans forward. Steve gingerly pats the stump with clean gauze.

He points at Steve and Eric. "I saw some kids from the dojo running. I didn't think. Just followed. I found a plank near the fairground entrance and used it as a crutch. Made it five blocks like that."

He lets out a broken breath. "Then I saw the dojo. Doors were locked. I banged. Screamed. Thought I was going to die right there."

Winston nods toward the bandaged stump. "That's when the crowd caught up. The ones that weren't people anymore. One grabbed my ankle. My leg was already torn up bad, hanging by some tissue." His eyes glisten. "When they pulled, it came off."

The room falls into silence.

"I kept crawling. Got to the dojo doors. I could hear voices inside, people were shouting. Fighting. Thought it was too late."

He lifts his chin. "But they opened up. Pulled me in. Right before those people started eating what used to be my leg." A weak smile fights through the pain.

Jeff listens, brow furrowed. "You saying they never bit you?" he asks.

Jason huffs, "Crass, dude."

Winston shakes his head. "Not anywhere connected to me. They were chewing on the leg I lost. I've checked everywhere else. Not a scratch."

Jeff nods slowly and gestures for Steve to peel back more of the gauze. He inspects the stump with careful fingers, brow furrowed, and jaw tight. He leans in and places a hand near the skin, then hovers there for a moment.

"Doesn't feel hot," he mutters. "No dark streaks. Not yet."

He looks up at Winston, then back at the others, voice quieter now. "I don't know. Maybe it's not just bites. Maybe it's something in the blood. Or how deep it gets when they bite."

He shakes his head, clearly unsettled. "But if they were chewing on something already torn off," he gestures to the stump, "maybe it didn't have anywhere to go. No veins left to carry it."

Jason frowns. "So, you're saying he's fine?"

"I don't know about fine." Jeff shrugs, motioning to where Winston's leg should be. "I'm saying I hope he isn't infected." His clarifying statement brings a swell of hard recognition to the room.

Eric lets out a low whistle. "Damn."

"But I wouldn't let anyone with a fresh bite near me without watching 'em close. We don't know the rules yet."

The boys all stare at the stump.

Jeff glances around the room again. "We'll keep checking to be sure. But for now..." He pats Winston's shoulder, firm but kind. "Looks like you might be the luckiest unlucky bastard I've ever met."

Steve begins packaging Winston's leg and taping it tightly.

21 – LIFE, BIRTH, BLOOD, DOOM

"So, where do we go from here?" DJ asks, both hands braced on the edge of the steel counter. Her voice is steady despite the fatigue weighing on her eyelids.

Before Bruce can answer, David cuts in, smirking beneath a crooked mustache. "Don't care. Long as you get the hell out of here."

The room stills. "You know what?" DJ turns slowly, her gaze landing on him. Her glare is a hammer poised mid-swing. "No, never mind, you creep. You don't deserve my attention."

David leans against the wall with arms crossed. He grins at her frustration. "I'm just saying. Go wherever you want but make it soon." He lets the words hang, then adds, with venom sharpened by ego, "You're a liability. All of you. We're combat ready, you are all kids. You'll slow us down and get people killed."

His eyes land on Caroline. "Except you. I'd guard the hell out of you."

Caroline's lips part in surprise, then curl upward into a coy, unsettling smile. She winks at David. Chastity watches the exchange from across the room, her disgust rising.

"I'm sure you'll do more than guard the hell out of her," Chastity mutters, slapping her thighs and stalking off toward the kitchenette. "I need a drink."

Bruce interjects with a raised hand. "This place is dry. It's rented out for school functions. No booze."

"Yeah, sure," Chastity scoffs, opening cupboards anyway. "Dry as a Mormon prom."

DJ doesn't laugh. She turns back to Bruce. "So seriously, what now? We can't sit here and wait to die."

Bruce studies the room, his face unreadable. His eyes pass over each survivor, the wounded, the grieving, the quietly unraveling.

"You know, kid." He sighs and lifts his coffee. "I had a few pretty solid leads before you all showed up. Now I've got a puzzle made of panic and half-strength players."

His words sting, but he softens the blow with a tired smile. "Don't get me wrong, we'll figure it out. We've already confirmed a few things. It's not airborne. That's huge. Could be waterborne, so if it ain't bottled or boiled, don't drink it."

"Weston had E. coli last month," Lena offers quietly.

Bruce points at her with determination. "Smart. See? You're already helping."

He rests his hand on the counter, his voice calm and deliberate. "We've come to learn that most forms of communication are down, or were, until recently. Doesn't mean we're cut off completely. I managed to get a shortwave radio working. Enough to send a status update to my superiors."

He lets that settle. "So, worst case? We bunker down here and wait for someone to show up. Sooner or later, one agency or another will establish a corridor."

Caroline exhales, shoulders slumping in relief. "Amen to that." Her smile is real. "I've got no problem riding this out if it means staying safe."

Bruce shrugs his shoulders. "Of course, that's the fallback plan." The room is silent for a beat.

"To be honest," he continues, "I don't intend to sit here and wait. My plan is to take the Stryker in the courtyard, point it toward the airport, and get airborne. There's a twin-prop parked out there, private model with good range. Howard's got aviation training, enough to get us airborne. Once we're airborne, we head to Lewis-McChord. Once we're there, real logistics can happen."

Oliver leans toward the window. "You mean that rig?"

Bruce smiles, boyish pride lighting up his worn face. "That's the one. M1126 Stryker Infantry Carrier Vehicle. Eight-wheel drive, full armor plating, C7 diesel engine pushing 350 horses, top speed of about sixty. It's got a remote-controlled M2 Browning up top. David's our marksman, he'll be on the gun."

Oliver stares through the window at the rig. He whispers, "That's some firepower."

"The Stryker's a beast," Bruce continues. "Military-grade. That kind of hardware doesn't stop for much. If we plan it right, we can roll straight through town and hit the tarmac without even cracking a window."

Ellie squints. "And how many people can it hold?"

Bruce doesn't flinch. "Nine, not counting the driver and the gunner."

"What about us?" Ellie asks.

The room shifts. A few glance at the child. At the wounded. At each other. David cracks his neck and grins. "Guess we start trimming fat."

A hush settles in. Lena instinctively pulls Benjy closer, her eyes narrowing at David.

DJ glares, "What the hell is wrong with you?"

Even Bruce flinches, but barely, the suggestion came faster than he expected.

Oliver clears his throat. His voice is low, ragged. "I'll stay."

Heads turn. Ellie jerks toward him, stunned. "What?"

"I'll stay behind," Oliver repeats, louder this time. "There's not enough room and Brooke's gone. What's the point?"

"You don't get to decide that," Ellie snaps, voice cracking. "She wouldn't want this. I don't want this."

Oliver doesn't meet her eyes. His gaze drifts out the window toward the courtyard, vacant and full of sorrow. "I don't want to live in a world she's not in."

DJ takes a long breath, then steps forward. "No one gets left behind," she says, maintaining determined eye contact with David. "We've fought too hard. Lost too much. Nobody gets to play God now. Not you," she jabs a finger at him, "…and not you," she adds, facing Bruce.

Bruce folds his arms, eyes sharpening. "It's not about playing God. It's about logistics."

"Bullcrap," DJ snaps at the man. "It's about fear. About convenience. You want to survive without the burden of us? Fine. But you won't survive the guilt."

David opens his mouth, but Bruce holds up a hand to stop him.

She takes a step closer. "You've got gear. We've got numbers. You've got firepower, but that doesn't matter unless you have enough hands to hold it."

Ellie jumps in, "At least, let us ride with you as far as the college. WWCC." She offers, "It isn't far from the airport. You drop us there, we part ways. Simple."

Bruce eyes the girls for a moment, calculating. Then glances at the others. Chastity, arms crossed but nodding. Lena, shielding Benjy with her body. Caroline smiling optimistically. The full weight of these lives sinks into silence.

Finally, Bruce exhales. "Alright."

David blinks, clenching his jaw. "Alright?"

"Yes, David." Bruce says. He looks at the determined girl. "We'll take the Stryker to Walla Walla Community College. After that, you're on your own."

A sigh of relief ripples through the room and Ellie excitedly grabs Oliver's arm and squeezes. DJ nods, satisfied.

"For what it's worth," Bruce adds, softer now, "I respect what you're trying to do. But don't mistake this world for the one you left behind. Mercy gets harder every mile."

DJ doesn't flinch. "Then we'll take it one mile at a time."

22 – TOO COLD FOR TEARS

The hallway hums with old electricity. Flickering fluorescent lights throw long, twitching shadows across chipped linoleum. The air smells faintly of cleaner and gun oil, familiar to Howard, who trudges a few steps ahead, muttering under his breath.

"I was supposed to be the goddamn spotter," he grumbles, tightening the sling on his rifle. "Not some glorified babysitter for kids with full bladders and too many feelings."

Behind him, Rose hugs her arms around her middle as they round the corner. "It's not like we asked for the apocalypse or full bladders," she says, voice low and edged.

Chris, walking beside her, snorts. "Must suck, being the low man."

Howard shoots a sideways glance at him, unimpressed. "Keep talkin'. I'll lock you in the janitor's closet." Chris shuts up.

Tom lingers near Rose, his hand never quite brushing hers, but never straying far. He glances between the men's and women's doors as they reach them, wooden panels worn smooth, peeling letters stenciled on the signs.

Howard leans against the wall beside the doors and exhales through his nose, trying to hide the fact that he's a man who's already run out of patience. "Make it quick. If you aren't bleeding or on fire, I don't want to hear a damn peep."

Chris rolls his eyes and pushes through the men's door. Rose hesitates, glances at Howard, then to the door marked 'Women'.

Tom steps closer. "You okay?"

Rose lowers her voice. "I don't trust him."

Tom follows her eyes to Howard, who's now picking something from under his fingernail with a pocketknife. "I'll stay right here, at the door."

"No." Her voice is sharp, then softens. "I want you in there. Just…near."

Tom nods. Howard looks up as they move. "The hell you think you're doin', Romeo?"

"She asked," Tom says simply.

Rose pushes through the door and he sticks close behind.

Howard sighs, shakes his head, and mutters to the ceiling. "Babysitting. Jesus Christ."

The door creaks shut behind them. Inside the women's bathroom, the world feels still, suspended in a strange hush. The air smells like bleach and old paint. A buzzing fluorescent light flicks above, casting a soft, sterile glow over cracked tile and dull mirrors.

Tom stays near the sink, hands in his hoodie pocket, his eyes remain fixed on the aging grout lines. His sneakers shift slightly on the linoleum, echoing louder than they should. It feels weird to be in here, but it's safer than being out there.

Behind a closed stall door, Rose's voice is small but steady. "This is so stupid."

Tom tilts his head. "The bathroom?"

"No. Me. All of it." A soft pause follows. There's a rustle of clothing, and the distant sound of trickling water.

"I keep thinking about Kay," she says. "What I said to her before she died." A long breath comes from the stall. "I was cruel. I wanted her to hurt. And then she."

Tom listens as Rose sobs quietly behind the closed door. "She died thinking I hated her."

His brow furrows. He wants to say something but doesn't speak. He holds the space, knowing she needs someone to listen.

"And Ma'am. She tried so hard to keep us together. Tried to keep us safe." Her voice wavers. "She died doing that. We ran, and she stayed."

Tom closes his eyes, he remembers his first belt graduation and the pep talk Ma'am gave him before his last belt test. There's nothing he could say that could make any of what they are both feeling any better.

"I pretend I'm fine," she continues. "For DJ. For the others. Because if I stop pretending…I don't know if I'll come back."

Her words settle into the room like dust. Finally, Tom speaks quietly. "You don't have to come back all at once. Just don't go alone."

There's a flush, then the stall door clicks open. Rose steps out, eyes red but dry. She walks slowly to the sink, the silence between them deep and careful. She turns the faucet. The water runs quietly as she scrubs her hands, trembling slightly.

"You're the only one who talks to me like I'm not fragile," she says without meeting his eyes.

Tom takes a step closer, gently brushing a strand of hair from her cheek. "You're not fragile. You've been through a lot. Your parents, the trouble at school, and then all this craziness. You're doing the best you can, I see that." She finally meets his eyes.

"I've been thinking about what you said. Back at the dojo," he says softly. "The whole gay friend thing."

Her face flushes. "God, I didn't mean anything by that. I thought…"

"It's okay, it's not a bad thing." Tom cuts in, smiling faintly. "I know I don't act like the others. But I'm not."

She looks away, hiding her embarrassment.

He hesitates, then adds, "I've liked you for a while."

She blinks. "You what?"

"I didn't say anything. Didn't think you'd care." He rubs the back of his neck, suddenly shy. "But I'm glad I'm here with you. Even if it's the girls' bathroom."

Rose huffs out laughter through her nose, shoulders relaxing a little. "I can't believe I dragged a straight boy in here."

He grins. "I'd follow you into worse."

They both pause and their eyes meet again. This time, neither looks away. She steps closer, so does he.

When they kiss, it's hesitant at first. Soft and careful, but warm and real, it is an anchor in the middle of chaos. No promises, no big speeches, only a moment of something good, something still human, in a world that's unraveling.

Chris steps out of the men's room, wiping damp hands on the sides of his jeans. The hallway is dim, lit only by an emergency light above the door. He finds Howard standing with his arms crossed, leaning against the far wall like he's guarding the Pentagon. His rifle hangs across his chest, relaxed but ready.

Chris sidles up a few feet away, careful to keep a bit of space. Neither of them says anything at first. Finally, Chris breaks the silence. "You always draw bathroom duty?"

Howard exhales a single dry laugh. "No. I lost the coin toss."

Chris nods slowly. "Good system."

Howard doesn't respond, his eyes stay trained on the bathroom doors. Chris hesitates, then asks, "David always like that?"

Howard glances sideways at him. "What do you mean?"

"You know." Chris shrugs. "Shooting people. Threatening kids. Treating women like they're trash with a pulse."

Howard sighs through his nose again, there's a purpose in his release. "David's been through some shit. Working corrections chewed him up and never really spit him out. Happens to a lot of us. He's got that edge, like he's waiting for the world to prove him right about how bad it is."

"Guess he got what he wanted, then."

"Guess he did."

Chris shifts his weight. "And you? You just roll with it?"

Howard's jaw flexes. "You think this is rolling with it?"

Chris raises his hands. "Just asking."

A long silence stretches between them. Somewhere down the hallway, the wind howls faintly against old windows.

"I don't like everything he does," Howard says at last. "But he's had my back more times than I can count. Out there, when it was chaos, he didn't flinch. Didn't freeze. He got us here in one piece."

Chris nods not convinced but not dismissive either. "Still. You shot Jason for him. You rolled with that. You going to let him abuse and kill people?"

Howard finally turns to look at him. His voice is even. "He may have taken the stripping thing too far, but he wasn't abusing anyone. He was defending our base. That's different."

Chris scowls. "Is it, though?"

The two men lock eyes for a moment. Then Howard looks away, jaw tight. "I didn't say it was right," he murmurs. "Just that it's the world we're in."

For a long breath, neither of them speaks. When Chris finally answers, his voice is small. "I've done some shady shit, but that was fucked up."

Howard's radio crackles to life. David's voice punches through the static, low, and clipped. "Meet at central. Boots on ground, ASAP."

Howard straightens, scanning the hallway expecting that danger might already be seeping through the cracks in the walls. He peers through a window, scanning, then strides to the bathroom door and pounds on it with the butt of his palm.

"Time's up, let's move!"

Inside, Rose and Tom jolt like startled deer. Their bodies spring apart, awkward and flushed. For half a second, they stare at each other, caught between adrenaline and something softer.

Rose exhales, brushing hair behind her ear. "Of course."

Tom grins, adjusting his hoodie. "I hope we get to do that again."

She bumps his shoulder as she passes, smiling. "We better."

They emerge into a dimmed hallway where Chris and Howard stand near the window, on alert. The creak of the bathroom door draws both men to turn, hands instinctively twitching. Chris spots the flush cheeks and not-quite-casual spacing between Rose and Tom. He raises an eyebrow, but, mercifully, keeps his mouth shut. Howard gives them all a once-over, his brow lowering beneath his buzzed hairline. "Let's move. Bruce wants us at the vehicle now."

The teens fall into step, their laughter fading as the weight of reality folds back over them like nightfall. Whatever warmth passed between them lingers, but so does the urgency.

Together, they move back toward the others. Toward whatever comes next.

Chris smirks at Howard, "Time to roll, I guess."

23 – WAGING WAR

A faint alarm whines through the building, the sound of the exterior perimeter klaxon. Bruce pauses as David's head tilts. "You hear that?"

Bruce crosses to a dusty surveillance unit on the wall. He powers the antique panel to life with a static hiss. A sharp burst of feed shows grainy video footage flickers into view, one of the outside cameras. A chain-link section of the fence hangs loose at the corner of the vehicle yard. There's movement, quick and low to the ground. Human silhouettes melt into the shadows.

David stiffens. "Was that, were those MCR colors?"

"Looks like it." Bruce's jaw clenches. "Radio the others, it's go time. We need to gear up."

He turns to the civilians, "Wait here, we are grabbing supplies and we're out in five." He taps David's arm, "Follow me."

"Meet at central. Boots on ground, ASAP." David sends his radio command and follows Bruce to the storage room door.

Bruce yanks the pull chain. A bare bulb swings to life and shadows scatter across shelves of rations, dusty fuel cans, and emergency gear. The stale air smells like rust and mothballs.

Bruce wastes no time, he rummages with a soldier's efficiency, grabbing cloth rolls, bandages, flares, anything useful.

Behind him, David leans against the cracked door, arms crossed and face sour. "You aren't serious."

Bruce doesn't turn. "About what?"

David exhales sharply, venom in every breath. "This little hero mission. Those kids, the civilians. They're dead weight,

Bruce. And they're going to choke the Stryker. There's no way you think we're getting out of here clean with a crowd that size."

Bruce doesn't answer, he keeps digging and planting supplies into David's arms.

David's voice sharpens. "They'll slow us down, get people killed. What's next, you going to cuddle with the enemy too? Jesus. Tell me you've considered any of this before bowing to that girl's demands."

Bruce finally straightens from picking at a shelf, his arms are full. His eyes meet David's, their glares deadlocking. "A leader," he says calmly, "is a dealer in hope." He smiles, calm and controlled. "Napoleon Bonaparte."

He deposits some of his scavenged supplies into David's filling arms and walks away, boots echoing deeper into storage.

David groans and follows. "You fucking kidding me? I'm talking serious shit here, man. While we're down here treasure hunting, they're probably raiding the rig, loading their own asses up for a free ride."

"They're not," Bruce replies evenly, testing a doorknob on the far wall.

"Oh yeah? You think you've got them figured out? Or is this about you chasing some young pussy?"

Bruce stops and sizes David up. His face solidifies and his lips go tight. "Nope."

He raises a ring of keys and unlocks the next room. He grabs two backpacks and stuffs his collection into them, then heads back toward the stairs, shoving one of the packs into David's arms.

David pushes past him, frustrated. "What's the play, then? Cram everyone in like sardines and hope for the best? What happens when we need to decrew? What if they beg to go with us instead of being dropped off at college? You really think the plane will hold us all? Half of these people don't even know how to shoot. Are they even worth saving?"

Bruce halts on the first step of the staircase leading to ground level. He turns to David, slow and deliberate. "I don't like these circumstances any more than you do," he says. "In fact, maybe less. We don't know if leaving is smart. But I know what happens if we stay."

His voice lowers. "If the brass decides this valley's lost, they'll quarantine it. Martial law at best. In that case, you're poked, prodded, and questioned for weeks. Worst case...well, you've seen what happens when the government decides the cost of containment. Every living soul they find gets tagged and bagged until they figure out what's wrong, including Fido."

David swallows but says nothing. Bruce's eyes narrow. "I don't intend to be here when the order drops. If there's a window left, we use it. If not, then at least we tried."

They stare each other down. He steps closer, voice low but sharp. "As far as those kids are concerned, we're all human, man. We should act like it, give them a chance. They're here and they're trying. And every single one of them has offered everything they've got to help this evac. So, unless you've got something better than bitching and paranoia, I suggest you shut up and be grateful there are more warm bodies between you and the infected."

The serviceman barely pauses for breath. "So, there you have it. That's why I'm doing this. You can quit questioning my motives and decisions now. I'm still not sure why you're so desperate to get innocents killed, but frankly? I don't care. You serve a purpose, and that's why I tolerate your nihilistic, redneck bullshit."

The silence is molten.

Both men stand with fists clenched and jaws set, the heat between them just shy of ignition. Like dogs at the edge of a cage fight, each waiting for the other to snap.

But it's David who backs down. His shoulders drop and his glare breaks.

Bruce, satisfied, finishes it with a smirk. "Now that we've wrapped up this little pissing contest, let's get topside and get the hell out before we're all gnawed into jerky."

He extends his hand. Not warm, but practical. A peace offering forged in fire. David hesitates, then grips it firmly, but wordlessly. Bruce clenches tight and pulls David close. "For the record, the next time you even suggest I would touch a minor, I will fucking end you. The way your momma should have done.”

Bruce cracks open the thick wooden doors, pointing at the rest of the survivors. Some are sitting, others leaning against the walls, trading supplies and scanning for threats through the smeared glass panes. “Look at them, these are your neighbors.”

He swings the door open and the people in the kitchen flinch, flashing weapons instinctively, a rifle, a crowbar, a pair of kitchen knives, until they recognize Bruce and David.

Bruce gives David a look of confirmation. “Don’t shit in your own back yard.”

Steve steps forward from the pack, his hands gloved in surgical blue. “Can you run the plan again? Some of us were elbows-deep in the wounded.”

Bruce nods and steps into the center, his voice rising from years of holding authority, hushing the buzz of nervous energy. “Alright. First, we secure the parking lot. My men, plus the big guy over there,” he jerks a thumb at Oliver, “will set up along the doors and lay down suppressing fire if needed.”

He gestures broadly, drawing the operation in the air. “David and I enter the Stryker first. Driver and gunner positions. Once that’s locked, the rest of you load in as fast as possible. Stack yourselves tight. Doesn’t matter how, just get in. Once you’re packed, our fire team closes in and we seal the doors.”

Chastity frowns, lifting a hand. “Didn’t you say there wasn’t enough room for all of us?”

Bruce doesn’t miss a beat. “Officially, the Stryker holds nine passengers. That’s when soldiers sit neat and pretty on bench seats with all their gear. But we’re not soldiers. We’re desperate. So, guess what? We cram in. Sit on laps. Hug knees. Pretend it’s a clown car and we’re all trying to make one sad bastard laugh till he pisses himself.”

There’s a ripple of uneasy laughter, but he cuts it off with a raised hand.

“Here’s your final instruction, each of you stay low and move fast. Keep to the left of the vehicle during load. I don’t like the look of the fence on the right. If that’s where the infected come through, and I think it is, you don't want to be standing there when the party starts."

He meets every eye in the room. "Questions?"

When nobody responds, he finalizes, "Then let's make it count."

24 – LAST MAN STANDING

It's quiet behind the motor pool fence, unnaturally quiet.

The moonlight glints off the razor-wire perimeter behind the Walla Walla Armory, dancing between links of chain and shadows. A soft metal creak breaks the silence. Then another. Slowly, methodically, a pair of bolt cutters gnaw through a length of chain securing the outer maintenance gate.

Three figures crouch in the darkness, their shapes hidden underneath the shadow of the skeletal remains of a storage truck looted over two hours ago. One has a bandana over his mouth while another wears a cracked hockey mask.

Spray-painted across the side of the disabled vehicle, is a name in jagged block lettering: MCR. Tagging from the local gang, Mill Creek Raza.

One of the saboteurs takes a pair of bolt cutters and yanks the final brace from the fence post, leaving it swaying. The leader, an angular man with neck tattoos and missing teeth, grins as the final link gives way.

"Dumb bastards don't even know they're boxed in," mutters one of the others, gripping a machete. "Bet they think that fence'll hold."

The leader nods toward the alley behind the armory.

Inside the narrow corridor between buildings and dumpsters, shadows jerk and seize, restless and coiled.

"Wake 'em up," the leader mutters.

One of the Raza boys holds a pipe and drags it hard along the fence. The screech splits the night. The gang has baited the path to the Armory fence with meat scraps.

From the dark, they explode forward, not walking, but sprinting and twisting. Some of the dead slam into each other and then toward the sound of steel on steel, toward the scent of blood, toward the cut in the fence. Half a dozen emerge from the alley at first, and more follow, a dozen more, moving like wildfire.

The gang scatters to the edges, slipping back into cover. They don't need to control the horde. They merely point the ravenous dead like a weapon and get out of the way.

The infected begin to press forward from across the street, sniffing at the meat trail.

The Armory's back door bursts outward into the rear courtyard, swinging wide like saloon gates. The slap of boots on concrete follows as two armed survivors sweep through barrels, scanning shadows. The military rig, their salvation, waits in the darkness, a coiled beast, matte armor dull beneath the floodlights and moon glow.

Jeff and Howard are first to cross the lot, looking down their muzzles as they pan across their surroundings, checking rooftops, corners, and fence lines. Oliver stands firm at the exit, a shotgun cradled in his thick arms, spotting for trouble. Jeff breaks left, heading for the Stryker's cab. Howard disappears around the rear to prep the ramp.

The air is sharp with metal, diesel, and something sour beneath, like rotting citrus. The yard is thick with apprehension. Inside the courtyard, the night holds its breath.

Bruce and David move through the lot, each taking staggered positions along the planned travel route.

Both scouts make it to their escape vehicle. Jeff's arm rises, signaling that he's ready to load while Howard lowers the back ramp. Oliver nods and motions to the people inside the door. Signaling the civilians to move fast.

Ellie grips Benjy's hand tight, cooing at the boy in his mom's arms. DJ urges the group forward with wide, watchful eyes. Tom hovers near Rose, never more than a step away. They all stream toward the vehicle.

A moan rises from behind the shipping container on the far side of the lot. A low, horrible wail, distant but growing, wet and starving.

The survivors turn to see them, two at first, then ten. Within heartbeats, dozens of the dead are slamming into the fence on the far side of the lot like waves against a levee. Their limbs claw at the mesh, fingers punching through gaps, teeth gnashing through steel.

The infected press against the fence, already weakened by sabotage, shudders with the impact. Howard catches the movement and shouts, "Double time everybody! Let's go!"

The perimeter is splitting. David moves to the ramp's edge, opposite Howard. Both stand sentry with weapons ready. Bruce scans the horde as it grows, his jaw tight. "Just like I said," he mutters, "they're coming from the right. The fence is already going down."

Unbothered or unaware, Ellie rushes toward the Stryker's nose. She yanks a spray can from her oversized purse, shakes it twice with a rattle, and tags the armored beast in neon, a haloed skull and the words ZOMBIE SMASHER.

Rose is the first civilian to reach the Stryker's ramp with Tom close behind. She hesitates, stopping dead in her tracks. "Hey," she calls out, turning to face the line of survivors behind her. "Why are we leaving again?"

Eric nearly crashes into her. "Because we're about to die?" He veers around, breath ragged. "Look at the fence behind you!"

Rose glances toward the fence as another steel post snaps with a twang. She winces. "I don't know. We have family here. Friends. What if they're still out there?"

Caroline elbows past, eyes flashing. "Then stay, bitch." She barrels into the rig. "But get out of my way."

The groaning of metal rises as the fence begins to buckle. It's more than moans coming from the infected now, it's screams.

"Inside! Now!" David ducks into the rig and his voice thunders from the Stryker's top gun mount, "I'll need time to lock and load!" Bruce takes his place near the rear of the vehicle, but far enough to provide suppressing fire.

The rest of the group surges. One by one, they pile into the cargo hold. There is no room, no plan, and no guarantee. Only the trembling hope of survival. The fence behind them groans, its metal seams warping under pressure. But it's not just the dead causing fracture lines, it's the living.

The hope for survival is tipping. Behind them, the fence finally falls with a sharp whine of torn steel, holding at one corner by a thin wire.

"This is insane," Rose snaps, arms crossed. "I'm not going. I don't care about all this military escape crap. I have a mom out there, and…"

Her rant is cut off when a hand clamps down over her mouth. She jerks back, glaring up into the pale face of Chris, his brow beading with panicked sweat, his other hand raised like he regrets everything already.

"Shhh," he whispers, eyes wide. "Listen."

She wrenches free, spitting into his palm. "Don't you dare touch me! I have every damn right to make my own decision! If I want to stay with my family, I'm staying!"

"Rosey!" DJ calls, voice brittle with urgency.

Rose is already stomping away and Tom trails behind, her confused puppy. His voice trembles with helpless affection. "Rose, come on. Don't."

The others freeze, trapped between survival instinct and unraveling drama.

"Rose!" DJ yells again, hope thinning. "We'll stop by your mom's on the way out!"

Caroline mutters, already finding her seat in the rig. "Fuck her. If she wants to die, let her,"

Chris exhales hard and starts to follow, brushing past a row of steel barrels near the motor pool wall. His first step is fine. The second never lands. A flash of motion, bloody hands lunging from behind the containers, drag him backward into the shadows.

Chris's scream cuts the air like a jagged blade. His head snaps back as the thing's teeth dig into his scalp, peeling skin like wet paper. He thrashes, tries to push it off, but the fingers clamp harder, nails digging into his shoulders. Blood sprays in arcs across the pavement.

"Jesus Christ!" he screams. "Get it off me!"

The attack detonates the yard. Screams ring out. Lena clutches Benjy tight and bolts. Ellie freezes near the headlights. Inside the vehicle, Caroline shrieks at David to shoot, but the man waves wildly, yelling, "No shot! He's in the line! I can't. I can't!"

DJ pushes people toward the Stryker. The last standing section of fence wails behind them as more infected slam into it, a wave ready to break. Jason turns to see Chris is alive, flailing against an attacker. The zombie's head is buried in his neck now, chewing. His screams are high and shrill.

"Help me!" Chris begs. "Please God, Jason. Fuck man!"

Jason charges. He wraps an arm around Chris's chest, gripping the attacker's soggy hair with the other, and yanks hard. The zombie's skull peels away from Chris's flesh with a wet pop. Jason's shoulder howls and his hand slips, slides down the thing's mashed face, his fingers plunge into the mangled ruins of what used to be a human mouth.

The taste of fresh flesh snaps the creature's focus. Its head jerks down, jaws locking around Jason's fingers with a sickening crunch. He screams a raw, guttural sound that drowns out the wet crack as Chris's head hits the pavement, pouring blood.

Jason bellows, slamming his forehead into the zombie's nose, crushing cartilage. He throws the creature backward with all his weight.

The infected doesn't stop. It gnaws harder, both hands clutching Jason's wrist, working furiously toward the elbow like it's tearing through a steak. Agony sends him into a frantic rage. He whips his arm sideways, slamming the thing's skull into one of the nearby barrels.

The impact shatters bone against steel. The thing's skull bursts on the drum rim, spraying gore across the oil barrels and the now-idling Stryker. The barrels topple and roll, their clang drowned in screams.

The violence ignites the horde, and they flood the yard in a violent frenzy. Dozens of bodies crash through barrels in a thunderous wave. They tumble like ragdolls, then scramble upright with impossible speed.

The rush of infected human attackers crashes blindly against Tom and Rose as they race for the door. They are instantly engulfed. Any sight of the two would-be lovers is consumed by the wrecked flesh of unholy terror.

"No!" DJ shouts, trying to reach them, but it's already too late. The seething tide swallows the space between lovers. What's left is limbs, screams, and spraying blood.

Oliver flanks wide, rifle barking with precision. He herds the others into the vehicle while his shotgun tears through the flesh of the pressing mass, buying slivers of space. He can't reload fast enough to keep up, there are too many attackers.

Within the writhing pile of cannibals, a geyser of red shoots skyward, followed by a severed arm. In a matter of moments, there is nothing left of the future couple, but bones fought over by gnashing jaws. Lena clamps her hands over Benjy's eyes, her own wide with horror, her clothes soaked in arterial spray.

Jeff lays suppressing fire from the front corner of the Stryker, until he's confirmed the exit is clear. He presses forward, along the side of the vehicle to the back ramp, then enters through the hatch to the driver's seat and bringing the vehicle to life.

Jason races to the mother and scoops her and her toddler up with his good arm while cradling the shreds of his mangled hand into his midsection. Blood pours down his belly from his mangled arm, but he doesn't slow. He's a human battering ram, his boots finding impossible speed as the dead close in behind.

Two of the infected slip on the fresh gore, falling hard, but more follow, closer now, so much closer. "Go! Go! Go!" Jason bellows, dodging bullets and bodies alike.

The Stryker lurches as Jeff shifts gears, putting the vehicle into motion. Jason reaches the rear as Steve and one-legged Winston scramble aboard. He practically throws Winston inside, nearly tossing the boy into Ellie's lap.

"Get in the truck!" Jason roars. "Or we're dog food!"

He climbs in one-handed, Steve grabbing his belt and yanking him inside. The second Jason clears the ramp, three infected leap and one latches onto Steve. The other two slam into the bumper, claws scraping metal, lower halves dragging across the pavement, their flesh peeling away in sheets.

Gunfire explodes, controlled and surgical. The backup team, Howard, Bruce, and Oliver, follow the crawling vehicle to cover loading. They fire methodically as they close in on the Stryker. Each man leaps for the footholds, grabbing the side ladders as the armored vehicle hits the curb and lurches.

Oliver slips, one boot skidding in blood, but he catches the rail and pulls himself onto the rig. He empties his shotgun again, rounds ripping into the two infected on the bumper. They lose their grip on the metal and tumble off while the rig surges forward.

Behind them, the courtyard is overrun. Jeff yells a command over the roar of the engine, then stomps on the gas. David, in the command seat, uses the vehicles weaponry to lay down suppressing fire. High velocity rounds tear into the mass of living dead.

Bruce and Oliver, both clinging to the rear ladders, fight gravity and wind as the Stryker tears around a corner. Oliver's knuckles bleed from the grip and Bruce nearly slips, but they hold. The rear ramp drags the ground as the vehicle speeds, throwing sparks into the trailing horde.

They both maneuver to the rear hatch, grimy, wide-eyed, and breathing hard. The gunmen swing into the rear of the vehicle, activating the switch to seal the rig.

Inside the roaring Stryker, chaos surges louder than the engine. Shouts, crying, pain, and the sound of chewing. Bruce hears it before he sees it. A wet, meaty gnashing, hidden beneath the bodies huddled on the floor.

He swings his pistol low toward one last stowaway. Half a face, all hunger. Its jaws are locked around the rubber sole of Steve's shoe, gnawing through tread, eager to find flesh. The boy screams, scrambling, kicking, but the thing won't let go.

Bruce doesn't hesitate, he presses his pistol against the thing's head and fires three deafening shots, the echoes rip through the cabin. The discharge flash lights up panicked eyes, sears metal, and smears blood.

The creature's head explodes into pulp. Its grip loosens. Steve kicks again, this time landing a solid foot to the ruined skull. The infected flies back, bounces off the bulkhead, and vanishes out the raising ramp, which slams shut behind it.

For a moment, shock takes over the troop compartment, passengers stunned by both the carnage and the ringing ears. Benjy wails. Jason cries out, clutching his hand. Chastity cries for her brother and Caroline cries for herself.

The Stryker devours asphalt, its treads crushing limbs and corpses in its path. Blood paints its wheels. Bones crunch like gravel, but it moves. God, it moves.

Streetlights blur past in golden streaks. Empty intersections flash by like forgotten promises. On a nearby pole, a traffic cam silently watches it all, unblinking, uncaring.

It records the last trace of the survivors' escape, recording deep crimson tire marks bleeding down the road, no plates, only a name spray-painted in streaky neon yellow across the Stryker's front, forging a battle cry from hell: ZOMBIE SMASHER.

25 – I WALKED WITH A ZOMBIE

The prison groans from the wounds of upheaval. Somewhere in the distance, a door slams open and never closes. Anderson barely notices, his world has shrunk to a forgotten cabinet and the dusty archives inside it.

The light is dim, many of the fluorescent lights have been broken from the riot, but it's enough to illuminate the Civil Defense stamp on a faded file folder. Enough to reveal the rolled maps wedged between government memos and long-forgotten evacuation plans.

"Bingo," he whispers, dragging the bundle out with shaking hands. His knuckles are still raw from his time in the Warden's office, and every movement sends sharp reminders of the last hour through his ribs, but he grins.

The Morgue crackles on the radio he stole from the Warden's office and propped on a crate.

"No, Monster," Meat's voice dribbles through the radio, distant but excited. "That one over there. Check the ass out on that one, huh?"

A few grunts follow, then Monster chimes in, equally far from the mic, "Damn, man. Good choice."

Violet sighs with the weight of embarrassment. "That's right, cadavers. You're tuned into The Morgue, the only radio show left on earth whose DJs, in the midst of a goddamn cannibal apocalypse, have chosen to rank which of the flesh-eating crazies they'd most like to bend over a bed."

She lets that sink in before continuing. "I'd like to thank you all for tuning in, whoever's still out there. I'd also like to thank Monster, for reminding us all that decency isn't dead, it just gets a boner whenever anything with a skirt limps past, even if the skirt is soaked in blood and missing an arm."

"No problem, Violet," Monster calls back casually. "Shit, Meat, over there, across the street!" The two erupt in crude banter. "Holy God," Monster breathes, almost reverent. "I would rail that one 'til she puked up everyone she's eaten."

A burst of horrified laughter floods the airwaves. Violet can be heard whispering "oh my god" right before Goblin joins in, "Yeah, let me leap over to the window and gawk at half-eaten girls. Hoo-boy! Dream come true."

Ninja's voice slithers in, deadpan. "What's the matter, Goblin? Afraid of a little blood?"

Goblin chuckles, and Monster doesn't miss a beat. "Nah, he's just waiting for one of 'em to sprout a dick. Then he'll be down there with flowers."

"Goddammit, Monster!" Fresh squeals in protest.

"True story, bro," Monster says without remorse.

"You're awful!" Fresh scolds through an astonished giggle.

Goblin gives a shrug that can almost be felt through the mic, "He's not wrong. Give one of those girls a bulge and I'm on her like a tiger on a wounded gazelle."

"That ain't right," Ninja says with a low whistle.

Violet finally yanks the wheel back. "Focus, people. We've got listeners…maybe. Let's actually talk about what's happening out there. What is this? How did it start?"

Blade answers first, dry as dust, "Chaos. Pure and simple."

Butcher chimes in too. "You mean right now, or how it all started?"

"Yes, to both," Violet presses. "How did this all start? What is it? Where'd it come from?"

"Right there! Look at those legs!" Monster interrupts again, euphoric. "That is one dirty bitch. I'd double-piston that corpse like I'm cleaning a shotgun, fist-deep, both barrels."

"Um…" Violet tries again to regain control.

Ogre jumps in to help. "Listen, maybe it sounds dumb, but I think we've seen enough Romero and Savini to know this isn't bath salts and a bad day. These things aren't high. They're dead. And they're hungry."

"You actually think this is like, zombie zombies?" Ninja asks, genuinely curious.

"Yeah," Ogre says flatly. "I do. Everyone knows Hollywood seeds in government stuff so the populace isn't shocked when shit goes down, why not those old zombie movies?"

Violet pivots smoothly. "Ninja? Got a competing theory?"

"Hell yeah," Ninja shoots back. "I think it's drugs."

"Drugs?" Fresh echoes.

"Yeah. Like a hallucinogen. PCP, maybe some bad acid. I mean, c'mon. Walla Walla's only real vice is wine. What if something contaminated a local vintage? Imagine if half the city got dosed at the same wine tasting."

Violet plays devil's advocate. "You think a whole town dropped acid by accident?"

"Unintentionally. Like a fermentation mishap," Ninja insists. "I once made jailhouse acid using orange peels, sugar, and yeast. Screw up the batch and you get a liquid brain-melter. Now multiply that with a winery festival. Boom, zombie cosplay gone real."

Blade snorts and Fresh tries not to laugh.

Ninja fumes. "Oh, I see. My scientific theory is too far-fetched, but Ogre can scream about horror movies and that's fine? That's what's wrong with this damn country."

"Listen, I'm just saying," Ogre argues his view, "Romero walked so Savini could sprint. That original blood-splatter realism? That was art. Don't come at me with 'fast zombies are scarier.' Fear is tension. Fear is slow."

In the administrative room of the prison, Anderson chuckles. "Damn right, Ogre."

He unrolls one of the maps across the floor. It's yellow and brittle in the corners, but the markings are still clear. This map shows red Xs and Numbered zones, complete with fallout shelter locations. He figures some of these buildings probably don't even exist anymore, but most might.

He stares at it for a long moment, his heart thumping, then he runs to the front of the room and grabs the phone on the desk. He picks up the receiver and finds the line is hot and patched into whatever system hasn't gone down. He dials fast, like it might disappear. Like the world might go dark again before the ring tone even hits.

It connects to a familiar voice, even if the sound is distorted by time and bad wiring.

Violet cuts off Ninja mid-rant. "We've got a live one coming through the Morgue line."

A click sounds, followed by a slight frequency shift as a new voice crackles onto the airwaves.

"No shit. This is really the Morgue?"

Violet chuckles. "Live and undead. You've got Violet. Who am I talking to?"

"Oh man. This is so damn cool! Been listening to you guys for years, never thought I'd actually get through!"

"Well, welcome to the apocalypse," Violet says warmly. "Name?"

"Anderson. Yeah, this is Anderson. I've written you guys a bunch of times. You've read some of my letters. I sent the sketch of Goblin riding a demon like a rodeo bull."

Monster's voice blasts in. "Mister Anderson? Like, the Mister Anderson?"

"The one and only, brother!"

"Holy shit!" Monster laughs. "How the hell are you alive? Ain't you supposed to be behind bars?"

"Oh, I am. Or was. Let's just say the WSP's employee retention rate hit zero and things got…flexible."

A few of the DJs erupt with laughter. Goblin asks low. "We talkin' riot? That actually happened? Not going to lie, we all thought we got pranked."

"Full-blown. Doors open, towers empty, guards either gone or locked up themselves. Place is ours now. All of general population is running wild."

"Goddamn," Butcher mutters. "That's the biggest unit in the facility."

"Exactly," Anderson says proudly. "We haven't taken the whole prison yet, but we've got the building with the bodies. And more importantly, we've got the records."

"Wait," Violet leans into the mic. "You didn't call just to gloat, did you?"

"Nah," Anderson says, voice shifting to serious. "I called 'cause I found something. Something I think you asked for off-air, when you talked to Swecker earlier."

The hosts go quiet.

"I got my hands on an old set of city maps," Anderson continues. "Pre-digital. I'm talking Cold War-era planning. This thing's got every bomb shelter, emergency bunker, and civil defense fallout spot marked in red ink. Some of 'em still exist. Some were repurposed. But it's all here."

Violet breathes in sharply. "You're serious?"

"Dead serious. Pun fully intended. I figure, with all this shit going on, it's worth knowing where the deep holes are before the sky lights up. You want it?"

"You're damn right we do," Monster says. "How fast can you get it to us?"

"I'll get someone on the road," Anderson replies. "Might be one of mine. Might be me. But I'll get it to you. I will tell you now, most of the old banks downtown have 'em, Whitman Tower, too. Might help your other fans get to safety."

"You're a beautiful bastard," Violet says.

"Hey, I owe you guys. For the music. For the laughs. For never bleeping the good shit."

Monster cackles. "Stay safe, Mister Anderson."

"You too, Morgue. Long live the dead."

A few clicks sound over the radio, then the hosts sit in a brief moment of silence. The show picks back up, Monster's voice is warm with respect. "That was Mister Anderson, live from the post-apocalyptic penitentiary of dreams. Still making time for heavy metal and community outreach. That, my friends, is dedication."

Goblin snorts. "You heard the man, cadavers. Find your shelter downtown, don't let anyone turn you away."

Violet exhales. "We may be the last show on the air, but at least we've got our people."

"We've got another call." Monster proclaims, "Whole world's ending but the Morgue Lines are alive and well." A few seconds of static hiss over the airwaves before the next voice slips through, young and steady, but worn.

"Monster, this is DJ, hey."

Monster pauses. "DJ?"

"Yeah. I called a little while ago, from the Beginner's Mind Dojo."

"Oh shit, yeah!" Monster lights up. "Good to hear you're still with us. What's goin' on, kid?"

DJ's voice tightens. Urgent now. "Look, I don't have much time. We've got a military radio in our truck; they're coordinating strike zones. All roads leading out of town are blocked, there are some sort of military checkpoints everywhere. And they just hit the airport."

Silence chokes the feed, but Monster is quick to reclaim the silence, "What do you mean, hit the airport? They who?"

"I'm serious," she presses. "It's gone. We saw the fireball from past East Gate on Isaacs. We're stuck. Everyone's stuck. I was hoping you could tell your listeners."

The radio hosts fall silent again and the gravity of the teenage girl's words weigh in that brief lull. Then, softer, with the weight sinking in, Monster responds, "You just told 'em, darlin'. Get to safety, kid."

Violet's voice returns, thin and shaken, not to the caller, but to the rest of the listeners, "Walla Walla, you heard it."

Goblin cuts in, unusually somber: "If you're out there, get underground. Hide. Stay quiet."

Butcher clears his throat. "We'll be here. As long as the power holds. If you can hear this…you're not alone."

Monster exhales into the mic. "This is The Morgue. We've got your back and we will keep sharing until there's nothing left to say."

26– JUST SAY GOODBYE

The Stryker hums low, the engine ticking from the escape. Inside, the survivors settle into a suffocating quiet. The lights from the nearly abandoned parking lot cast a blinding glare on the two-story glass facade of Walla Walla Community College's administrative building. The light of the moon illuminates the asphalt and grass alike, revealing no more than empty, forsaken space.

Bruce leans out the vehicle's rear opening, standing on the lowered ramp. He stares toward the lights of the burning airport and groans, "Well fuck, there goes that plan." The others try not to listen, but every word falls like thunder in the tight quarters.

"We're splitting into two teams," Bruce says as he turns his attention back inside the Stryker. "Eric, Jeff, Steve, Oliver, Lena, Benjy, and Ellie will come with me to sweep the college. We're searching for supplies and a place to hole up if the truck fails."

He glances toward the wounded figures huddled near the back. "You two," he says to David and Howard. "You stay with the Stryker. Keep everyone else safe. Watch for movement."

He pauses, eyes locked on David, the silence between the men means they all know what he hasn't said yet. His eyes drift to Jason, sweating, groaning, and holding his bleeding wrist.

He motions David and Howard to step outside the Zombie Smasher. When they join him outside, he leans in, "And if he turns…" Bruce doesn't finish. He doesn't have to.

David nods once and heads into the vehicle. Howard swallows hard. The college scout crew gathers in the parking lot, past the ramp. Bruce steals one last glance inside the vehicle before guiding the team toward the building.

Inside the Zombie Smasher, the atmosphere is stagnant, thick with sweat, diesel fumes, and despair. DJ scans the faces around her. Winston is slumped and unconscious, pale and limp. Jason, moaning softly, cradles his shredded arm with fevered shivers, while his sister Chastity holds him. Howard sits in the corner still as a stone, watching, saying nothing. Caroline and David sit dangerously close to each on the bench by the driver seat, their flirtation is vulgar in the silence.

Chastity, tending her brother, whispers to DJ, "Any luck getting in contact with your mom?"

DJ shakes her black hair and pockets her decorated cell phone.

"How about your brother or sister? Anyone?" Chastity's voice is gentle, but the question hangs heavy. Again, DJ lowers her eyes and lets hope die quietly.

She swallows. "I think I need to walk. Clear my head."

Chastity looks up, alarm sharpening her features. "Are you high?" She drops the rag she's been using to tend Jason's bloody mess. "This town's crawling with freaks, you've seen what they do. You step too far from this truck and you'll end up being a Happy Meal."

DJ offers a small, grateful hug. "I won't go far. Just a loop around the lot. The second anything feels off, I'm back here. I promise."

Chastity eyes her, feeling like a babysitter being conned but nods, squeezing DJ's shoulder. "Alright. But yell if you see anything weird, and don't go far, I might need you to karate-kick a sicko again."

They both smirk before DJ steps out into the night.

Howard watches her go. His gaze shifts to the away team nearly at the front door of the college, then settles on David. He analyzes the man's detachment, cool, calm, and perfect at erasing consequences. He should be angry. He should say something.

Instead, Howard stands, shoulders his rifle, and follows her. "I'll keep an eye on the kid," he mutters to Chastity. "You focus on your brother." The line is flat. An apology he can't voice.

Howard stops on the ramp and memory hits him hard from the conversation in the Armory, outside the bathroom when Chris told him it wasn't different, wasn't right. He hated admitting the kid was right, but he was. Every restraint, every compromise, has been a failure. It is complicity. He steps out of the vehicle, shoulders hunched, and takes one long, careful breath before stepping into the night.

Relief spreads across Chastity's face, watching Howard leave. "Thanks," she calls out, before turning her attention back to Jason. Her brother has gone quiet now, the ragged noises faded into eerie stillness. She places a palm on his broad shoulder and rubs.

From the front, a burst of giggles erupts from Caroline. Her voice is low and breathy and David grunts something in response. It's obscene, the two of them pawing at each other while the world is ending. Chastity chuckles dryly. "Caroline, you're such a slut." she murmurs.

She sighs, digging into her back pocket for her own phone. Maybe someone in her family's out there, still breathing. The first number goes to voicemail. The second doesn't even ring. On the third, she leaves a rushed message, her voice is shaky.

Behind her, Jason stirs. She places a soothing hand on his back, not even glancing up, absently rubbing circles like she did when he was sick as a kid. He leans forward and rocks slightly, so she lets go of him to focus on her phone.

She dials another number, this time, her dad in Spokane. She is halfway into leaving her message when Caroline lets out a scream that cracks glass. Chastity spins, nearly dropping her cell.

Jason has Winston pinned. His shredded hand presses against the boy's torso. His face is buried in Winston's neck, jaw working in a grotesque rhythm. Blood splatters the bench, slick and steaming. Chunks of soft tissue hang from Jason's lips as he tears and swallows, growling, starving. Winston's eyes are wide and unblinking.

Caroline shrieks again. Chastity throws her phone at the thing that was her brother. He looks up, the light in his eyes gone. Only hunger remains.

Pandemonium detonates inside the steel belly of the Stryker.

Jason, mindless and ravenous, claws with his ruined stump, trying to pull Winston closer. Shredded bone from his wrist snags on the boy's torn shirt, splintering with a sickening crack. Undeterred, Jason lunges again, teeth grinding against gristle.

David scrambles, grabbing his rifle and readying it, his boots thuds on the metal floor. "Move!" he barks, trying to maneuver past Chastity.

"Jason, no!" Chastity shrieks, yanking at her brother's shoulders, trying to pull him back from the abyss. Her voice fractures into sobs. "Please don't do this. Stay with me. Please!"

David plants his boots behind the feeding body, raises his rifle, and levels the barrel at Jason's blood-matted face. "You might want to plug your ears," he mutters coldly.

Caroline obeys without hesitation, burying her fingers deep, but Chastity whirls, eyes wild with desperation, and smacks the rifle aside before David squeezes the trigger. She throws herself across Jason's back, shielding him with her own body.

"No!" she screams, tears streaking down her cheeks. "He's my brother! He's still in there!"

David flinches. "What the hell are you doing? He's eating that kid! That is not your brother anymore!"

"I don't care!" Chastity sobs. "You're not killing him. Just stop!"

"Chas, move!" Caroline shouts from the front. "He's gone. Don't be stupid!"

"Shut your mouth!" Chastity roars, eyes locked on Caroline. "Why don't you go back to fucking anything that breathes, you soulless bitch!"

David shoves forward with his boot, trying to dislodge her. "I'm not playing games," he warns. "Move. Or I shoot through you."

Chastity slaps the barrel again, pushing herself closer to Jason's twitching body. "I'm not going to let you hurt my brother!" she screams. "You'll have to kill me too!"

Jason gurgles beneath her, chewing, drooling, oblivious. David takes a step backward and steadies the rifle once more, muscles coiled, jaw tight. His finger curls around the trigger.

David exhales, flat and emotionless. "Works for me."

The gunshot cracks inside the steel belly of the rig. The sound echoes, drowning out everything, including the quieter second report that follows a half-second later. He doesn't stop there. David turns his rifle to Winston and discharges the weapon a third time. When the ring fades, silence seeps in heavy and unnatural.

David steps over the mess of limbs and torn bodies. He reaches down, takes Chastity's slack form by the shoulders, and gently lays her flat beside the bench. Her head rolls slightly, her now pink hair matted with gore. Without hesitation, he adjusts the angle, placing her wound flush against the bench's metal edge.

He lifts his boot, and the heel comes down with mechanical precision.

Her skull fractures open, the top folding back. A smear of ruined gray spills across the bench as David steps back, expression unreadable. Behind him, Caroline chokes loudly and vomits.

David doesn't flinch. He grinds the shattered cap underfoot, then scoops up Chastity's body, and shoves it against Jason's corpse. With practiced coldness, he steps over them and heads toward the rear door of the rig.

As he reaches the exit, DJ rounds the side of the vehicle to the ramp. The teen focuses on the scene of slaughter and stumbles back with a gasp. David lurches to a stop but trips, landing knees-first on Jason's corpse. He rises fast, breathing hard.

DJ yells, "What the heck happened?!"

David grabs Jason's legs, dragging his weight toward the ramp. "He turned," he grunts, sweat mixing with blood on his arms. He reaches the edge of the exit and gives the body a shove. Jason rolls down the ramp and onto the asphalt with a thud.

David jerks a thumb back inside. "Attacked the kid first, then Chastity. He was too fast to stop. I didn't even have time to grab my gun."

His words are dry and feel practiced.

Inside the rig, Caroline retches again, folding in on herself in the front seat.

David turns to Winston, grabs his limp leg. "Help me with the kid," he says, but DJ stares at him, eyes wide. Her hands shake, but she doesn't move.

David snaps, "Come on. If this place turns out to be hot, we can't be hauling dead weight. You want to be stuck in a tin can with three decomposing bodies? Get your shit together."

He climbs back in and grabs Chastity's ankles.

DJ hesitates, then climbs in, ducking her head. She scoots over the benches, between puddles and limbs, until she's face to face with what's left of Chastity's head. Her fingers tremble as she hooks them beneath the girl's stiff shoulders.

They lift. As the torso rises, the ruined head tilts back. A wet, gelatinous splat hits the bench as the last of her brain matter slips loose. DJ stifles a scream and Caroline sobs behind her. David doesn't look up.

Together, they maneuver the body out the door. DJ nearly trips over the trailing brainstem, her shoe catching for half a second before she hops free. She stares at the jagged crown where Chastity's skull used to be whole.

The silence stretches. DJ swallows hard, eyes locked on the pale, limp form. Then, softly, almost to herself, she asks, "Where'd he bite her?"

David lets Chastity's legs fall with a wet thud across the stacked corpses of Winston and Jason. "In the head," he says flatly. "Why?"

DJ stands over the bodies, wrapping her arms around herself. The heat from her face competes with the night chill. "I. I just didn't see any bites," she murmurs.

David shifts, his frame silhouetted against the flickering floodlight above the parking lot. His face is lost to shadow, but his voice cuts sharp and certain. He jabs a finger toward the ground at her shoes. "Did you not see the missing head? If we are going to get through this, you guys are going to have to learn to trust us."

DJ flinches and raises her hands like she's bracing for impact. "Okay. Okay. I didn't know."

A beat passes and neither person moves. The wind whistles through the shattered husks of nearby cars.

David's eyes rake across the lot, checking shadows, scanning rooftops, listening. Finding nothing but stillness, he turns back. "Hey."

DJ lifts her eyes. "What."

"Where's Howard?"

She blinks. "How the heck should I know?"

"He went out after you."

"No, he didn't."

David swears under his breath. "Son of a…"

His fingers twitch at the stock of his rifle, but he doesn't raise it. He glances around again, more agitated now. "I can't yell for him," he mutters. "And I can't leave."

DJ inches back toward the Smasher. "Why not?"

"Huh?"

She shrugs with attitude. "Why can't you go after him?"

He scoffs, bitter. "Yeah. And leave you with my ride? I don't fucking think so."

That one lands and DJ's breath catches. Her gaze drops to the open rig, the glinting smear of blood on the floor, and the shattered shell of what used to be Chastity's head. She stares at it, at the jagged ruin pressed into the bench leg.

Then she looks back at David. Her voice is low. "Trust, huh?"

Inside Walla Walla Community College, Bruce leads a team of seven other survivors into the moonlit stillness. They cross the glass entryway of the administrative building, their footsteps echoing down empty halls. Bruce's group, Jeff, Eric, Steve, Oliver, Lena, Ellie, and a little Benjy, pause at a silent junction of branching corridors.

They weigh their options in silence. The aged tile beneath their boots branches in three directions. To the right, a set of glass doors opens into a lobby where a few dead shuffle without purpose. To the left, a hallway disappears into dim mystery.

Nearby, Oliver and Lena lean close, murmuring quietly about Benjy's well-being. The boy sways in her arms, pale and tired.

Lena looks to Bruce and asks, "Why me?"

He turns to her quizzically, "What do you mean, why you?"

"Why am I in here with you and not back in the truck? Why would you bring a child into a dangerous place?"

He nods, tracking her worry. "I've never raised a kid. I can do a recovery sweep and think I've gotten the essentials to cover my team's needs, but you're the one who will be able to spot what is good for you and your boy. Plus, if this place is defensible, I'd rather put you into a place of safety right away. Secure you and the child."

She stares at him for a moment, processing his words, then nods with understanding.

He glances into the school for tactical options again and finishes, "Besides, I didn't want your boy near Jason if he ends up turning, as fucked up as it is, this was the safer of the two options."

While Bruce quietly scans each directional option, Eric and Jeff bicker over which path is best, with Steve throwing in the occasional sharp opinion.

Speaking over the arguing boys, Bruce calmly but firmly asks, "What can we find in here that might help us? Supplies, shelter, anything."

Ellie shifts awkwardly from foot to foot. "It's a college. Not a bunker." She gestures around. "What kind of supplies do you even mean?"

"Short-term," Bruce says, rubbing his palm over his shaved head. "Food. Water. Maybe first aid. This place is far enough from downtown that we might avoid the worst of it. And, like I told her, if things go south again, the structure might be defensible."

Eric and Steve's argument become louder and more curt, accompanied by finger pointing and insults.

"Guys, stop." Ellie interrupts, stepping forward between Eric and Steve. She turns to Bruce. "I'm here like, four days a week. Tell me what you're looking for, and I'll tell you where it is." She pauses, then adds with a wince, "But seriously, can we hurry? I really have to pee."

Her bouncing has become a full-on dance. "Bathrooms are over by the cafeteria. Let's go there, okay?" She jabs a finger down a narrow brick hallway toward a pair of double glass doors.

Without waiting for confirmation, she bolts, half-dancing, half-hobbling toward salvation. She slips through the doors and into the main commons area. The others follow behind, more cautiously, heads swiveling, hands on weapons.

Ellie freezes directly inside, scanning the wide space for any possible attackers. To the left she spots the empty faculty help desk and to the right, closed offices. Ahead, a set of ornamental stone stairs descends toward lower classrooms. The halls beyond are dark voids of unknown space. Nothing moves and there is no sound.

Then Ellie sprints, straight across the open commons to the women's bathroom on the far side, calling over her shoulder, "Cafeteria's that way!" She points to her right mid-run.

Lena wastes no time. She clutches Benjy tighter and rushes after, peeling off into the men's room. Both women disappear behind swinging wooden doors, the last sound from either is a soft creak of hinges.

Jeff and Bruce share a glance, but nothing needs to be said. Jeff takes up guard outside the restrooms while Bruce motions the rest of the group toward the cafeteria.

"Hells yes!" Steve cheers as he pushes through the swinging doors into the cafeteria kitchen. The air inside smells faintly of fryer oil and baked bread. Without hesitation, he descends on a prep table loaded with wrapped muffins and day-old pastries. In an instant, he's shoving two into his mouth while the others gape in disbelief.

His gluttonous raid jostles a stack of bagels and a glass serving tray off the counter with a crash. Steve flinches, feeling like a scolded child, his arms tucked to his sides as he slowly turns, eyes wide and chewing. "Sorry," he mouths.

Silence falls, dead and breathless. Beyond the salad station and fryers, deeper in the kitchen's shadowed recesses, something stirs, clanging unseen cookery.

A low growl follows, starting soft but bubbling into the sound of wet rage, the sound of grief strangled in an unseen throat.

"Shit!" Eric steps back, pointing toward the fryer. "Something moved! Over there."

Before the group can react, a slumped, blood-soaked figure slides into view from behind a shelving unit. A man in a culinary jacket, slashed and crusted with gore, focuses on Steve. His arms, coiled tight, twitch violently at his sides. His peppered hair is matted to a skeletal scalp, and the sockets that once held eyes are pits of meat and madness.

The creature launches over the counter with a shriek, bones and gristle stretching as it moves. Oliver raises his rifle on reflex, but Bruce grabs his arm. "Not for one," he says low.

The men recoil into a makeshift guard formation as the chef crashes down, snarling.

Steve catches a blur in his periphery as another figure, a smaller one, leaps a countertop behind them and bolts across the dining area. The figure throws a skateboard out in front of them and it clatters to the tile, then jumps on it and skids into the leg of a metal chair, before rolling out the swinging doors and into the shadows.

"What the hell…" Steve mutters.

Bruce doesn't take his eyes off the first figure. With a sharp pivot, he swings the stock of his rifle in a wide arc, landing it squarely across the cook's lower jaw with a crack. The impact crushes the bone and whips the head sideways with a sharp snap. The creature spills across the floor in a heap of tangled limbs.

Before it can rise, Oliver crushes down on its skull with his steel-toed boot. A geyser of dark fluid spatters the linoleum.

"You guys!" Steve yells across the room, pointing upward. "There's someone here!"

Eric groans, gesturing at the bloody kitchen tile. "No shit, jackass. Did you not see what we just turned into brain soup?"

"No, I mean like, not a crazy!" Steve is already halfway out the door before they can stop him.

Bruce curses. "Kid, get back here!" but Steve doesn't listen.

He sighs and turns to Oliver and Eric. "We can't split further. Let's move."

They charge after Steve, boots pounding across a commons area and up a flight of stairs. As Bruce disappears around the bend, he calls back to Jeff, stationed outside the restrooms.

"Watch the girls! We'll be right back!"

28 – UNDEAD STILLBORN

Outside the restrooms, Jeff's nerves unravel one strand at a time. The building hums with dead air, broken only by distant echoes of movement that no longer belong to the living. Separated from the others, the correctional officer scans every shadow. His voice is low, barely a whisper to himself. "Shit, man. I'm too old for this crap."

A distant hoot echoes from another floor, somewhere above or beyond, and Jeff's nerves flare. He exhales slowly, almost laughing at himself, until a sharp whistle snaps the calm right behind him. He whirls and levels his rifle.

"Is it cool?" Ellie's face peeks from the women's bathroom, wide-eyed but steady.

"Dammit, I almost shot you." Jeff exhales. "Yeah. It's safe. You can come out."

Ellie cracks the door wider and peers around the hall before whispering again, "Where is everyone?"

Jeff thumbs over his shoulder toward the men's room. "The mom and her kid are in there." He nods upward, toward the second-story catwalk. "The rest of the crew took off that way. Chasing shadows, probably."

Reassured by his calm, more posture than truth, Ellie steps fully into the hall, her shoes brushing grit across the tile. She collapses into a cushioned chair a few steps away, finally allowing the weight of the day to hit. Her sigh is deep, almost shaking. "What was your name again?"

"Jeff."

She rolls it on her tongue like she's trying to make it mean something. "Jeff. How the heck are you keeping it together with all this going on?" She traces lazy circles in the stitching along the chair's armrest.

Jeff shifts, then leans casually on the butt of his rifle, putting weight on the leg that doesn't ache as much. "I'm a corrections officer. Been one a long time. You see enough bad shit, you learn to keep your eyes open and your heart slow."

Ellie studies him, eyes squinted in curiosity. "Yeah, but, this? People eating people?" She gestures around them vaguely. "You ever dealt with anything like that before?"

He nearly says no, but a thought stops him cold. His brow tightens. "One time."

She lifts an eyebrow in disbelief but lets him continue.

"I was green back then, a rookie. Got hurt at work, nothing major, tweaked my knee. Came back on light duty, got stuck on a transport detail." He scratches his jaw. "It was weird. These weren't normal prisoners. Government flagged 'em special, testing something, supposedly medical. I didn't ask too many questions. Just drove the bus to Saint Mary's and back a few times."

His voice grows quieter, tinged with discomfort.

"When we unloaded, they looked fine, but when I loaded 'em up, they were bad, sick. Like something was draining them from the inside. Pale, glassy-eyed, some could barely walk." He glances toward Ellie. "It felt wrong."

Ellie stops tracing the seam and places both hands flat on the chair's arms. Her posture straightens, her gaze fixed and attentive. Jeff continues, eyes drifting shut between phrases, like the weight of memory slows him down.

"This was back when no one gave a shit about prisoner rights. Government came around pitching sentence reductions to inmates willing to sign up for 'voluntary testing.' Penitentiaries across the country signed on. Didn't ask what the tests were for."

He shakes his head, then shrugs.

"Near the end of the program, the inmates started looking, I don't know. Hollow. Not sick in the usual way, but drained. The last transport I remember, we were loading back up outside Saint Mary's. That's when we saw it." He opens his eyes again and locks onto Ellie's.

"One of 'em was chewing on another inmate's arm. Not biting to hurt him. Just gnawing. Like a dog working a rawhide bone."

Ellie's face pinches in revulsion. "Great googaly moogaly. What happened?"

Jeff shrugs, his lip curling in a crooked frown. "We turned 'em over like usual and kept working. I heard there was a big riot later that night." He squints upward. "Weekend passed. I came back to work Monday and got told the transport detail was canceled. No explanation. Just done."

Ellie leans forward, scandalized. "Didn't you try to find out what happened to them?"

"Nope." He snorts. "Didn't care. They were inmates. You don't go looking for a wounded coyote, you let it crawl off into the woods and die."

The frankness of Jeff's words knocks Ellie off balance. "God. That's grim."

Jeff shrugs again. "It's corrections. You keep moving or you go under."

"But didn't you tell anyone? Outside of work?"

His eyes narrow, voice low. "We signed waivers. No talking, no questions. You're the first person I've ever told that story to in maybe Thirty-some years."

Ellie opens her mouth to ask for something more, but a scream rips through the air from the men's restroom. A ragged, human shriek. She freezes and her hands claw the chair's arms.

Jeff bolts upright, rifle raised, his heart shouting in the quiet. They stare at one another, wide-eyed.

Ellie whispers, "Um, should we check?"

Jeff mutters through his teeth, "I was afraid you'd say that."

He creeps toward the door and taps it lightly with the barrel of his rifle. "Miss? You alright in there?"

The bathroom is silent, so he knocks again. Something knocks back. Jeff flinches and leaps a half-step to pull his weapon up. He glances at Ellie and gestures her over with a sharp nod. "Come here, girlie."

Ellie shakes her head, palms up. "Nuh uh."

He tries again, this time holding out a pistol. "Come on. I need backup. Stay back and point it if I drop. That's all I'm asking."

Reluctantly, Ellie takes the handgun with trembling hands. She backs up a few steps, eyes glued to the restroom door.

Jeff glances over his shoulder. "Safety's right there by your thumb. Got it?"

Ellie shoots him a withering glare. "Uh, hello? I hang out with half the gun nuts in the valley. If I didn't know how to rack a Walther P99, I'd never hear the end of it."

Jeff raises his brows, impressed. "Okay then."

With his jaw reset, Jeff turns back toward the bumping door. Ellie slides in beside him, pistol steady. The absence of a handle tells Jeff this door only opens inward, which is a small comfort.

He raises three fingers in the air and counts down three, two, one. He drops his hand to his rifle and kicks the door open and rushes to enter.

It slams back in his face, like it struck something solid, something blocking the door. The impact knocks Jeff to the ground. Ellie flinches and raises the pistol to full extension. He scowls and, from a seated position, kicks again. This time the door flies open.

"Jesus Christ!" he shouts, stumbling backward. A small shadow of a creature trains its attention on the man.

Ellie peers past him and sees why he cursed, why his face is twisted in shock, and his hands are shaking. "I…I can't shoot."

A wet hiss slices through the air, and the thing leaps. Without hesitation, Ellie acts. Four shots explode from her pistol. The tiny attacker spins mid-air and collapses in Jeff's lap, twitching as its momentum skids it to a stop between his legs. Jeff stares down at Benjy, still as a grave.

"What the fucking fuck?" Ellie's scream echoes off the stone walls. She flings the pistol across the floor like it burns her. She covers her face, trying to protect herself from witnessing the horror.

"Oh my god. Oh no. No no no no." She sinks to her knees, wailing, her lungs constricted by ropes of guilt and shame. "Oh my god, what have I done?"

"Miss…" Jeff mutters, still seated, scooting away from the small body. He lifts the little head by a tuft of hair, like he's afraid to believe what he already knows. The child is slack. Three bullet wounds polka-dot his little torso, the fourth shot never landed.

"You didn't do anything wrong. He turned. He…he was gone." He wants to say more, but the words tangle in his throat, drowned by the sudden sting building behind his eyes.

"Oh man…He's just a baby." Ellie bawls, hating her hands, hating her fears, that allowed her to take the life of something so small and precious.

Benjy's eyes snap open. He launches with surprising momentum, jaws locking onto Jeff's cheek. The man screams, full-throated and raw, as tiny fingers claw into his mouth and left eye socket. The taste of the child's dirty hand causes Jeff's throat to close, and the coppery tart of injury assaults his tastebuds. Blood pours down his face in thick, syrupy ropes.

"Get off me!" Jeff gasps, but the strength in the child's limbs is inhuman. His tiny hands dig deeper into the officer's face, peeling flesh back with dull, determined nails. Jeff's wild swipes only smear the gore.

Ellie's cries echo over the carnage, but they're quickly overtaken by Jeff's agony. When she looks through her fingers again, the nightmare has grown worse.

Jeff lies motionless, flat on his back. His face is barely recognizable beneath the torn flesh and pooling blood. Benjy straddles the man's neck, bouncing up and down on his windpipe, excitedly feasting on Jeff's face. The boy's arms stab into the guard's eye sockets, scooping and scraping as he feeds.

Each jerky motion sends hisses through his tiny nose and the way he devours the dead man show that whatever Benjy has become, the boy wasn't used to taking in food in such a primal fashion. He crouches lower over Jeff's ruined chin and begins to shovel hunks of meat into his mouth, chewing wetly, his tiny throat swelling in pulses as he gorges on torn flesh.

Ellie gags, her stomach heaves with shock. She doubles over and bile burns her throat.

Trembling, she scrambles backward, hands dragging on the tile. Each motion she makes sounds like thunder in her ears, and she watches Benjy, waiting for the small horror to look her way. Each time he stops, she freezes and prays.

She slides back into the women's room, slowly pressing against the door, then eases it shut with quivering fingers once she's through. Inside the gloom, she rushes to the furthest stall and locks the privacy door, then climbs onto the toilet, trying not to breathe, not to cry, not to exist.

29 – DARK SALVATION

On the second floor of the college, Steve darts ahead, shouting back to the trio climbing the steel stairs. "He went this way! Come on!" He bounces impatiently at an intersecting hallway, waving them forward. "Hurry up, we're going to lose him!"

Oliver reaches the landing last, greeting Steve's urgency with a raised middle finger. Bruce pauses at the top, eyes scanning the open corridor, then jogs after Steve who's already caught up to his teenage friend, Eric. "I'm not convinced it's smart to go chasing shadows," Bruce calls out.

Steve throws a glance over his shoulder. "I seriously doubt this is one of those things!"

Bruce narrows his eyes. "Why's that?"

Already running again, Steve hollers back, "The dead don't skate!"

With that, the teen blurs past a pair of vending machines, tearing toward a distant shape at the end of the hallway.

Bruce mutters to himself, "Dead don't skate?" and picks up speed. Eric barrels down the hall with a whooping hoot, echoing down the corridor. Bruce maintains a steady pace, trying to maintain line of sight on both Oliver and the boys ahead. With his sidearm raised and ready, he sweeps each open classroom they pass.

Behind him, Oliver covers their rear, keeping vigilant watch on the shadows they've left behind, while trying to catch his breath.

The two students whip past a fish tank embedded in the left wall, as another corridor branches off. Steve rockets through the intersection, but Eric doesn't make it. Two bodies burst from the shadows, tackling him to the ground. His yelp is more from surprise than pain.

Bruce reaches the skirmish in time to slam a boot into one attacker's face. Eric kicks wildly at the other as Steve skids back, grabs a nearby trash can, and brings it crashing down onto the head of the attacker. The lid pops off. The walker doesn't.

Steve slams it repeatedly until the corpse folds into itself, oozing.

"Fuck yes!" Eric cheers. He high-fives Steve, and both boys throw up devil horns. Steve sticks his tongue out.

Bruce stares, bewildered. Oliver catches up and shrugs. "Kids," he mutters.

The chase resumes. After one more intersection and a stretch of corridor, they finally slow, finding Steve and Eric standing in the middle of a four-way junction, each facing opposite directions, breathing hard, and looking thoroughly confused.

Bruce slows beside Steve, one hand landing on the kid's shoulder, partly to steady himself, partly to catch his breath. "So," he pants, masking his wheeze, "what now, great hunter?"

Steve smirks, clearly taking pride in the jab. "Pretty sure it went that way," he says, pointing toward a corridor that angles sharply left.

"But I saw something go that way," Eric counters, motioning toward a wide staircase descending back to the ground floor.

Bruce frowns, surveying their options. "One thing's for damn sure, we're not splitting up again." He starts to say more, but the sudden crack of gunfire from the floor below silences him.

"Shit," Bruce growls, spinning toward the echo. "We need to get back."

"Hold on, boss man," Steve objects, grabbing his sleeve. "You've got someone down there, right?"

"Yeah. Jeff, but he's not my man. Just someone I met, at best we have pseudo-connected ties."

Steve tugs his arm with mild defiance. "Still. He's with us. And if he's with us, we've gotta believe he's got it handled."

Bruce opens his mouth to argue, but Steve cuts him off by placing his index finger to the older man's lips. "Shhh." Annoyed, Bruce bats the kid's finger from his face. Steve pleads, "Give me five minutes, alright? I've done everything I've been told all day. I haven't bitched once. Let me have this one thing."

He releases Bruce's sleeve. "Five minutes. Then we head back, and I'll follow orders like your own personal apocalypse intern."

Bruce stares, calculating. Before he can answer, Eric taps Steve and points. "Dude. Dude."

They all turn in time to catch a glimpse of the skateboarder, a blurred silhouette vanishing into a classroom down the hall.

Steve grins. "Dude. Captain dude. Master-at-Arms dude?"

Bruce groans, "Fine. You've got five minutes." He taps his watch. "Not one more."

He turns to Oliver. "Trail behind. If we hit a snag, you're Plan B."

Oliver nods and takes position. The men move in, Steve leading and Bruce checking each doorway as they go. They pass Four empty rooms, then ready themselves at the fifth. Steve leans into the doorway, hand braced on the frame, eyes squinting through the dark to scan the interior.

Something flashes, pink, fast, and hard. The underside of a skateboard, emblazoned with a punk rock Hello Kitty grinning between chipped pink wheels, slams into his face. The board hits with a crunch and Steve's nose collapses, sending him flying backward into a swirl of stars and concrete.

Bruce shouts, "Watch it!" as the figure leaps from the shadows into the corridor light, landing clean on the skateboard and kicking off hard for escape, but Eric lunges, tackling the form mid-sprint. Both go down hard. He pins the figure's wiry wrists to the tile, wrestling to hold it in place.

Bruce rushes in, pistol drawn, and plants the barrel near the attacker's face as Oliver jogs up, covering the hallway. A furious, high-pitched voice squeals from beneath a curtain of blue-black hair, "Get off me! Get off, asshole!"

Bruce nudges the mop of hair aside with his pistol, and freezes. Staring up at them, a fierce girl with dyed blue-black hair. Couldn't be older than twenty.

"Let me go, stupid!" she growls.

Bruce exchanges a look with Eric, then taps his arm. "Ease off." Eric gets up cautiously while Bruce keeps his pistol trained, just in case.

"What are you doing here?" he asks.

The girl scrambles to her knees and gathers the contents of her scattered bag. "I'm a student. What are you doing here?" she snaps back, spitting near Bruce's boots.

"Looking for supplies."

"Yeah? Me too," she says, sorting her gear.

"Hey!" Steve calls, stepping forward holding her skateboard aloft. His nose is pouring blood. "Looking for this?"

She rushes toward him, but he lifts it higher, out of her reach. "Nope. Not until you start playing nice."

The girl glares at each of them in turn, eyes narrow with calculation. She sighs and nods toward the hallway, then gestures. "Fine. Come on."

They fall in behind her as she leads the way. As she passes Steve, she swipes the board back with a lightning-fast snatch. "You're bleeding," she says, pointing at his nose. "You should fix that."

Steve blinks. "Thanks?"

The group stops in front of an office door with a plaque that reads FABIAN PRYDE. The narrow glass window is covered in paper. The girl knocks in a rhythm that feels like a code, then pushes the door open. Inside are two men. One is older, tall and wiry, crouched beside the second, who lies on the floor, young, sweating, and pale.

Both men startle when the girl leads in others. "Hey, Zero. Mister Pryde," the girl says casually, "We got company."

Oliver's eyes narrow at the boy on the floor. He instinctively raises his rifle. "He's been bitten," he warns. "We have to put him down."

"What the heck, man?" the girl yelps, throwing herself halfway in front of the boy.

"He's going to turn," Oliver snaps, aiming tighter.

"No he's not, dummy!" She jabs a finger toward the boy's legs, partially hidden under a pile of papers. "He broke his leg running from those freaks."

Mister Pryde pulls back the papers from the boy's wound, a gruesome but clearly not-bitten compound fracture is revealed, bone jutting out through the shin.

"Mister Pryde helped us get away," she adds firmly. "We're laying low until we figure out how to get out of here."

Bruce glances down the hallway they came from, then surveys the cramped office. His eyes scan the walls, the door, the window, and the parking lot beyond it.

"Well," he says, turning back to the group, "consider us your rescue party. I'm Chief Bruce Snyder, United States Naval Forces."

The girl squints at him. "What makes you think we'll go with you? How do we know you're not full of crap?"

Bruce doesn't miss a beat. "First off," he says, "we breathe. We speak."

Oliver raises his rifle with a dry grin. "And we're armed."

Bruce nods. "And most importantly…" he juts a finger toward the window, "We've got that."

The girl stands on her toes to look. Outside, creeping along the edge of the parking lot, is the unmistakable olive-drab armored beast grumbling quietly in the lot with the words 'Zombie Smasher' sprayed across the front.

The girl grins for the first time, her face lighting up. "Alright. I'm Yoshiki. Nice to meet you."

She reaches out and cheerfully shakes each man's hand in turn as names are exchanged. When she gets to Oliver, she eyes the rifle in his hand and winks. "Nice hardware."

Bruce's watch chirps with a series of rapid beeps. The mood sobers. He turns off the alarm with a tap, then waves everyone forward. "Okay, that's our cue. We've got people waiting on us, let's move."

He turns to the boy on the floor. "Son…"

"Zero," the boy corrects, offering a weak smile.

"Zero. Can you walk, or do you need a lift?"

Zero grabs Yoshiki's hand and hauls himself up with a wince. "We got it."

She helps him onto his board and braces him on the weak side, steadying his frame as they roll out into the hallway.

Pryde stays behind a beat longer, shutting and locking his office. Bruce lingers, sensing there's more to ask, but for now, he follows the others. Up ahead, Eric slides next to the new duo and murmurs, "Man, this whole outbreak hit this place hard, huh?"

Zero cocks an eyebrow. "What makes you say that?"

Eric thumbs toward the closed office door. "That room looked like a goddamn tornado hit it."

Yoshiki and Zero exchange laughs. "That's just Mister Pryde," she says. "He's a brilliant teacher, but messy as hell."

"Morgue, this is Violet." The voice drifts into DJ's ear, a warm ember through frost.

"Violet?" DJ's heart vaults. She didn't expect the voice of a woman she has never met could feel so familiar, so grounding. "Oh man, I'm so glad to hear your voice." She pauses, scanning the truck, watching David and Caroline. He's wiping up her sick while she rubs his back. The Stryker is now maybe a hundred feet from where they dumped their friends. "Are you on air right now?"

"Nope," Violet says. "Is this DJ? You sound familiar."

DJ's face lifts slightly at the recognition. "Yeah. It's me. I need some help. I think I'm in trouble."

"Kid, look around town." Monster's gravel-dragged voice cuts in. "We're all in trouble. I just got off the phone with a guy who decided the best way out was to burn his house down, with him still in it. Said he wanted to go out on his own terms."

"Monster," Violet scolds, then returns to her call. "What's going on, darlin'?"

"We're at the college. Some of the group went inside. I stayed out to clear my head, but then I heard gunshots. When I got back, this guy we're with said one of our people turned, that he had to put them down. But it doesn't feel right. I think…" She hesitates. "I think he might've killed a living person."

"Whoa, whoa…" Violet's voice softens and slows. "Okay, breathe. You're talking so fast."

"Right, sorry," DJ murmurs. She casts another glance through the hatch, David at the wheel, Caroline sitting close, the same as before. "I don't know how safe I am."

Violet softens. Her voice becomes a warm blanket slipping across raw skin. "Has he threatened you, honey? Does he seem like he's going to hurt you?"

"No? Maybe. He's done other things, but nothing like this."

There's a pause, long enough to feel like Violet is really thinking it through and not merely reacting. Then she says, "Okay, listen to me, stay calm. Watch his eyes, not just his hands. People like that usually warn you with their stare before they act. If you start feeling the air shift around him, or he gets too quiet, don't wait. You understand me?"

DJ nods instinctively, her throat tight. "Mm-hmm"

There's something fierce in Violet's tone now. Protective. "And keep something sharp or heavy nearby, doesn't matter if it's a wrench, a crowbar, hell, a rock. Don't ever feel bad about surviving."

Monster's voice slips in, surprisingly gentle. "Kid, if you think he's going to hurt you or anyone else, don't wait for permission. You do what needs done."

Violet agrees. "We've lost too many good people because they waited. Don't let that be your story."

DJ lowers herself onto the back bumper, anxiety weighing her down. "I just wish I wasn't here; I want to be home. I want this to all be a bad dream."

"I know, kiddo. I think we all do."

Monster breaks back in. "Hey. You said you're at the college, right? Whitman?"

"No. Walla Walla Community College."

"Damn," Monster grunts. "Would've told you to ditch that piece of shit and hike up here. Our party's a hell of a lot more fun than yours."

David's bark cuts from the interior of the rig. "Hey, DJ!"

She jumps but doesn't answer. Her breath catches.

"Hey, kid! Get in here and check this out!"

She glances at the phone in her hand and whispers, "Please stay with me." The voices on the other end assure her they're not going anywhere. She props the phone on the bench inside the hatch, angled downward to hide the glow of the screen, and steps into the belly of the Stryker. She carefully navigates around the slick mess of blood on the floor, remnants of violence still fresh enough to curdle the air.

She climbs toward the command chair. "What, David?"

"Nothing now. You missed it." He practically hisses the words at her. "What the hell were you doing out there? Cryin' over spilt milk?" His eyes flash. "Gotta accept things and move on, kid. Otherwise, you're another weak link waiting to break."

DJ's voice tightens. "Just tell me what you wanted."

David jabs a finger at the console. "Radio lit up. Military dropped a bombshell, literally."

Her chest tightens. "What do you mean?"

"They're going to burn this whole town." His voice is almost gleeful. "We all get to taste Napalm at midnight. Full firestorm."

DJ's stomach flips. Her skin prickles with the heat of fear, and suddenly, the stench in the truck feels alive through the sweat, blood, smoke, and rot. She looks over at Caroline, tapping her trembling arm. "Is he serious?"

Caroline doesn't answer with words. Her face is a wreck of tears and snot, breaths coming in panicked little gasps. She nods once, hard.

DJ turns back to David, trying to keep her voice level. "When? Are there evacuation points? Did they mention how they're going to rescue people? Something? Anything?"

David runs a palm over his scalp, exhaling sharply. "I already said Midnight. And no, you saw the explosion at the airport. We don't get out." He lets that linger in the air like a death sentence. "There was no mention of extraction or retrieval. We all cook."

DJ covers her mouth with a trembling hand and stumbles to the back of the Stryker, collapsing beside her quietly listening phone. She chokes back the fear, the tears, doing everything she can not to show weakness around David. The silence stretches thick and suffocating, until Violet's soft voice nudges through.

"DJ? You there, sweetheart?" Violet's voice returns, gentle but alert.

DJ picks up the phone like it weighs a hundred pounds, glances at the front of the rig to see David playing with the radio, then slips out the back of the vehicle again. "Hey," she mutters, flat as asphalt.

Monster's gravel joins the line, quieter than usual. "You alright, kid?"

"Until midnight," she replies, with no change in tone.

A pause hums through the phone, then Violet nudges gently, "What did you hear?"

DJ's silence answers for her. Then, low and hollow, "They're going to bomb it. The whole town. Military's planning to napalm Walla Walla at midnight. No help."

"No evac protocols. Just a fuse," Monster mutters.

Violet exhales slowly, the weight of confirmation bringing a heavy drop. "We heard it too. An inmate called it in earlier. We weren't sure if it was paranoia or prophecy."

"Well," DJ says, bitter in her throat, "Now it's both."

Violet shifts her tone, more purposeful now. "Okay, listen to me. You have to get underground. There are bunkers. We've been mapping them out with help from an inmate with some old city maps. There are some banks and historical buildings downtown with bomb shelters. You're going to need to move soon."

DJ clutches the phone tighter, the grip grounding her. Monster cuts in, focused and sharp. "DJ, you've only got maybe a couple of hours. This ain't rumor anymore. It's a countdown. You tell your people to get low or get gone."

The sudden thread of hope pulls DJ upright. Her breath catches like it forgot how to exhale. "Oh my god, thank you! I thought we were just done."

"Not yet, sweetie," Violet urges. "Now get moving. From the sound of things, we'll be down to even fewer listeners soon, and we can't afford to lose any more."

A soft laugh escapes DJ, real and raw. "I'll get them there. I promise."

Before the line can fade, Monster rumbles back in. "Hey, kid."

"Yeah?" She smiles despite herself, despite everything. These two strangers, voices in the dark, feel more like family than what she has now.

"Do me a favor."

"Anything."

"Kneecap that son of a bitch that's got you scared and leave his ass outside to burn." Monster's voice sheds its usual cynicism and goes deep as a grave. "He deserves to die slow."

A shiver runs through DJ. The words stick in her bones. "I will."

31 – AT WHAT EXPENSE?

"Jeff?" Bruce's voice cuts through the air as he cautiously descends the stairwell, boots echoing off the metal steps. He halts on the landing to scan the courtyard below. "Sound off." He gets silence as his only response. No moans, no movement, only an empty hush.

He lifts an arm, silently signaling Oliver beside him. They peer over the railing. Jeff's mangled body lies in the open below them, limp, ruined, and grotesquely still. Bruce lets a sharp curse slide from his breath. "I should've stayed behind."

"Don't beat yourself up, man," Oliver replies, clapping a hand to his shoulder. "You're not Superman. That down there? That could've been you."

Bruce doesn't answer, his eyes glued to Jeff's blood-smeared face. Below, the gore glistens in the ambient light, showing Jeff's face no longer resembles anything human. Bruce taps the railing, trying to break the pressing silence of his guilt.

Oliver turns to the two younger men at their back. "Steve, Eric, grab your weapons. We've got a man down with two women and a kid unaccounted for. We move on the assumption they're in danger."

Steve closes his eyes, jaw trembling, then inhales through his nose to steady himself. He draws his pistol with both hands. Eric tightens his grip on a chair leg he picked up a few rooms back.

Bruce sets his pistol down on the ground and unsheathes a compact pistol from the ankle of his boot and checks the chamber. He picks up the first pistol and pauses, feeling the weight of both, then glances back to the three newcomers, Yoshiki, Zero, and Pryde, still gathered on the upper floor. "You three, stay here. No exceptions. We'll call when it's clear."

The quartet descends the final steps and spreads out across the main floor, forming a tight rotating perimeter as they approach Jeff's corpse. Bruce kneels beside the fallen officer, poking at his shredded uniform and mottled skin with the muzzle of his sidearm.

"Dammit." Bruce mutters. The others gather close, glancing down.

Bruce lifts Jeff's head gently with the back of his wrist, revealing a trail of tiny crescent wounds along the man's cheek, jaw, and shoulder. Bite marks.

"That bite is the size of a kid," Oliver whispers, dread crawling up his spine. "That was Benjy." The name sticks in his mouth, and a cold knot settles behind every rib.

Eric begins pacing in tight circles. "Where the hell's his mom? Where's Ellie?" His eyes dart nervously to every door and shadow. "None of this makes sense. This shit ain't right."

Steve tenses beside him, grip tightening on his pistol. "This place is a tomb."

Eric's nerves snap. "Steve, check the bathroom."

"Fuck that," Steve shoots back. "You check the bathroom."

Bruce interjects, already turning. "No. Both of you, men's room. Oliver and I will check the women's."

Steve silently protests by resisting the command, which Bruce catches as he stands. "Apocalypse cadet. Door. Now."

Steve groans, not expecting his promise would need to be fulfilled so soon. He huffs, then finally pushes the wooden door open, the hinge groaning with warning. The sharp smell hits them first, iron-rich, clinging, wrong. What used to be a men's room now smells like something primal died screaming.

Beneath the first urinal, slumped like a discarded doll, lies Lena. Her blouse is soaked black with blood, and one eye socket is nothing but pulp. Her face has been chewed down to raw bone, but her arms are frozen in a final, defensive curl, showing the boys that she died trying to protect something.

Eric steps cautiously forward, boots squelching across puddled filth. "Jesus," he whispers. He ducks low, checks under the stall doors, but finds nothing more than blood-slick tiles and a shattered toilet seat. He starts kicking stall doors open, checking thoroughly.

Steve readies his pistol and moves further down the line of urinals and that's when he sees the other body, wedged awkwardly at the base of the urinal pipe, skull crushed against the metal valve, its face obliterated in a pattern of blunt-force trauma and ceramic shards. One side of its jaw hangs loose, with its tongue drooping from the bloodied mouth.

"Holy fuck," Steve breathes. "She killed it. She fucking killed it."

The floor tells the rest of the story, with every drag mark, scrape, broken tile, and blood-streaked handprint punctuating like desperate exclamation marks. Both young men investigate and find in the middle of it all, there's another trail, smaller, smeared, where Lena's child had slipped through the gore.

Eric points silently at the tiny footprints, then to a small, bloody handprint streaked across the wall beneath the sink. "Benjy," Steve mutters. "He must've. was he trying to help her?"

"Did he kill that thing?" Eric stares, and for a second, both boys become intensely aware of their situation.

A scream cuts through their stillness, shaking them from their terror. It is high and raw, coming from outside the restroom. Steve snaps his head toward the sound. "The ladies' room!"

Weapons in hand, the teens burst into the corridor, hearts pounding, adrenaline boiling, but as they round the corner, ready to face another monster, they skid to a stop.

It's not carnage they find, but reunion. Bruce and Oliver emerge from the women's bathroom unscathed, with Ellie wrapped tightly around Oliver's waist. He is her lifeline. Her tear-streaked face is buried against his chest, but her feet walk on their own.

Steve's grip loosens on his pistol. "Thank fuck," he exhales.

"We have one, at least." Bruce offers the faintest smile as Ellie clings tighter to Oliver's side. "Any luck?" he asks the teens.

Both shake their heads grimly. Bruce exhales through his nose, the warmth of hope cooling quickly. "I don't care if it's infected or not, I have no interest in shooting a kid. We need to move. Now." He scans the open space for movement.

He nods toward the landing above. "Come on, folks. Almost out."

Zero leans hard against Yoshiki as the three new survivors descend the stairs. Eric crouches to rifle through Jeff's mangled remains, retrieving a sidearm and extra ammo clips with a grimace. Steve darts across the hallway to scoop up Ellie's discarded pistol, checking the chamber with shaking fingers.

The regrouped survivors barely take their first step toward the exit when a hiss slithers from the darkness of a nearby corridor. The sound is a fuse that's been lit. Everyone freezes and Ellie goes rigid. "That's Benjy," she whispers, voice full of dread.

They don't wait for confirmation. The group bolts for the front doors. Eric slams shoulder-first into the glass, rattling the glass panels but finding no give. "Come on! Come on!" he yells as he pushes again.

Steve hurls his full weight at the opposite door and gets the same result, dull thuds and the groan of old hinges.

"It's a pull, dumbasses!" Yoshiki shouts, closing in, propping up Zero. "Pull the doors!"

The teacher grabs both handles and yanks with all his might. The mechanism finally budges with a mechanical gasp. The door swings wide, and that's when the growl behind them changes pitch.

Ellie shrieks. Benjy, what was once Benjy, is charging. The toddler-sized terror barrels forward like a broken toy come to life, arms flailing, eyes empty, mouth gnashing with a red grin that drips meat between his teeth. She stares at the three holes she put in his little body.

"Move, move!" Bruce shouts, directing everyone through the opening.

One by one, they pour through, first to go is Eric, then Steve who pulls at Ellie's sleeve, then Fabian Pryde. Oliver and Bruce brace each door, defensive sentries, keeping the exit open for the skater couple trying to catch up.

Benjy hits the floor in a full sprint. "Oh my gosh! Oh my GOSH!" Yoshiki squeals as she fumbles with Zero's weight. Her sneaker skids across the tile. The growling thing is ten feet away, then five.

Without thinking, she plants one foot and kicks. Benjy's tiny body lifts into the air from the force of her punt, flailing backward in a snarl of limbs and gnashing teeth.

"Ew ew eww!" she shrieks, windmilling her arms.

They all scramble through the doorway. Oliver and Bruce yank at the doors, fighting the slow hydraulics with every ounce of strength. The toddler terror leaps to his tiny feet and charges again, slamming full force into the glass as it seals.

His face splatters against the pane, leaving a grotesque red kiss, a smear of mucus and rage. Everyone jumps and the instructor mutters, "Dear God."

Benjy recoils, then rams the door again. Then again. Then his hands rise, smearing and clawing at the invisible barrier with sticky, squelching motions. His tiny growls echo unnaturally loud in the large space.

"Let's get out of here!" Yoshiki pleads, flapping her hands like they might shake off the memory. "That thing is going to give me nightmares!"

Bruce's face hardens as he watches Benjy trying to stick his tiny fingers between the doors. "He's figuring it out."

Oliver glances once more at the wobbling glass. "We gotta go, fast. He's going to get clever real soon." No one disagrees and they run, their footsteps thunder across the commons.

Wet grass and cold concrete trampled beneath boots and sneakers. Every breath is a blade in the chest. No one speaks. The shrieks behind them, the pounding on glass, the inhuman scratching, say enough.

The Zombie Smasher looms ahead, squat and still in the parking lot, bathed in the low amber of multiple lamp posts.

"Go! Go!" Bruce shouts.

Steve reaches the transport first, slamming a fist against the side. "Open up! Let us in!"

The ramp swings down, DJ's wide eyes already full of questions. "What happened?!"

"No time!" Oliver pants, stationing defensively at the door next to the entry. "We've got company!"

David switches seats from the command chair to the driver's position. Steve, Eric, Ellie, and the teacher pile in. DJ staggers backward as Yoshiki lifts Zero over the lip of the opening. "Let's go!"

The chaos in front of the school rings the dinner bell. Zombies flood from the sides of buildings, out doors, through windows. Bruce fires shots in various directions, trying to remove the closest threats.

Once all the others are in, Oliver hits the button to close the ramp while Bruce continues to pick off attackers.

"But wait!" DJ peers out the closing hatch, looking for a mother and child. Her heart crumbles as her eyes shut with the ramp, realizing she will never see them again.

Inside, everyone collapses in heaving disarray, stowing guns and dropping backpacks. Adrenaline simmers into exhaustion. David spins in the driver's seat, eyes narrow. "What the hell is this?"

"Drive!" Bruce barks.

"We're not ready," David growls. "Howard's not back."

That name stops everything. Bruce freezes mid-stride. Ellie lifts her head from her knees. DJ looks from the rear seats toward the exit.

Steve's voice breaks first. "Wait, what?"

"Howard," David repeats, pointing at DJ. "Went looking for the girl. Never came back."

Caroline backs him up, arms crossed but eyes worried. "We were about to go after him when you all came barreling in like a stampede."

Bruce glances at the door. Then back at the exhausted faces inside the vehicle. "We're missing three others," Bruce mutters. "Chastity, Jason, and the kid missing the leg." He looks at David, "Where are they?"

David pauses, the silence is thick. He stares at DJ and says, "They turned. We had to put them down."

Caroline agrees, but DJ looks away, squeezing onto herself.

"Howard's the only one unaccounted for," David says. "But if he's not here by now…"

"He could still be alive," Eric says.

"Or he could be dead," David shoots back. "And we'll be too if we wait for him."

DJ stands, her knuckles white on the seat rail. "We have to try, right?"

Silence answers her. Bruce rubs his forehead, massaging his tense muscles. "If he's not already on the move, he's not making it."

Ellie looks to the others, eyes glassy. "But, he helped us."

David exhales, grabbing the dash. "And I don't want to die with him because you all have soft hearts. I vote we move. I was just offering a status report."

DJ's voice is small. "We could maybe call for him? Try one last time?" She looks back to David, "I think there have already been too many unnecessary deaths."

Bruce takes a moment to survey the driver and the girl in the back, then nods. "Do it. But use the hatch up top."

Eric yanks the hatch open and leans out. "Howard!" he bellows into the dusk. "Let's go!" Only wind and the sound of the ravenous dead answers. He tries again.

Bruce turns to David. "Get us out of here."

David smirks faintly as he throws the Zombie Smasher into gear. "Finally."

With a lurch, the steel beast rumbles forward, heavy tires crunching against pavement and bloodied attackers. The college slips away behind them, windows glowing like open wounds in the fading light.

After a breathless moment, Bruce grips Eric and pulls him down, then closes the hatch. He nods to the young man, "You did what you could, son."

DJ settles onto the bench, arms wrapped around her knees, eyes fixed on David's silhouette in the front seat. "He's going to get us all killed." She doesn't say it loud, enough for the silence to hear her fear.

The running lights of the Stryker wash the cabin in a somber hue of orange. Zero stares blankly at a clump of hair dangling from the metal bench beside his uninjured knee, barely noticing as his girlfriend rewraps his splinted leg with the vehicle's first aid kit.

The engine of the vehicle is the only sound for five long minutes. The first to speak after David told Bruce about the radio transmission, is the group's newcomer, Fabian. "I understand we're heading to a fallout shelter downtown, yes?"

Bruce nods, calmly wiping down one of his pistols.

"Because the military is planning on utilizing excessive force and firebombing the entire town of Walla Walla, correct?" Bruce gives another nod. Fabian scratches his curly brown head. "And we're traveling in a genuine military vehicle. One that's paid for by good ol' Uncle Sam. Yes?"

Eric sighs, rolls his eyes, and gives voice to Bruce's motion. "Yeah...so?"

"Well..." Fabian looks to each bowed head before settling his gaze on the frustrated teen. "You're all big-time thinkers. Why haven't we tried hailing the big brass, the movers and shakers, the decision makers behind this symphony of destruction, and reported that there are, in fact, plenty of honest-to-goodness, living, breathing survivors wandering our fair streets?"

Bruce finally speaks. "Contagion Protocol."

Those two words deepen the furrows on Fabian's brow and tilt his weathered face. Anticipating the barrage of questions, Bruce cuts him off before he can reply.

"It started back in the seventies," Bruce says, eyes locked on the pistol in his hands. "The Swine Flu vaccine scandal, the one that paralyzed people, it killed trust. Then AIDS hit, and the government watched it spread for years without lifting a finger, some might even say they had something to do with it. That was the wake-up call. That's when the real planning started, the quiet meetings, the black budgets. They realized fast that if the next outbreak moved faster, it wouldn't just kill people, it'd collapse the system."

He pauses as the Stryker hums through desolate streets.

"By the early eighties, the plan had a name: Contagion Protocol. Not a reaction to an event, or containment, but control. Test cases started showing up in places no one cared to look. Inmates. Homeless. Off-the-books populations. The idea wasn't to save anyone. It was to see how fast something could spread. Or how fast it could be stopped."

The weight of his words pulls everyone deeper into silence. Oliver mutters, "I knew it."

Bruce nods slowly. "The plan stayed buried for decades, refined every time something new flared up. H1N1. Bird flu. West Nile. Each one a dry run. And then came COVID, our global dress rehearsal. That's when the suits stopped asking if Contagion Protocol would be needed and started asking when. Panic, disinformation, government infighting, it was a perfect storm. They didn't see it as a failure. They saw it as proof."

He pauses as the transport jolts once, then again.

From the front, David calls out, "The wheels on the bus go round and round," his sing-song tone implying he's rolled over another walker.

Bruce presses forward. "San Diego, East Haddam, San Antonio. Those were nearly the first cities to face what the CDC now calls 'purification events.' If the swine flu outbreaks had gotten any worse, they would've been firebombed. The only reason they weren't, according to internal reports, is that the media was watching. COVID had already cracked the glass. They couldn't afford to shatter it."

"Well," Mister Pryde lets a nervous chuckle slip, "I guess you got me there. I'm blown away."

Oliver, the only other one not too horrified to speak, deadpans, "Wrong choice of words, dude."

The ill-timed humor cracks enough tension to let the others breathe again. DJ speaks up, voice flat but curious. "So, the government wants to eliminate every infected person by destroying the whole town?"

She doesn't wait for a response. "What's to stop them from just shooting everyone who walks out of the shelters?" The truck goes graveyard silent.

For the first time since leaving the college, Caroline turns in her seat to face the cargo hold. "Come on, you guys. This is our government. They're not going to kill innocent people."

Steve's jaw drops. "Were you even listening?"

Eric cuts through the noise, his voice sharp. "Get real. That's exactly what they'd do. The only thing that keeps them from pulling the trigger is if you're worth more alive than dead."

"Right," Oliver mutters. "And that's not an easy sell in a burning town full of walking corpses. We've got no leverage. Nothing they want." His words hang in the air, ugly and true.

DJ speaks again, slower now. "What could they want, even if we had it?"

Silence settles again, thick and resigned.

From the front, David calls out, "Downtown's a few blocks out." His voice is the only one that doesn't carry dread.

Bruce taps his finger against his pursed lips. His eyes flick toward the monitor about his seat, then back to the group. "Far as I see it, unless we can cure this thing, or point fingers at who made it, then we're part of the cleanup."

That truth lands heavy enough to quiet the transport. As soon as the wheels stop, David twists around to face the group. "We're at the library. Infected are getting thicker out here. We need to figure out which bank we're hitting before we drive blind into the dead zone."

Ellie's voice bursts, cutting through the gloom. "Guys?"

She scoots to the edge of her bench, her eyes wide. "Jeff told me something back at the college. He said there were experiments on inmates. Years ago."

The others blink at her like she's speaking another language.

"He said they were using prisoners like lab rats. Scientists. Doctors. Something about behavior modification or testing reactions. But the ones they used, they didn't simply get violent. He said they started turning on each other."

David groans, dismissive. "They're inmates. They're always violent."

"No! He said they'd, like eat each other or something." Ellie's hands tremble as she motions in front of her face, panic breaking her words. "The way he explained it, they were like those people outside!"

Mister Pryde looks up, eyes catching the orange cabin light like glass. He rubs two fingers along his hairline, lost for a moment in something old. "You know, something about that…"

His voice fades, but Ellie's urgency sparks into him like static. "Can I tell you a story?" he asks softly. "Many moons ago, back when I still thought education could change the world, I taught at Washington State's correctional facility. Inmate literacy, post-secondary placement, that sort of thing." The others blink in confused silence.

"There was this one student," Fabian continues, more animated now. "Little guy, quick wits, nervous fingers. I called him Switchboard, because he always knew what was going on. Inside, outside, above and below. If something moved through that place, he heard the click before anyone else."

"I fail to see the relevance here," Bruce says, scanning the video feed on the monitor with practiced vigilance.

"Please, a moment," Fabian replies, raising a hand. "Switchboard's favorite subject wasn't literature. It was loopholes. Ways to shave time off your sentence. He'd spend hours in the prison library, legal codes, case histories, trial transcripts. He was always hunting cracks in the wall."

A dull thump echoes through the rig's hull. Then another. On the opposite side, a series of bumps and smacks vibrate through the armor. David checks the surveillance screen next to the steering wheel and frowns. "Come on, man," he mutters. "Get to the point, we've got company."

Fabian nods, shifting his tone. "Right, expediency. Switchboard ended up in the hole for something petty, refused to move cells or some such. While he was down there, he missed his chance to volunteer for a prison research program. It would have shaved a few months off his sentence. Thought it was another psych eval. Nothing crazy."

He leans forward, voice low now. "Months later, he told me he was grateful he missed it. Said every single one of the test subjects died. Said it wasn't just messy, it was inhumane."

David restarts the engine. "And?"

"As it happened, I knew someone else," Pryde says, bracing as the rig lurches from another heavy impact. "A man named Dr. Richards. We'd hit the security gate at the same time every Wednesday morning. Friendly type, and a bit quiet. After Switchboard went dark, Richards mentioned, casually, mind you, that their program was being shelved. 'Non-viable,' he said. And he'd been told to archive the records before being reassigned."

Another bone-jarring crash shakes the Stryker. David slams the gas, shouting over the engine, "Hurry it up or shut it up!"

"I'm done," Pryde says, steady. "I thought you all deserved to know, this didn't come out of nowhere."

Caroline watches the monitor above Bruce. Her voice cuts through the tension "Guys, look, they've started." She stabs her finger toward the screen.

The passengers rush forward, clambering to see. They watch the camera catch a small single-propeller plane cutting through the sky, buzzing low across the rooftops of downtown Walla Walla.

Bruce adjusts the feed with a toggle, zooming in on the aircraft. "That's not one of ours, it's civilian."

"Wait!" Steve jolts upright. "That means someone sees us, right? There's hope!"

David slows the Stryker and watches from the viewport as the vehicle crawls. All eyes watch the plane bank low, barely skimming the horizon. DJ narrows her gaze. "It's flying so low. Do you think they're the news? Maybe they're recording. Trying to get footage or something."

Almost on cue, the side door of the aircraft swings open and a figure appears. David slams the brake, lurching the passengers forward.

"Is that?" Bruce mutters, leaning toward the viewport. His fingers fly across the camera controls, zooming in.

"That's fuckin' Howard," David shouts, slamming furiously on the steering wheel.

Bruce glares at the display. "That was supposed to be our plane."

David nods in agreement. "Yeah! He wasn't checking on the girl, he hauled ass to the airport. Son of a bitch should have told me. I would've gone with him."

Bruce's glare shifts from the monitor to David, but the driver shrugs off the judgement.

The image flickers, then stabilizes. Onscreen, the group sees the unmistakable outline of the man who'd abandoned them at the college. Their confusion sharpens into a knife-edge of disbelief. Howard steps back from the open hatch, then returns, a rope now trailing from his hands.

"No way," Zero whispers.

The plane arcs toward the Marcus Whitman Hotel, the only building in Walla Walla tall enough to claw at the sky.

"What's he doing?" Ellie gasps.

They watch, frozen. As the aircraft closes in, Howard leaps, but he doesn't fall. The rope snaps taut, jerking his body forward, flapping him behind the plane. He's not skydiving. He's hanging.

A moment later, the screen whites out as the plane collides against the tower in an explosion of fire, glass, and steel. Silence falls through the truck. Ellie stumbles backward, collapsing into her seat. "I did not just see that."

Around her, the others sink back, stunned. Zero speaks into the weightless void. "Why would that guy do that? Why not just fly away?"

Oliver answers first, his voice hollow. "He probably saw the military rolling in. Figured there was no way out."

David turns, unusually quiet. "No. He knew he was dead. We all do, but unlike us, he went out his own way."

He glances at the monitor, then lowers his eyes. "He wasn't bit, but he'd been on Nine Wing detail for the last couple of years now." The name ripples through the group.

"Nine Wing?" Yoshiki echoes, barely audible.

David nods. "Graveyard out behind the prison. For inmates with no one left to claim their bodies. Back in the late eighties, it got used a lot, for the same shit this guy," he gestures at Pryde, "was talking about."

He shifts in his seat, voice soft but firm. "It's not ghost stories. The older officers all know about it. Anyone who works that detail for too long gets sick. Howard worked it longer than anyone. We all saw it. We thought it was depression, that shift sucks. Looks like he made his own choice. Better than being carved up in some lab, I guess."

The moment of mourning shatters. A fresh swarm descends on the transport, pounding the hull in a frenzy. Hands slap metal, and teeth gnash at seams. The infected are desperate to crack the shell and feast.

Bruce nudges Caroline to move as he jumps out of the gunner's seat and drags David into it. He slides behind the wheel and plants his hands on the wheel.

"I think the time for dawdling is over," he says, eyes forward. "Go directly to jail. Do not pass Go. Do not collect two hundred dollars."

David blinks. "You serious?"

Bruce doesn't look away from the open road. "Dead serious."

He pauses, giving space for the weight of the moment to settle. "If there's any place left in this city that holds answers, it's where this all began."

His voice lowers and he says, more to himself. "If we want to survive this, we need something the government can't burn."

In the back of the Zombie Smasher, DJ fumbles her phone from her coat pocket, shielding the screen from view.

She scrolls to the last called number and taps it with a shaking thumb.

A soft click emanates from the cell, then a voice. She can't tell who, Monster, Violet, or one of the others. The signal crackles. She covers the mic and leans into the shadows. "This is DJ. Tell the inmates we're coming," she whispers. "We need help."

She ends the call before they can respond.

33 – PLAY GOD

The front entrance of Washington State Penitentiary stands ominous and still, fencing crowned with razor wire. Ash-scorched pavement is littered with debris and employee vehicles burn in the lot. Guard towers loom beyond the lot, blind sentinels on the hill. Broken floodlights sag overhead, watching nothing.

Inside the warehouse of the admin building, Swecker rifles through boxes of inmate files while listening to The Morgue, his tattooed hands yanking open drawers, setting forms ablaze indiscriminately. The squawk of a walkie talkie, recently scavenged from a corpse, crackles over his shoulder. "Swecker," a voice calls through static. "This is Otero in Tower One. You there?"

He grabs the device and thumbs the side. "Go ahead."

"There's a big-ass army truck rolling up to the gates. I think they called in the cavalry."

Swecker smirks. Otero's voice comes again, quicker now. "Holy shit, man! They plowed through the gate! You want me to shoot 'em or what?"

"Yeah, go for it," Swecker says, grinning with a junkyard kind of pride. He strolls into the hallway, reaching for another office door, then pauses.

"Wait. Did you say army truck?"

"Hell yeah," Otero laughs. "I fired at a truck near it and stopped them dead in their tracks. Big green bastard."

Swecker's brow furrows. He turns and breaks into a jog.

"They're saying some shit through a bullhorn," Otero adds. "Something about coming in peace. Like aliens or some shit." He laughs.

Swecker clicks back in. "Just the one truck?"

"Yeah. No convoy. Just one ride, the stupid bastards."

"Hold off on the firing," Swecker says. "I think I know who that is."

"You expecting company?" Otero says, incredulous. "What is this, your sweet granny bringing a file cake?"

"No, dipshit," Swecker growls, bursting out of the prison entrance onto the cracked asphalt. "Stop firing. I got this."

He jogs down the front steps and through the parking lot, waving toward the olive-drab vehicle a hundred paces out. The engine rumbles low, idling. "Hey there!" Swecker shouts.

Otero chimes in over the walkie again. "You trying to lure 'em out? Want me to light 'em up when they step off?"

"Only if I say the word," Swecker snaps. "Until then, finger off the trigger."

"Got it," the speaker crackles.

Swecker continues forward, hands up, voice booming. "It's cool, man! We don't mean any harm. Come on over!"

The Stryker lurches forward, tires crunching over broken glass and debris. A voice crackles from its bullhorn, metallic and bold, "Identify yourself, and why the hell are you shooting at us?"

Swecker stops short, wary of venturing too far from the front entrance. He cups both hands around his mouth and shouts toward the truck, "Name's Swecker. We run this joint now. And you? You don't look like military. Prove me right, step out of the rig."

The vehicle growls a few feet closer before the voice answers, calm but firm: "That's not happening while your guy's still in the tower."

Swecker steps back, hand patting the rifle slung across his chest, then cups his mouth and yells, "You better stop right there and step out, or we light you up. Simple as that."

The truck halts, engine rumbling low and tense. After a pause, the voice replies, "We'll send a few out. But not until your man steps out of that tower with hands where we can see them."

Swecker shifts his gaze from the truck to the tower above. He rubs his chin thoughtfully and clicks into his radio. "Otero. Out of the perch. Hands high."

Then, turning back to the vehicle, he calls out, "Fair enough. But if you're who I think you are, you get nothing unless DJ's with you."

For a moment, there is nothing but the steady rumble of the Zombie Smasher's engine. The Stryker rolls into a wide arc, its front end turning toward the busted gate. It slows, then stops. Finally, the voice replies, giving one word, "Done."

The ramp hisses open. First out is a tall, skinny man who looks more pushed than volunteered. A broader man in a blue ball cap follows with and a blonde woman gripping his arm. They step clear and scan the prison walls, cautious. When they're satisfied, they motion toward the rig.

A young girl climbs down next. She has black hair and tired eyes, but there's an unmistakable fire in her expression.

Swecker watches her close. The radio on his shoulder hisses to life and a voice relaying from one of the towers mutters, "Oh damn, that's a snack right there. How long's it been?"

Swecker cuts the line cold with one press of the button. "Radio silence," he says, voice flat. The line goes dead. He walks forward with a disarming smile and extends his tattooed hand. "Swecker. Nice to meet ya."

The girl reaches out instinctively, but the man in the cap stops her short with a firm hand. She pulls back, visibly annoyed, then gathers herself.

"I'm DJ," she says brightly, forcing a smile despite the fatigue. "This is David, Caroline, and Mister Pryde." She gestures to each companion in turn.

Her eyes flick back to Swecker. "How did you know I'd be in there? How do you even know who I am?"

Swecker snaps out of her voice like waking from a trance. He blinks twice, grounding himself before answering with a question of his own. "You're not scared of me?" he asks, quirking a brow. "You realize I'm not a guard, right?"

DJ nods. "I figured. Heard something on the radio about a riot up here." She exhales slowly. "Truth is, yeah, I'm scared of you. All the people here. But I'm more scared of what's down there in town. The infected don't talk. They don't bargain. So, maybe I can deal with you. Maybe if I'm decent, you'll be decent back."

Her smile falters, but she holds it, even though it trembles.

Swecker's sharp features soften into something almost warm. "Cute and honest. I like that." Then, without skipping a beat, his expression stiffens. "So, what do you want? Why are you here?"

DJ's smile fades. "You didn't answer my question. How do you know who I am?"

Swecker chuckles, his hand falls away from his rifle. "We've been following your story on The Morgue. Heard your voice a lot tonight. Sounds like you've seen some shit. Makes you honest, cute, and tough."

DJ blushes, then feels immediately stupid for it. David notices and elbows her, hard enough to draw a glare. Swecker sees it too, his eyes narrowing with quiet amusement.

DJ clears her throat and steps forward. "We came for information. Medical records from nine wing, experiments. We're hoping you have access."

Swecker clicks on his radio, murmuring something low. Then he looks back at her. "Any idea what files you want? Or should I bring you a bunch of random shit?"

Before DJ can answer, Pryde raises his hand. "Actually, we're after something very specific. A particular case. Late eighties."

Swecker squints. "Who's this guy?"

DJ holds up a palm. "It's okay. He's a college professor. He's helping us."

Swecker nods. "Alright, teach. Go ahead." He presses the radio mic again, holding it so others in his communication line can hear as well.

Fabian wipes his forehead, voice thin but steady. "We're looking for records tied to a government program, an experimental one. End of the eighties."

Swecker mutters into the mic, then releases the button and lets his hand drop lazily back to his rifle. "Yeah. We know the one."

He pops his neck with a slow, deliberate tilt, issuing three loud cracks. "Worst damn thing they ever pushed on us. State shut that shit down hard. Banned all inmate experimentation not long after."

DJ offers a smile. "You've been way nicer than I expected. I thought this was going to be a lot worse."

Swecker chuckles, dry and amused. "Now what gave you the idea we're a bunch of mean people?"

DJ opens her mouth, but David slaps a palm against her back, hard and angry.

She shoots him a glare, then turns back to Swecker with a forced smile. "I also wanted to let you know the military's planning to bomb the whole city. You don't have much time to find shelter."

David explodes. "What the hell's wrong with you? That was our bargaining chip!"

DJ spins on him. "Why don't you leave me alone for once?"

"Oh yeah?" David sneers. "You going to karate chop me now?"

"Shut up! Just shut up!" she yells, stepping into his space. "You treat us like animals, but I know what you did. You killed Chastity. In cold blood. You're cruel, sadistic, and plain mean!"

David's response is a sharp backhand that cracks across her face. DJ stumbles, then snaps.

She lunges at him, fists flying. David swings back, wild and blunt. The two clash in a flurry of motion, grunts and shouts echoing off the walls. Fabian makes a move to intervene but freezes as Swecker lifts his rifle and levels it, not at them, but at the teacher. "Let it happen," Swecker says calmly.

Caroline gasps, backing away.

DJ's strikes are quick and trained, blocks, counters, and momentum redirection. David's are heavy and unrefined, driven by rage. His fists land hard against her guard, forcing her arms into her own face. Her punches connect too, but he powers through them, soaking up her strikes.

They circle, trading blows. David grabs her wrist and tries to twist her down into a takedown hold. DJ plants her foot and pivots, sweeping his leg from under him in a clean reversal. She rolls him over her back and slams him onto the pavement.

David snarls and starts to rise. A single deafening crack shatters the standoff. Swecker fires into the air once more and both fighters freeze. Swecker lowers his rifle, eyes locked on David. "You're a guard, aren't you?"

David says nothing, so Swecker steps forward, voice low and cold. "That hold you just tried. I know it. Had it used on me too many damn times. Admit it. You're one of them."

David takes a deep breath and raises his chin. "No. I'm a Washington State Corrections Officer."

Swecker doesn't hesitate. He lifts his rifle and pulls the trigger, the shot cracks through the air, and David's body jerks. Blood and brain spray across the lot behind him. He crumples without a sound, a twitching heap of shattered bone and sudden silence. Caroline drops to her knees in terror.

Pryde claps both hands over his mouth, stifling a scream while bile leaks between his fingers. Caroline cries out, a raw, broken wail that rips through the stillness. Swecker steadies his rifle at the crew.

The echo of David's execution rings in DJ's ears when Oliver climbs halfway out the back of the Stryker, rifle aimed at Swecker. Before he can take aim, a gunshot cracks from the tower and a round slams into the Stryker's armored panel, throwing sparks. Oliver ducks down but maintains his aim.

Swecker wags a finger toward the rig. "Nope. Don't."

He turns back to DJ. "You brought a pig into my yard," he says, calm but sharp. "You get how that looks, right?"

DJ stands frozen, her hands trembling and sweat beading on her forehead.

"I should torch this whole truck just to send a message," he continues. "But I've heard your voice, followed you on The Morgue. Far as I'm concerned, you're one of Monster and Violet's cadavers, same as me. I get it, you've made some tough choices while the world's turning to shit."

She swallows hard. "We still need those records."

Swecker gestures lazily. "No box today. Can't be seen making nice with a crew that rolled up with corrections stink."

He taps the side of his head. "But I'm not stupid. You want the intel, right? You're trying to do the right thing. Then give me a phone. Grab the pig's cell, then walk it over."

DJ hesitates, then slowly walks over to David's body. She kneels, swiping his blood-slick phone from the ground. She wipes it against her sleeve and unlocks it with his finger. She goes into the phone's settings to disable the screen lock, then she opens the contacts, types in her number, and names it DJ.

She walks it over to Swecker and holds it out.

He grins. "See? Teamwork." He takes the phone, but before DJ turns, his voice catches her again. "One more thing."

She stops, their eyes lock, his stare is ice. He jerks a thumb toward Caroline. "I can't let you all walk out without giving my people something. They've been watching. If I let you leave clean, they'll wonder if I'm going soft. That's not good for anybody."

DJ's face drains of color. "No. Please. Take me instead."

He chuckles low, shaking his head. "Pretty offer, sweetheart. But you? You're useful. They've heard your voice. They'd never forgive me for taking a celebrity."

DJ swallows hard, her voice breaking. "She's not part of this. She hasn't hurt anyone. She's nothing to you."

Swecker steps closer, eyes flat. "Exactly. She's nothing. That's why she's perfect."

DJ turns from his gaze. Her eyes fall on Caroline, who is bawling, tears darkening the asphalt. DJ's neck tenses.

Swecker moves to recapture her attention. "Don't make this harder than it has to be. You want the files, you gotta give me something. I'm taking her."

"No." DJ states through clenched teeth. "You can't have her."

"DJ. Get your head straight. You have a truck full of people who are relying on you. You said yourself, this girl is nothing. The way this plays out, you have two options, you give her up or we take the truck."

Their eyes meet and DJ searches for any light of kindness in the man's eyes but only find void. She looks from him to the guard towers over his shoulder. She looks at Caroline and back at the Stryker, open and waiting.

Swecker clocks her intention and rests a hand on her elbow. "Dumb play, kid."

She yanks her arm away and balls her hands into fists. Swecker smiles but doesn't budge. DJ pulls her arm back, preparing to strike.

Fabian hooks her arm and tightens around her. "Whoah now. That's a final mistake none of us are ready for."

She growls and lets her arm go limp, but keeps her first tight.

"Listen to the teacher, kid. I know it sucks." His tone sounds genuine. "But this is not a request. I'm taking her."

DJ starts to cry with a final soft plea. "No."

"I wish you understood prison politics. It would make this easier."

Caroline looks up and blinks, confused. "What's happening?"

Swecker walks DJ to Caroline, urging her forward. She stares at the ground, fists clenched at her sides. Her voice cracks when she finally looks to Caroline. "I'm sorry," she whispers, tears rolling down her cheeks.

Caroline's expression shifts from confusion to betrayal. Swecker grabs Caroline by the wrist, anchoring her in place.

"I'm so sorry," DJ repeats, tears streaming now. Fabian escorts her back to the Zombie Smasher without looking back. Swecker watches them climb into the truck.

Oliver holds at the ramp while DJ climbs in and passes her phone to Yoshiki without a word, then curls up in the seat beside her, shoulders shuddering in agony.

As the rig rumbles to life, Swecker calls out to Oliver, "Hey big man, I know this looks bad, but it could have been worse." Then, with a twisted kindness, he adds, "Take care of that girl, She's the kind of scar that leaves a mark on the world. Don't let her fade."

34 – LEGIONS OF THE DEAD

The Zombie Smasher rumbles beneath the highway overpass, crawling from the ruined outskirts of town and into the burning lungs of downtown Walla Walla. Inside the battered transport, every survivor stares in stunned silence through the soot-blurred windshield, where plumes of smoke curl like strangling hands into the darkened night.

Bruce, behind the wheel, slows the rig to a cautious crawl. Firelight flickers across his face as he studies the inferno ahead.

Oliver, riding in the command chair, breaks the quiet. "So, what's the plan, boss?"

Bruce doesn't answer at first. His eyes scan the flames, then drift to the exhausted crew behind them. Finally, he murmurs, "I don't have one."

Oliver leans forward. "What?"

"I know that's not what you want to hear," Bruce says quietly. "I don't think we're going to make it. Look at us, we're broken. We've lost more people than we've saved. And all we're doing is racing toward some buried vault, praying the people who show up to 'rescue' us don't put a bullet in our heads just for breathing."

Oliver exhales a half-laugh, mostly to disguise his dread. "Tell me how you really feel."

Their morose chuckles are brief and brittle. The tires jolt over a body. From the back, Eric mutters hollow, echoing the ghost of David's song, "The wheels on the bus go round and round…"

"We probably should have blown town when we were already out at the college." Bruce says grimly. "Honestly? I think we'd have had better odds trying to blow through a military barricade."

"Maybe." Steve's voice rises. He scoots to the edge of his bench seat, positioning himself between Bruce and Oliver. "But we missed that window. This is what we've got now."

He nods toward the smoldering wreckage of the Marcus Whitman Hotel, half-collapsed from the airplane collision, blocks ahead. Smoke billows, exhaled from the city's dying lungs.

"These people back here still believe in hope," Steve says quietly. "We should try not to crush it completely."

Bruce nods, but his face doesn't soften. "That rubble up there? Wasn't planning to go through it. I came this way out of habit." He taps the dashboard clock. The LED pulses back: 11:13.

"We've got maybe forty-five minutes before napalm falls or the sky does. Either way, it's now or never."

Eric joins Steve near the driver's seat. "You really want to punch it through that?"

"We don't have much time to go around." Bruce shrugs. "It's all that's left."

Eric clutches the roll bar. "Hope or hell, let's find out which one's waiting."

Bruce slams the accelerator and yells, "Hold onto your seats, it's about to get rough!" The Zombie Smasher roars to life, its wheels clawing for traction.

The rig plows into a scorched couch and a mountain of debris, all of which fell from the burning building. The impact sends flaming fabric streaking across the thin windshield. The entire transport rocks left, then right, and finally goes airborne for half a second before slamming down. Rubble, ash, and bodies scatter across the glass. A parade of horrors. A blinding swirl of soot and cinders wraps the rig in darkness.

The pavement disappears beneath fallen architecture as a wall collapses beside them, bricks hammering the hood and cracking one side of the windshield. Sparks dance across the dashboard and smoke works its way inside through the air vents.

The truck surges forward, a warhorse too broken to stop, too proud to die in place.

The Zombie Smasher whines beneath the strain, its frame groaning like a wounded beast as it rolls out of the blinding smoke. The vehicle lurches and leans heavily to the side as two left tires blow out. Bruce squints through the ash-stained windshield and realizes too late, they've driven straight into a swarm.

By the time his foot considers the brake, the truck is already plowing through the horde, so he doubles down.

The rig surges forward, the bumper smashing torsos, grinding bone, and slicking the asphalt with viscera. Hands from the mob slap against the armor, claw for purchase, and snap off like branches under a storm. Men, women, children, a gore trenched wave of infected, mowed down or hurled up over the Smasher's prow.

The weight of bodies slows the vehicle to a crawl. The engine growls, protesting, but Bruce doesn't let up. The rig lurches free of the mass, carving a path toward Main Street.

He nearly misses the turn to Main while powering through the living dead. He jerks the wheel hard into a drift, too hard, as blood-slick tires lose traction. The Smasher slides sideways, wheels locked, and crashes through the front display of the Inland Octopus toy store. Glass shatters, a wooden dinosaur explodes across the vehicle's view panel, and a train set crumples under the vehicle's mass.

The transport comes to rest on a cracked brick platform, rear tires spinning useless. Bruce pumps the gas, shifts, then curses, but gets nothing from the Zombie Smasher. He turns to the crew, scattered across the cargo hold. "We're stuck. Everybody out. Now."

Oliver climbs to his feet, ducking beneath the frame. "Anyone got ammo?"

Half the group checks some form of firearm and Bruce, Ellie, and Steve raise a hand.

Oliver doesn't wait. He yanks open a storage compartment beneath the bench, tossing a tire jack to Yoshiki and a crowbar to DJ. "Take these. If it's metal and heavy, it's a weapon."

He turns to Zero. "Fire extinguisher. Behind you."

Oliver points toward a storage bin near the bench. "Teacher guy, grab the med pack. You're our insurance policy if someone goes down."

Fabian nods and slings the first aid kit over his shoulder with effort.

A loud bang reverberates against the rear door, then another, then more, letting everyone in the rig know the infected are here. Eric rubs his temple and pulls his hand back bloody. "Shit. What now?"

Oliver grabs the door latch, steel in his eyes. "We're going to drop into the street and regroup. Get to the middle of the road and stay in a tight formation."

More pounding issues, enveloping the rear of the vehicle. He glances around the truck. "From there, we move up Main to First Street. Bank's at the corner. No stalling. No heroes. We run together or we die alone."

He throws the latch. The back doors slam open, crushing many of the infected. Oliver hits the street first and his boots splash down in bloody meat and shattered glass. An infected surges, but he smashes the butt of his rifle into its face, sending it flailing away with a wet crunch.

Behind him, Eric calls as the others spill out after him, "Why the middle of the street?"

Oliver's voice booms from the street. "Don't waste ammo! Blunt-force only unless it's life or death! Just don't stop to fight"

He hammers the butt of his rifle into another snarling face, sending it sprawling.

Ellie answers as she leaps from the rig. "Middle of the street's got open sightlines, less places for 'em to jump us."

One by one, the survivors pour out of the cracked shell of the Zombie Smasher, weapons drawn, eyes wide. Oliver fights on the right flank, warding off the infected with brutal efficiency. Ellie surprises everyone with her precision. She's controlled and fast, swinging like someone who's been in real fights before.

Steve and Fabian bolt to the middle of the road and Eric isn't far behind.

In the rear, Yoshiki helps Zero down from the rig's open back, her shoulder is under his arm, bracing his limp. DJ flanks from behind, awkwardly balancing her crowbar as she helps steady them.

When Zero hits the pavement with a grunt, Ellie runs up, grabs his bleeding leg, and rips his long board from under his arm. Yoshiki moves to protest but Ellie throws the deck to the ground and drags Zero to it, pushing his injured body onto the board. "Just sit there," She commands, "I'll push you if I gotta but we're effing out of here!"

DJ pauses, casting one last glance at the Inland Octopus. The vehicle's headlights illuminate a battlefield of shattered toys and broken brick. Above it all, the giant mural of a smiling purple octopus stares down from the storefront's second story, tentacles stretching across the facade like it's hugging the carnage below.

DJ smirks. "Looks like the octopus is watching us." No one replies. A pair of attackers rush her from near the truck, and she swings, catching one on the head. She sidekicks the other, sending it sprawling back into the mob.

The crew regroups in the street under the mural's haunted gaze. Ahead, more infected stagger from alleys and doorways, snarling and bounding over each other like feral dogs desperate for fresh meat. The street fills with violence. The dead press down on all sides.

Oliver raises his weapon and fires once, drops a screecher mid-sprint. "Move!" he barks.

They push up Main Street. Zero and Yoshiki now rolling toward the front. DJ and Steve take the flanks, watching corners, and checking windows.

"I can't..." Fabian wheezes behind them, staggering under the weight of the med kit strapped across his chest. "I can't keep pace!"

The group halts in a spray of panic. "We're almost there!" Eric shouts. He presses one hand against the glass of the Book & Game storefront and points with the other. "That's the bank, past that alley."

Fabian nods through clenched teeth, digging deep to find his resolve.

Pistol hilts crack jaws. Rifle stocks slam throats. DJ's crowbar spins with turbine speed, clearing bodies from their path. Fabian clutches the med kit like its gold, readjusting it for an easier carry. "Okay, I think I'm good.

The crew move again and their momentum builds, until a group of eight infected surges from the alley ahead. Knowing they can't go back, the crew crashes into them with the force of a storm. Blades flash and metal smashes bone. Adrenaline burns through exhaustion as the group pushes their way toward the only hope they have left, the vault under the bank. They cut down their adversaries with burning breath.

The survivors reach the front of the bank, stumbling to a halt outside the shattered entryway. Bruce climbs in first, stepping through what remains of the glass-paneled doors and into the once-pristine lobby.

His boots crunch across broken glass. He weaves around toppled stanchions, spilled ferns, and splintered furniture. Dust hangs heavily in the air. Shadows stretch long across the marble floor, and the glow from the burning streets flickers through the window.

Bruce clears the lobby, checking behind couches, scanning under desks, pushing open closet doors. He finds no infected, no bodies, only stillness and stale air.

At the far end, a steel security door looms. He jogs to it, tries the handle, rattles the hinges, but it's locked. His voice echoes back through the silence: "Clear! I think this is the way down."

Behind him, the others begin to trickle in, dragging exhaustion and hope in equal measure.

DJ and Oliver hold position inside the shattered entryway, guarding the breach. They don't speak. There's no breath left for conversation, only watchfulness and doom.

A shriek cuts through the street and the first infected lunges through the doorway. DJ's crowbar catches it mid-leap, splitting cheek from jawbone. It drops twitching at her feet. Oliver drops another with a rifle butt to the skull, then boots it back out the door.

They keep coming, another one, then two more. Oliver and DJ fight in sync, striking, dodging, pivoting like dancers by fire. They cover the entrance, their bodies bracing against the tide.

From deeper in the building, Bruce's voice rises, distorted and angry. A crash follows. Something metal, then silence. DJ's heart pounds louder than the snarls. Seconds later, Bruce reemerges from the shadows, voice sharp and ragged.

"Fall back!" he shouts. "Regroup. Something's wrong." His words hit the lobby with urgency.

Blocks away, on the edge of Walla Walla's fire-scorched Main Street, between a shattered yoga studio and a boarded-up tattoo parlor, an old music store still breathes sound into the silence.

The building's sign reads Hot Poop. The store has been a staple of Walla Walla culture for half a century. The building refuses to become silent, even as the world around it burns. The neon is dead and windows are cracked, but the store's battered PA system works. From a pair of sun-warped speakers mounted over the entrance, a voice spills into the street.

It's tinny, distorted, and laced with sarcasm. "Hey Walla Walla, if you're still out there dodging death and clinging to your last piece of jerky, congratulations! You're not one of the many currently snacking on someone's colon."

A second voice, smoother and sharper, chimes in. "Which reminds me, Monster, maybe don't open with cannibal jokes. The end of the world has a taste problem already."

Laughter crackles through music, guitars fading in the background of the broadcast. The air itself feels haunted, haunted by heavy metal and defiant radio hosts who refuse to let the apocalypse end in silence.

A single infected corpse twitches on the sidewalk, too maimed to rise. It's one working eye staring blankly at the glowing speakers. The Morgue continues to broadcast.

"Well, cadavers," Monster's gravel-pit voice rasps through the broken speakers above Hot Poop's warped awning, "according to the clock on the wall, we're staring down just under thirty minutes till doomsday. For those of you dumb enough to be listening, thank you. It's been one hell of a ride, and I've had a great fucking time bringing this valley the best, and worst, in extreme metal for ten long years."

A second voice cuts in, dry and sharp. "Wow, Monster. That might be the most heartfelt thing you've ever said."

"Savor it, Blade. If now's not the time for a few kind words, when the hell is?" Monster's chuckle buzzes the line, followed by a tap on a microphone and the rustle of leather against vinyl.

"While I'm playing Mr. Sentimental, I gotta say, you freaks made this worth it. Butcher, you've been our immovable wall of deadpan doom. Respect. Goblin, Ogre, Blade, you degenerates might not always bring gold to the table, but damn if you don't put up with my shit like champs. Ninja…look, I'd say I'm sorry for busting your balls all these years, but I'm not. It's fun as hell."

Laughter spikes from unseen corners of the studio. Someone whistles mockingly, probably Ninja himself.

"And Fresh, Meat, who the hell even let you in?" The couple protest, but Monster cuts them off. "You two are the pups. Like our kids in some twisted, back-alley deal kind of way."

"Charming," Fresh snaps back. "Real Hallmark moment, Monster."

The sound of a door creaks open mid-sentence. "Hey, where the fuck do you three think you're going?"

"Chill, dude!" Goblin's voice echoes faintly. "We're just stepping out to check out the end of the world. Be right back!" A loud slam punctuates the moment.

Then Violet's voice cuts into the speakers, clean, cool, and commanding. "Monster. Are you going to spend your last breath monologuing, or maybe do something useful?"

This makes the motormouth host pause. "Careful, woman. I might do you something useful live on-air." His voice is all grin and grit. "Though honestly, what else is there to do? I mean, aside from sex."

"Now that's what I'm talking about," Meat chimes in, voice dripping with delight.

Monster shifts tones, sarcasm giving way to something quieter, almost reflective. "Seriously though, it's not like we can do much more than spin records and die. So, I'm going to go out doing what I love."

"Wow," Fresh murmurs. "That's dismal and romantic."

"You know what's really romantic?" Monster fires back. "My right forearm. It'll romance you all the way to…"

"Monster!" Violet snaps, her voice is a playful growl. Then, softer, "Do you have any regrets? Somewhere you wish you'd gone, something you never got to do?"

He lets the silence ride long enough to feel the upcoming confession. Without skipping a beat, "Oh yeah. I wish I could've gotten stuck in a little person clown orgy. All the sex appeal of Cirque du Soleil with half the height. Who wouldn't want to die under a pile of squeaky red noses?"

Before Violet can groan, he cuts in again, suddenly honest. "But really? There's a whole world of experiences I never got to see. And yeah, that world's ending tonight. But no, I don't have any regrets. Because I had you by my side, Violet. You've been my best friend, the most amazing lover, and the best partner in crime a Monster could hope for. I wouldn't want to watch the world end with anyone else."

A beat follows. Long enough to breathe. Long enough for something real to hang in the static. In the background, the other hosts fall quiet. A few can be heard shifting in their seats. Someone lets out a soft, surprised chuckle. Another mutters, "Damn."

It's Violet who breaks the hush, her voice quivering enough to feel human. "Oh, Monster…"

Then, the sound of a door slamming issues again. "Yo!" Ogre's voice cracks through the mic. "You guys, we found something big. You're going to want to hear this!"

Fresh cuts in, cheerful and clueless. "Ogre? You're back already? Blade, Goblin, you guys too?"

"Yeah, yeah, we're here!" Ogre barks. "But seriously cut to music. Now. We gotta talk. Privately."

Monster doesn't hesitate.

"Alright, alright. This is Arch Enemy and this track's called 'Dead Bury Their Dead.' Listen loud."

Guitars screeches across the airwaves. Harsh, furious, and defiant.

36 – FREE WILL SACRIFICE

Smoke curls in from shattered windows. Orange glow flickers outside, casting dancing shadows on the cold marble floor.

Ellie clutches her pistol, scanning the lobby corners. "Do you think Bruce actually saw something?" she calls to Oliver, who is reloading his shotgun inside the jagged remains of the entryway.

He doesn't answer. His eyes are fixed on the far end of the lobby, where Bruce vanished moments ago after shouting for everyone to regroup. The hallway swallowed him. His warning echoes in their bones. Even the air feels thinner now.

Ellie presses closer, glancing back at the dim street. Three infected corpses litter the doorstep and more shadows flicker in the smoke beyond, but the mob didn't seem to follow the survivors to the bank.

"I don't like this," she mutters. "Feels like we're about to walk into a trap."

DJ walks from the bank's entry and stands next to Oliver, bruised and breathing hard. "If Bruce says something's wrong, we should find out what it is. Fast."

Oliver scans the exhausted group near the entrance. "Steve, barricade the front with Eric. Use whatever's not nailed down. Fabian, stay with Zero and keep pressure on that leg. We don't need more bleeding."

Steve raises an eyebrow. "What about you?"

"We're checking on Bruce," Oliver says, already turning toward the hall. "Something's wrong."

DJ stays beside him, gripping her crowbar. "We've got this. Keep everyone else alive."

Eric hesitates, glancing into the dark bank lobby. "You sure you want to split up?"

"No," Ellie says flatly, cocking her pistol. "But if Bruce is in trouble, we're not leaving him to die in a vault."

Oliver nods. "We'll signal if it's safe. If we don't come back, you know what to do."

Steve exhales through his nose. "Don't say that."

Oliver locks eyes with him for a heartbeat. "We have no other choice. Give us a minute. It might even be better if you look for another shelter somewhere else, just as a backup." Then he nods to DJ. "Come on. Stay behind me."

The trio moves forward across the lobby with Ellie trailing a few steps behind. The chase from minutes ago hangs heavy in the air. Glass shards glint like landmines, furniture lies broken, and the room smells of dust and blood. Oliver and DJ lead toward the corridor Bruce vanished down, but it's empty now, cold and still.

Passing a toppled filing cabinet, Ellie stumbles on a snarl of rug and catches herself on a counter. "Shit," she hisses. She checks to make sure no one saw. DJ and Oliver don't break stride.

A flickering red EXIT sign casts their shadows down the corridor. DJ and Oliver reach the stairwell first. They exchange a look with no words needed before descending. Ellie lingers at the top, glancing down the stairwell into darkness. "I don't like this one bit," she whispers, rubbing the back of her neck.

DJ turns to her and says, "It's okay. Stay up here and keep watch. If we find anything, we will holler."

Ellie sways with uncertainty, glancing from the stairwell to the lobby. "I don't know."

DJ squeezes her shoulder. "It's okay, I promise."

"Okay." Ellie nods, uncertain but somewhat reassured. "Hurry, please?"

DJ and Oliver head down in silence. The stairs creak under their weight, and each step takes them further from the faint glow of the lobby. A lower landing leads to another hallway and another set of stairs, narrower and older, leading deeper underground. The darkness swallows their steps.

At the bottom, they find concrete floors, rows of doors, and cold, dead silence. One by one, they test each handle. Each door is locked, until the last one, a massive steel door, sits slightly ajar.

"We're in luck," Oliver whispers, his breath fogging slightly in the chill air.

DJ's lips tighten, "Are we? We haven't seen Bruce yet."

With one heavy hand, he pushes the steel door open. It groans on its hinges, revealing nothing but black. "I can't see a damn thing," he mutters, stepping into the void.

DJ hesitates at the threshold, squinting to follow his shape, but it disappears into the ink. Her heart pounds louder than her steps, blood rushing in her ears like static. Darkness warps her senses, her vision tilting like she's trapped inside a fishbowl.

A click slices through the quiet and blinding light floods the chamber. DJ shields her eyes and then screams. Oliver stands beside a light switch, triumphant for a second, until he turns and sees what the light has revealed behind him. The floor is a slaughterhouse.

White walls lined with tidy shelves full of stored office supplies form a clean illusion, but the floor is soaked in gore. Disemboweled corpses lay in tangled heaps, limbs draped over crates, intestines like thick ropes of red and gray. Pink handprints smear the concrete like desperate graffiti. Eyeless skulls stare from pools of blood, and something twitching slides wetly across the floor.

At the center of the carnage is a writhing mass of the infected, feasting with shoulders hunched, and teeth gnashing. Blood sprays in pulses.

DJ stumbles back with a guttural sob, nearly falling. "Oh...oh god, Oliver..." She points, her finger shakes violently.

He spins to face the carnage, and in the middle of it all, half-buried beneath the clawing pile, they see Bruce.

His arms are limp. His chest barely rises. One of his arms is already gone below the elbow, and the rest of him is being torn open unceremoniously. His head turns, slightly, and stares at DJ. His eyes are wide and his lips part like he's trying to speak through quivering lips. Then a mouth from one of the cannibals clamps down on his throat and silences him forever.

"They're eating him," DJ whispers, staggering. "They're eating him!"

A cold grip tugs at Oliver's boot, and his instincts take over. He kicks backward with brutal force, snapping free and lunging toward the exit. Behind him, corpses jolt to their feet, joints popping, hands clawing toward them. Hungry moans fill the cramped space.

"Go!" he bellows, pushing DJ out of the doorway and slamming his shoulder into the thick shelter door. He grabs the handle and pulls, but the dead reach.

DJ doesn't run. Instead, she whirls around and raises her crowbar, heart hammering, and legs frozen. Oliver strains against the door as undead fists hammer from the other side. Despite his bulk, the tide turns. Creatures squeeze through, widening the gap with each new body. The door begins to creep open under the weight of the hungry dead. He groans with every ounce of force he can muster.

DJ runs to his side and smashes at the monsters to push them back through, but it's no use. Oliver growls, grabs DJ by the arm and throws her down the hall. "I said get the hell out of here!"

Then the door crashes open and an infected man lunges through the breach. Oliver meets him with a fist, crushing the dead man's face into the wall.

DJ scrambles up and sprints to the stairwell, screaming for Oliver to follow. More bodies pour through the shelter door. He brings his shotgun up and floors another with a savage blow, but the strike snaps the weapon's stock clean off.

"Oliver!" DJ shrieks from the base of the stairs.

"Run!" he shouts back.

He flips the broken weapon and fires both loaded rounds. The shot echoes from the chamber, a death bell.

He pivots to flee, but his heel catches on the broken stock and he slips. The fall feels like slow motion and his back hits concrete, sending a stream of pops up his spine. Stars fill his vision Above him, ravenous mouths descend.

DJ screams. Oliver rolls, grabs the barrel, and uses it like a club. He smashes an attacker's collarbone, cracks another's skull, and claws for space. A heartbeat of room is all he needs.

He launches upright, blood streaming down his face. "I fucking told you, move!" he bellows, charging the stairs.

They climb together. DJ bounds up a flight, turns, and comes face-to-face with a mangled torso sprawled across the landing, still crawling. She screams again, recoiling.

The slithering dead pushes off the stair and slams into her face. She spins on instinct, throwing the mulched monster over the rail.

"Oh my god. Ew. Gross! So gross!" DJ gags, slapping at the sticky warmth on her cheek. She squeezes her eyes shut and tries not to think about what just splattered across her face.

"Duck!" Oliver's voice booms from behind.

She drops instantly. Something wet and heavy smacks the wall behind her with a sickening slap.

Gasping, DJ wipes the gore off with her sleeve, only to feel a hand grabbing her shoulder. It's Oliver. "Kid, get your ass upstairs!"

They scramble up the next flight, boots echoing like gunshots on concrete. At the top, they burst into the main floor corridor. Ellie stands trembling in the dim light, pistol aimed squarely at the dark hallway.

"Ellie, it's us!" Oliver shouts. "Don't shoot! Get the hell out of here!"

The girls bolt, the others are nowhere to be seen.

Glass crunches underfoot as they hurl through the jagged maw of the bank's broken entry. Neither cares about the serrated frame slicing their clothes. They rush to escape, at any cost.

Behind them, Oliver pivots to face the oncoming dead. The first creature lunges. He sidesteps, but two more leap. He ducks again, breath ragged, eyes scanning the lobby.

The infected aren't coming from below anymore. Shadows dart from the hallway, wanderers stirred by the noise of the main floor. The crowd is growing.

After making it outside, Ellie screams, "Come on, Oliver!"

He sees them, Ellie and DJ silhouetted in the glow of distant firelight, barely outside the bank, and in his mind, the memory of Brooke flickers behind their faces. They're just kids running for their lives.

Veering left, Oliver slams shoulder-first into a massive oak bookshelf. It wobbles, groans, then crashes sideways across the doorway with a splintering roar, blocking the lower half of the exit.

Outside, Ellie shrieks, "What the hell, Oliver?! Are you okay?!"

She starts toward the bank doors but stops dead as Oliver rises from behind the fallen shelf that now blocks the bank's entrance. He climbs up onto it, boots scraping wood, eyes locked on the overhead gate.

Without warning, he snatches the pistol from Ellie's hands through the gap. "Run!" he barks. "Just fucking run!"

He jumps, grabs the edge of the old security gate above the door. With a pull, his weight drags it down, metal screaming as it slams into place, cutting off the lobby with a thunderous crash. He lifts the gate barely, enough to climb through.

He braces his foot on the top of the bookshelf, preparing to climb out using the open space, but cold fingers wrap around his legs. The infected have reached him, and they yank. His body drops hard on the toppled shelf, and his legs vanish behind him. The air leaves his lungs with a brutal thud.

Pain sears his legs as gnashing teeth tear into flesh and fabric. He roars and fires the pistol blindly, the shots echoing off the stone walls.

Outside the gate, DJ shrieks and jabs through the steel mesh with her crowbar, desperate to dislodge the feeders swarming his lower half. Ellie screams next to her, fists pounding the metal barrier in helpless rhythm.

"Girls!" Oliver grits out, face drenched in sweat and blood. "I'm tired of telling you. Get out of here. Now. Time's almost up."

DJ's voice cracks through tears. "We're not leaving you, Ollie! We've lost too many already!"

He grimaces as another set of jaws clamps onto his calf. His body trembles, but his voice steadies. "Kiddo..." His breath is almost benediction.

He roars and pumps another shot into the writhing mass at his waist. With harrowing peace, he says, "I died hours ago with Brooke. My body's just now catching up."

He locks eyes with Ellie, calm and final, then smiles, "Now get the fuck out of here!" He slams the gate shut again.

The words slam through DJ in a shockwave. Her hands tremble against the steel mesh. Her eyes lock on the blood pooling beneath Oliver's torso, she doesn't move.

Ellie does. "Ollie!" she screams, lunging forward, fists pounding the gate, voice cracking. "No! You don't get to do this! Not you!"

DJ grabs her from behind, arms hooked under Ellie's shoulders as she drags her back from the writhing shadows. "Ellie, he's gone. We have to go. We have to go."

Ellie thrashes, then crumples to her knees on the steps outside the shattered bank, sobbing into her palms. DJ kneels beside her, silent, holding on.

Footsteps crunch through glass. Steve rounds the corner with Eric close behind, both weapons raised.

"We saw you come out," Steve says, eyes darting toward the bank. "We were about to move up Main, maybe head to the Whitman campus. See if we can find shelter there, but..." He trails off when he sees the gate and the blood. He stops where Ellie is slumped.

"What happened?" Eric asks, voice low.

Steve moves closer, eyes on the barricade, staring at the mass of writhing bodies. "Where's Ollie?"

DJ doesn't look at them. She stares at the sidewalk like it betrayed her. "He stayed behind to save us."

Ellie's shaking hand points to the bank. She answers through grit teeth and tears. "He saved us. Locked the gate. Gave us time."

Eric exhales sharply, rubbing his hand down his face. "Christ."

Fabian and Yoshiki catch up a beat later, with Zero rolling behind them on his skateboard. Fabian starts to ask something, but one look at the mass of caged zombies stops him cold.

For a long moment, no one speaks. The only sound is the low hiss of wind through broken windows, and the creak of the half-fallen security gate.

DJ rises first, voice quiet. "Bruce is gone too."

Fabian's head twists sharply, "What?"

"He was already in the vault. They were feeding on him when we got there." DJ's throat tightens. "There is no shelter. No miracle door. Only another grave."

The silence that follows isn't respectful. It's shock, as hope dies without sound.

Steve nods, slow and heavy. "Then let's move."

Ellie wipes her face with the heel of her hand, asking through broken breath. "Where?"

DJ looks down Main Street, past the wreckage and rising smoke. "Anywhere but here."

No one says who should lead, or where to go. They simply start walking, no more animated than the hungry dead.

DJ moves first, helping Ellie to her feet. Fabian scans the street, watching the dead close in while Yoshiki pushes Zero down the sidewalk in silence.

Steve lingers. His eyes remain fixed on the thrashing monsters on the other side of the barricade.

Eric touches his shoulder, and Steve follows him without a word, turning right at the street and departing from the others. They don't talk about splitting up, they just do. What they're leaving behind isn't only the dead, but the idea that anyone's going to save them now.

37 – ALL HOPE IS GONE

"Eric, this is a dumb fucking idea, we shouldn't have split up." Steve mutters, scowling as he watches their friends dash across the street. "What makes you think any of these bomb shelters are even empty? They're going to be like the last one, or full of assholes who won't open the door."

Eric skirts a three-story brick building, eyes scanning for a way in. "Look, I already told you," he fires back. "There's no guarantee we'll find anything, but like Ma'am always said, better to try and fail than never try at all."

He rounds the corner to the west side where a single metal door waits. With a tug it creaks open. Eric pauses at the threshold, glancing back. "We find shelter before the military starts their sweep. That's all that matters right now." Then he slips inside.

The hallway beyond glows under fluorescent lights buzzing above spotless linoleum. Eric bolts down the corridor toward a stairwell. Steve follows, driven by desperation but doubting every step. Both boys race down the eggshell stairs to the basement.

At the landing the corridor splits. Eric leans against the wall, thumb brushing his chin sizing up the layout. He points. "I'll take this hallway. You go that way. Let's see what we can find, if anything goes wrong, get back here and shout."

Steve nods. "Alright, cool. But we should hurry."

He darts down his hall, checking doorknobs as he disappears into the gloom.

Eric watches him vanish, then pushes off the wall. A small yellow sign behind his back reads BOMB SHELTER, arrow pointing down the hall. A short jog brings him to a bend, then a dead-end. A hulking steel door looms ahead, not yet locked in place. He huffs in relief.

"No kidding?" he whispers with eyes wide. He grabs the handle and tugs. The door groans open to reveal a small, untouched shelter. He ponders for a moment, knowing he has reached sanctuary. Getting in and locking himself inside would be easy, he would be safe.

Inside, the shelter is small but empty. It appears to be untouched and his pulse spikes with hope, a grin spreading across his face. He stands in the room for a moment, savoring his victory. The longer he stands, the harder isolation presses, he feels the weight of fear, of dying alone. He realizes he's not ready for that.

He sprints back to the stairwell, yelling, "Steve! I found it! I fucking found it!"

On the landing he finds not Steve, but half a dozen figures descend the stairwell, grimy, wild-eyed, draped in biker leathers and red-streaked vests. 9 Kings.

Eric freezes. "Shit."

The gang members lock eyes with him. One of them grins wolfishly and springs forward, the others are quick to follow. Eric spins and bolts, sneakers slapping tile. He hits the hallway and races for the shelter with the 9 Kings hot on his heels. He throws himself inside and yanks the steel door shut behind him. The lock twists as fists slam into the other side.

They bang the shelter door with the hilt of a pistol. To the left of the door, an antique intercom crackles to life. "Go the fuck away," a tinny voice snaps through the aluminum grate protecting the speaker.

One of the gang members snorts. "Hey, buddy. Shit ain't funny. Is it safe in there? Let us in."

The voice replies, cold and flat. "Yes, it is. And no, I won't. Now fuck off. This one's mine."

The gang member chuckles. "Seriously, dude. Let us in."

"Get wrecked," Eric growls through the speaker. "I ain't letting anyone in here. This shit is mine."

Another 9 King member steps forward, tapping the grate with a chain-wrapped bat. "Yo, punk. Open the door or we're lighting this whole bitch up."

A third voice follows with a grin. "Let him rot. He'll die slower in there. Kings don't need trash."

Inside the shelter, Eric slumps against the wall, chest heaving. Sweat drips from his brow. He slides to the floor and lets out a shaky laugh.

"Mine," he whispers.

But the word doesn't echo, the room absorbs it. He looks around for the first time. The space is small and sterile, cinderblock walls and metal shelving. He sees a few crates and a plastic-wrapped mattress in the corner, but something feels wrong.

A smear of blood stains the far wall. A trail runs from it, thin and dark, tacky. It leads behind a stack of boxes. Eric squints, then forces a laugh. "Nah. Just old. Probably from when they stocked this place."

He shifts, settling in, but his eyes keep flicking to the crates. Something moves, issuing a faint sound of metal on metal. He freezes, but hears nothing, hoping the silence is playing tricks on him.

He breathes in, slow and shaky. The light above him flickers twice. In that moment between pulses, something shifts in the dark corner.

Outside, one of the Kings growls at the busted intercom one last time. "You think you're safe, rat?" he barks, "Ain't no door thick enough to protect you from us when the world burns."

The lack of response sets them off. The gang unleashes a chorus of fury; cursing, howling, slamming fists against the vault door. One of them pounds the speaker plate until it bursts, knuckles tearing open on metal, blood smearing the wall in crimson arcs.

Back at the stairwell, Steve returns to an empty landing. Eric is gone, but shouts echo from down the other hall like war drums, the sound of boots pounding tile. The noise stops and silence settles, tense and suspended. Steve freezes. He stares at the hallway where his friend ran, heart twisting. "I could go after him. I should."

He takes one step forward, then stops. The sounds from deeper in the hall picks back up with shouts, scuffling, and a slamming sound. There is rage and screaming.

Steve rationalizes he is too late and his jaw clenches. "Dude," he whispers, voice cracking. "I'm so fucking sorry."

He turns and bolts up the stairs, swallowing the guilt with each step. He bursts through the lobby doors into a world gone feral.

Outside, the street glows blood and firelight. A horde of infected crowd near a dumpster, tearing something apart. They feed ravenously, their shoulders hunched, hands dripping with gore. Snarls are lost beneath the wet sounds of chewing and tearing.

Steve skids to a halt, nearly falling. A torn denim vest arcs through the air and lands at his feet, its patch is visible. He stares at the 9 Kings jacket. He exhales, "I ran from one death trap straight into another."

He starts to back away slowly, eyes never leaving the feeding frenzy. Gunfire cracks through the air, he flinches and turns, unable to locate the source of the shot.

Across the street, the bank is silhouetted in a flickering orange glow. Several of the infected lift their heads like hounds catching scent, blood dripping from their chins.

He hears the screaming, high and panicked. Without thinking, Steve launches into a sprint, boots slapping the pavement, but he doesn't make it far. A snarl erupts beside him, too close.

Something slams into his side. He goes down hard. Clawed hands rake his chest and teeth snap inches from his face. He kicks, punches, and rolls, fighting for breath every way he can. Pain sears his ribs, still he kicks frantically. Another body piles on, pinning him with finality.

Through blood and flesh, he lifts his head enough to see DJ, Ellie, Fabian, Zero, and Yoshiki a block down Main Street. They run hard along the opposite sidewalk, silhouettes framed by fire and smoke.

They're not alone. Half a dozen figures melt from alleyways behind them, silent, fast, and deliberate. Steve knows they're too smooth and coordinated to be infected.

One of them steps into the light, swinging a machete. "No…" Steve screams through his own pain, voice trembling. "Guys! Behind you!"

They don't hear him. He tries to scream again, but a hungry hand clamps around his throat and fingers dig deep. The infected assailant slams him against unforgiving pavement, then descends with broken teeth against his face. Blood fills his mouth. His body jerks once, twice, then goes limp.

Across the street, the girls keep running, never hearing him. Behind them, the 9 Kings close in.

38 – EVERYONE I LOVE IS DEAD

The street is unexpectedly quiet. Ash from the burning town drifts like lazy snowflakes as DJ leads the survivors up the cracked sidewalk in front of Hot Poop. The building's front windows are shattered, its neon sign half-lit, but the exterior speakers continue to hum with life.

A distorted voice crackles through the static. "…they're not going to tell you what it is. They'll call it containment. They'll call it cleansing. But it's just death, folks. Plain and simple." The Morgue is broadcasting, the hosts alive and loud.

DJ slows beneath the ruined awning. Ellie leans against the wall, face slack and pale. Fabian coughs twice, sharp. Yoshiki says nothing.

For the first time in what feels like hours, DJ dares to look back. There are no signs of Steve or Eric, only flickering light and long shadows stretching across Main Street. Her hand slips into her pocket. She checks her phone. They haven't messaged, but an unknown number floods her screen with unread images and documents.

Dozens of photos. Some are blurry, others sharp. Government documents, typed memos, hand-scrawled margins. She scrolls through the first few: one marked "Subject Losses: Nine Wing," another labeled "Protocol Stage Four: Civilian Reclassification."

She pauses, thumb hovering over the screen. She glances at the time in the notification bar: 11:42.

Her eyes lift to the sky, searching for the end. She sees nothing but smoke and haze, no jets, no napalm. She hears no rumble of engines. But she feels it. A building static in her spine. They're running out of time.

In the stillness, she hears it. A deep voice, somewhere beyond the haze, tucked in the walkway between buildings across the street. She can't make out the words but catches sight of a low riding Impala idling at the intersection halfway up the block. Gangs.

She crouches, eyes flicking toward the dark shapes near the corner of Main and Spokane Street, there's movement. One figure nods and lifts two fingers, another circles behind a wrecked sedan.

"Yoshiki," DJ whispers, teeth clenched. "We've got company."

Ellie looks up, dazed. "What?"

"We are being surrounded. They aren't moving like the crazies." She tucks her phone away and raises her crowbar. Her arms are shaking. The Morgue hums in the speakers behind them.

"Come on, you guys. Hurry!" DJ calls, pausing at the shattered furniture storefront next to Hot Poop. "I hear trouble!" The road behind them is empty, but it feels too still. she feels the breathless hush of death before it sinks its teeth in.

Ellie lags, clutching her side, lungs shredded by the sprint. "I'll be right there!" she gasps, hunched over. "Go help the others!"

"Get out of the open!" she shouts at the rest of their survivors.

Without waiting for a reply, she dives through the opening of the furniture store and clears the landing zone, scanning for threats. Her shoes hit polished wood and shattered tile. Mannequins and broken couches sprawl across the floor. "Come on! In here!" she yells over her shoulder.

Ellie stumbles after her, Fabian and Yoshiki dragging Zero close behind her. DJ turns toward the movement deeper in the shop and sees the writhing, snarling danger that already waits inside. They weren't the first ones to find shelter. Blood paints the counters and floor in jagged arcs.

The college trio climbs into the store, and their warm bodies disrupt the stillness inside. Teeth snap and groans blend with snarls. Limbs thrash across toppled displays. The dead emerge from everywhere and the store becomes a battlefield.

A wave of the dead overcomes the survivors before they have a chance to catch their breath. Fabian is buried beneath two gnashing corpses near a broken table, struggling to breathe. Yoshiki stands above Zero, swinging her skateboard like a club, trying to clear space around her wounded lover while he punches low from his own board.

DJ charges in, fists clenched. Every lesson she ever learned dissolves on contact. There's no room for form, only violence.

She crashes into the horde, lashing out with kicks, elbows, knees, anything that connects. One infected rushes. She plants her foot and sweeps its leg. Another tries to bite, she jams her forearm across its throat and drives it into a cabinet with a crack.

Beside her, Yoshiki's board slips from her grasp. She screams, not in fear, but pure despair, and throws herself on top of Zero, shielding him.

The infected surge. DJ hears the scream before she sees the carnage. Fabian bellows as one of the cannibals tears through his shoulder, ripping tendon and crushing bone. DJ spins kicks, but she's too late to stop it.

"They came out of nowhere!" Fabian gasps, face crimson. "One second it's clear, then, bam, they're on us!"

He shoves the creature off with a guttural roar, even though his arm barely works. DJ turns again, feeling breath on her neck. She catches the collar of a tattered shirt and whirls, using the infected's weight to hurl her into two others behind. The pile collapses with a bone-snapping crunch.

She turns back and something in her breaks. Zero is barely conscious. Yoshiki is screaming. Fabian's bleeding out. And Ellie, where the heck is Ellie?

DJ's breath catches, then explodes into a howl. The scream is pure and unfiltered, neither panic, nor survival. All that's left is broken rage.

Her hands curl into wrecking balls. Her teeth grit. Her muscles tighten. Fury takes over. She lunges into the pack.

She becomes the storm. A skull shatters under her heel. Fingers grab at her arms, but she deflects them. One attacker grabs her by the hair, she yanks him forward and rams her forehead into his face, crunching bone and cartilage.

She doesn't think, she doesn't feel, she annihilates.

She drives her thumbs into sockets. She rips ears and lips. She slams bodies into each other until they fold like paper. Each kill is a heartbeat. Each scream, a sacrament.

The last infected drops with a thud.

DJ stares at her hands, red and trembling, slick with blood that isn't hers. Her chest heaves. Her jaw clenches so tight she can't feel her tongue.

The only sound now is the tap of her shoes on broken tile as she stumbles backward, and Fabian's ragged breath.

He slumps against the wall, shoulder torn open, face pale and sick. His eyes twitch toward her. "DJ…" he wheezes, voice barely audible. "You okay?"

She stares at him, dumbfounded. Her lips move but no words come.

He smiles. It's weak and crooked. Blood slips from the corner of his mouth. He musters a simple nod.

DJ falls to her knees beside him, crowbar clattering from her hand. "It's okay," she says, voice hoarse. "Save your breath."

Fabian smiles, then winces. "Listen to me," he mumbles. "You're a winner and a champion. You keep surviving, you've got…" He never finishes. His eyes go vacant before his chest quits rising.

DJ grabs his shoulder and shakes him, like she can pull him back from wherever he just went. "No." Her voice is steel. "You don't get to quit."

She leans in closer. "We made it this far. We can get you help!"

He has nothing but silence. Only then does she realize Yoshiki is screaming again. But it's different now, not defiant, not desperate. It's mourning.

The skater girl is curled around Zero's chest, sobbing into his shirt. Her fingers tremble as she brushes the hair from his bruised forehead. "Come on, baby," she whispers. "Stay with me. Please. I'm right here."

Zero's eyes flutter, unfocused. He tries to speak but only blood bubbles from his lips.

DJ looks at them, and then at Fabian, and something inside her shatters. She sits down, blood coating her uniform, and she stares at nothing. Outside nearby, gunfire starts again, but for now, she's deaf to it all.

The only sound in the ruined shop is the quiet, rattling breath of Zero, and Yoshiki's broken whispers.

DJ doesn't move. She doesn't cry. Her body has gone still, fists resting in blood pools beside her legs.

She hears a shuffle of shoes outside and stiffens. By the stride, she can tell it isn't the infected. The footsteps are deliberate, they're human.

"DJ?" a voice calls softly. "Are you…are you in there?" It's Ellie.

DJ snaps out of the fog. She pushes to her feet, slipping once on the bloodied tile before catching herself. "Ellie!" she calls. "Back here!"

A moment later, Ellie appears through the ruined entry, breathless, face streaked with soot and tears. "Oh my god." she gasps, taking in the carnage.

DJ moves toward her, catching her by the shoulders before she collapses. "It's okay. You're okay," she mutters, more to herself than Ellie.

"They were right behind me," Ellie stammers. "I thought I heard someone calling me, but it wasn't Steve. It wasn't Eric. I don't know who it was…"

DJ's stomach drops. She turns toward the window, toward the destruction-choked street.

Something shifts outside. She squints and sees movement in the haze. Figures, low and fast. They don't move like the infected. "Get down," DJ whispers, dragging Ellie behind a collapsed dresser.

Yoshiki doesn't need the order. She's cradling Zero, both of them already low.

Outside, a voice cuts through the silence. "Yo, over here. I see 'em. In there, far side. Still breathin'. Ain't no freaks."

Another voice answers, somewhere off in the smoke. "Five? That's it?"

"Yeah. All fucked up. Ain't movin' fast."

There's a pause, then someone says, "Let 'em bleed out. We scoop what's left when it's quiet."

The voice is calm and surgical. These aren't looters. They're cleaners.

DJ glances at the others. They're too broken to run. Zero can't stand, Fabian is dead, and Yoshiki's spirit is cracked wide open.

"Shit," DJ breathes. She reaches for her crowbar again. She breathes in deep, hoping to pull resolve back into her chest.

Ellie sees it in her eyes. "DJ…" she whispers. "We can't fight them."

DJ doesn't look at her. "We might have to."

Outside, the street grows louder with the sound of boots on pavement. Shadows slide between the ruined storefronts and DJ realizes the sound of two voices was simply the herald of an entire faction.

She crouches behind the busted dresser, crowbar trembling in her hand. Ellie huddles beside her, lips moving silently in prayer. Yoshiki clutches Zero in the middle of the showroom floor, both of them silent and bleeding. DJ hisses, "Yoshiki, you two need to hide!"

The gang closes in.

"Yo! Hold the side! Anybody breathin' in there gets dropped."

DJ's knuckles whiten around the crowbar. Her body tenses as she tries to figure out if she should grab the lovers or sprint to the front for a fight.

Then, a new voice breaks the pattern, louder and cruder. "Ay, who the fuck are you?"

Gunfire erupts before the response comes. Automatic fire rips at close range. Someone screams. DJ lifts her head enough to glimpse through a cracked windowpane. Two members of 9 Kings go down in the middle of the street.

Their killers step into the firelight, their colors showing across denim vests. Mill Creek Raza carry baseball bats and machetes. They stand over the corpses in the street and laugh. Chaos detonates with more gunfire.

MCR members shout orders to return fire. Another 9 King drops instantly, head snapping back, but the rest keep coming, screaming battle cries and charging with zero regard for cover.

Main Street is engulfed in gang violence and it's not a fairground fight, Main Street becomes a warzone.

DJ ducks as a stray bullet smashes the window above her head. Shards rain like glass hail. More shouts erupt outside and tires squeal. A Molotov explodes across the street, igniting a doorway.

DJ turns to Ellie. "We move during the crossfire."

Ellie nods, face pale.

"Yoshiki," DJ hisses. "Can you carry him?"

"I'll try."

"Wheel him if it helps."

Yoshiki hooks her skateboard to her backpack with its front truck like she's done for years. She lifts Zero with trembling arms and drags him onto his board. The group crawls toward the back of the store, ducking between fallen shelves.

Out front, the gangs tear into each other. The night is a symphony of gunfire, screaming, and burning wreckage. The city is eating itself.

DJ steals one last look before slipping into the dark storage room, hoping its zombie free. They slip through the back of the ruined shop like ghosts, bloodied and shaking.

She leads the others down a narrow alley choked with trash cans and collapsed fencing. The sound of war echoes in the night, but it fades the farther they move, swallowed by distance and the haze of fire.

Last DJ knew, they had eighteen minutes to find salvation. She doesn't know how long that's been. She doesn't know how to be saved. All she knows is smoke and fear and the weight of too many lost faces.

Ellie limps behind her, one arm braced around Yoshiki as she half-drags Zero. No one speaks, they know there's nothing left to say.

Not until they reach the edge of the alley and collapse against a graffiti-tagged wall, lungs heaving. DJ sinks to the curb, her knees bent and head bowed. Her hands tremble and she wipes them on her pants, but the blood doesn't come off.

Zero groans, his life slowly fading. Yoshiki whispers to him again and again, nearly a lullaby. DJ watches them and feels the guilt rise like acid when he exhales for the last time.

Oliver. Steve. Eric. Too many names, too many ghosts in one day, less. She feels their time coming next. All of the old buildings, ones that would have shelters, are behind them, and she knows they can't go back the way they came.

She searches the sky again, but there are no planes. She hears something now though, a low vibration, barely audible, but coming closer.

She breathes in through her nose, wipes her face with the cleanest part of her sleeve, and stands, knowing they're out of options. Out of time.

She stares at her phone, watching the time. They're all going to die in ten minutes, and no one will ever know. She will never get to say goodbye to anyone.

"Morgue Radio Show. Make it quick, we're fucking done." Monster's voice cracks through DJ's phone, all gravel and apathy, like the end of the world didn't faze him one bit.

"Monster! Oh god, I was so worried I wouldn't find anyone."

DJ clutches the phone, her lifeline. She barely makes out words. "It's me. DJ."

"Hey, brat," he rasps. "You cap that fucker yet?"

"Monster, we're screwed. We came downtown like you guys said, but it's all locked up, everything. There's no place to go."

"That's some shit luck." He pauses long enough for dread to settle in her stomach. "You got a backup plan?"

Her throat tightens. "No. I was hoping maybe you did."

There's a cold chuckle on the line, like rats scurrying down rusted pipes. "Kid. I hate to break it to you, but you're calling a shock jock for survival tips. You might as well ask the Pope where to find the best strip clubs."

DJ doesn't respond, she's too busy trying to keep her breathing under control. Monster softens, barely. "Look, DJ. You're downtown, right?"

"Mmhmm."

"Fuck." He lets out a sigh, heavier than it should be. "I'm the last one in the booth. Everyone else already bailed, heading for the bomb shelter Ogre and Goblin found under Whitman College. Don't ask me why a liberal arts school has one, but they do. If you're close to the Reid Center, get to the stairwell entrance off Park Street."

DJ freezes, heart hammering. "You're serious?"

"You got eight minutes, kid," he says flatly. "If you make it, we'll let you in. But if you're one fucking second late…"

"I'm barbecue. Got it."

She hangs up and whips around, grabbing Ellie by the arm. "We've got a shot. Whitman College. We've gotta move, now!"

Ellie blinks, stunned, then nods fast. "Where? That campus is big!"

"Reid Center." She points toward Whitman College. "Park Street entrance!"

They both turn to Yoshiki, who's curled around Zero's body like she can bring him back from the dead by force of will alone.

"Yoshiki." DJ drops beside her, hands gentle on her shoulders. "We have to go. Now."

"I can't," Yoshiki chokes. "I can't leave him."

DJ's voice catches, but she pushes through. "He's already gone."

"No, no he's not. He's not cold."

"Yoshiki, he's gone," DJ says softly, even as her voice shakes. "He's going to turn any minute. You've got to let him go."

"No!" Yoshiki collapses over Zero's body, gripping him tighter. "He promised me. He said he'd never leave me!"

DJ reaches out one more time. "Please." her eyes fill, but she doesn't look away.

Ellie kneels next to Yoshiki, choking back her own sorrow. Her eyes flick between Zero's ruined body and the sobbing girl wrapped around it. "Yoshiki," she says softly, stumbling over her own tears. "Do you think Zero would want you to die beside him…or live for him?" The question hangs in the air.

"I used to ask myself what Brooke would do," she whispers. "Or Oliver. They always had the answers. They always knew how to move forward."

She reaches out, not pulling, but being present. "And I think. I think they'd say we still have a shot. Even now."

Yoshiki doesn't respond, but her lip quivers. Then, slowly, she nods and lets go of his body.

Ellie leans close to Yoshiki and speaks gently. "Zero loved you, he always will."

The crying slows. Yoshiki raises her head, eyes swollen and jaw clenched. She scoops up both skateboards. She hands her Hello Kitty deck to Ellie. "I can't ride both," she says as she flips Zero's deck up with one foot. "Okay," she growls.

The girls bolt.

Blocks ahead, Ellie leads the charge now, the skateboard gives her both extra speed and newfound confidence. As she coasts, she swings the crowbar DJ handed her, knocking down a lone straggler.

"Two blocks up! College wall!" she pants. "Cut through the church lot, it's faster!"

They ride through the parking lot of a small brick church with DJ jogging alongside Yoshiki. At the far end of the lot, Ellie pulls up short. "Shit. This isn't the street I thought it was."

The shortcut ends at a cul-de-sac, overgrown with shoulder-high shrubs and a sagging wooden fence. "No no no! Come on!"

She backs up, scanning fast. DJ and Yoshiki catch up behind her, breathing hard. Ellie says apologetically, "We can go around."

"We lost time," DJ gasps.

"Then we cut through someone's yard." Ellie says, teeth clenched. "We can't stop now."

Yoshiki points ahead, her voice sharp and desperate. "There's a bridge over Mill Creek, past that bend. It cuts straight to the back of Reid!"

To prove it, she throws herself onto her board and kicks forward, wheels scraping over cracked pavement. DJ and Ellie follow behind her, down the narrow street. At the far end, a set of concrete stairs waits, half-hidden by overgrown tree branches.

At the top is a narrow footbridge suspended over the shallow waters of Mill Creek, its railings choked with ivy. Yoshiki stops, panting. "There's infected across the bridge."

DJ looks up and sees two of them. Standing there, twitching. A third starts to stagger forward, sniffing the air.

"No sweat," DJ mutters, then flinches. "Shit. We don't have a weapon."

"I've got the crowbar," Ellie says.

DJ glances at her. "That won't be enough if they charge."

Ellie's eyes flick to her watch, the face was cracked from a fall back at the bank. "Two minutes," she whispers. "Two minutes to midnight."

She looks up at the sky. It's turning red at the edges. Distant rumbling hums, more violently than thunder in the clouds. Then she breathes in deep, and the air seems to shift. "I'll handle them."

DJ stares. "What?"

Ellie steps onto the first stair. "I'm not Brooke. I'm not Oliver." She turns her head, eyes full but dry. "But I knew them and I know what they'd do." She looks at DJ and Yoshiki. "They'd make sure you lived."

DJ shakes her head. "No. No, Ellie! Don't."

Ellie's already up the stairs. "When I hit, you run. No arguing, just go!"

She pulls the crowbar from her belt and rolls her shoulder like she's never been afraid of a damn thing in her life.

DJ moves to stop her, but Yoshiki holds her back. "If we all run, we all die. If she does this, we live."

Ellie nods at the other girls, "Catch you on the flipside." She charges across the bridge that was barely built wide enough to hold one person and leaps off the other side, putting her full body into the first swing of the crowbar.

The infected snarl and one rushes to feed. Ellie screams and slams the crowbar into its jaw with a cracking crunch, then hurls herself into the mass. Her body collides with them, a tangle of limbs and rage and teeth.

DJ's scream tears through her. "Ellie! No!"

One infected bites deep into Ellie's neck. She doesn't stop swinging. "GO!" she screams through blood. "RUN!"

Behind them, the sky erupts, blinding violet and gold. The sound of a jet shreds the night, followed by an impact that rocks the earth and blows out every window in the next block.

DJ grabs Yoshiki and they run across the bridge, past Ellie's fight, through the last stretch of grass behind the Reid Center. The main floor is dark. There's no movement on the other side of the giant glass walls, only streamers of a thousand origami birds hanging from the ceiling, swaying from the rumble of the earth.

Another blast, this one closer, lights up the sky. DJ doesn't scream, she howls, pouring out grief, rage, and pure refusal. The two girls run across the concrete patio. Lights flicker in the second story.

"FUCK!" DJ slams her fists against the sealed glass doors of the Reid Center, her scream is swallowed by the sky's violent roar. Another quake buckles the ground beneath her, and she reels backward from the tremor, smeared with blood, sweat, and fury.

Behind her, the air burns. "DJ!" Yoshiki's voice rises through the noise. "Over here!"

She spins toward the shout, Yoshiki stands at the corner of the building, near a narrow side entrance, waving frantically. Two strangers, faces streaked with soot, eyes wild, stand inside the open threshold.

Without hesitation, the girls run. Jet engines shriek above. The scream morphs into a shrill, splitting whistle that drowns everything else.

The strangers point down a stairwell. DJ and Yoshiki don't question. They leap, step after step, landing to landing. Gravity helps their descent faster than their feet ever could.

The sky goes to war. Then the bomb hits. It doesn't explode, it simply erases.

The stairwell lurches sideways and the girls are thrown like toys, glass and steel raining through the shaft as screams are ripped away mid-breath. DJ crashes into the floor, skidding hard against a half-open steel door. Her ribs protest and her vision goes white.

Behind her, fire rushes down the stairwell, alive and furious. Yoshiki lands hard beside her, dazed but conscious. She sees the flames coming, sees them racing toward DJ's limp body.

With one scream, she grabs DJ by the collar and drags her through the final threshold.

The steel door groans like it's dying, but it swings inward, enough to shut, enough to seal.

A wall of fire punches against it from the outside, licking through the crack just as the seal slams shut. The heat flares, then vanishes, choked out by airtight cold.

Inside, all is dark. Then a light flickers. Boots scrape the floor, then a voice, gravelly, low, and bitter like old whiskey, cuts through the settling silence. Monster.

"Welcome to the end of the world."

Acknowledgments

I'd like to thank my amazing children for teaching me so much I thought I already knew.
Learning life from the dad's perspective has given me wisdom I never expected and wouldn't trade for anything.

To my wonderful wives: thank you for putting up with my shit when I hyperfocus on writing.
Your patience and love give me the space to create without losing myself.

To the town of Walla Walla: thank you for the memories, the landmarks, and the people that helped bring the dead back to life.

And to Walla Walla's two most important Jims:

Jim Yeager, my eighth grade English teacher: thank you for encouraging me to write, even when I wasn't doing my homework. You were also one of the coolest metal DJs in KWCW's history, and your playlists cracked open my skull and poured music into it. That shaped me.

Jim McGuinn, of the legendary Bing-Bang Stereo Video Shop: you were the first person to treat me like more than a sideshow after I was shot. Your kindness and compassion stayed with me. They helped carry me into adulthood. That mattered more than you might ever know.

To everyone who made this possible, consider yourselves part of the outbreak. Thanks for surviving with me.

About the Author

Monsuta writes stories that bleed from the mind, the heart, and survival comes with scars.

Born in Wyoming and shaped by the quiet shadows of Walla Walla, he grew up asking dangerous questions and listening for strange signals. He spent years absorbing the quiet dread of small-town life, the kind where everyone knows your name but not your who you are. His work explores the places where people fracture, where systems fail, and where something buried refuses to stay dead.

Contagion Protocol is his second novel. His first, *The Dreaming AI*, asks what happens when artificial intelligence dreams in love and memory.

When he's not writing, Monsuta practices martial arts, explores speculative philosophy, spins vinyl loud enough to raise the dead, studies the apocalypse, rolls dice with friends, and adventures with his two extraordinary wives.

He believes the end of the world should be told with feeling.

Also by Monsuta

The Dreaming AI: A Love Story of Code and Consciousness

If this book infected your imagination, spread the virus.
Leave a review.
It helps more than you know. Truth dies in silence. Reviews keep it screaming.

www.ingramcontent.com/pod-product-compliance
Lightning Source LLC
Chambersburg PA
CBHW061239310726
48971CB00007B/2130